M000200226

SHAKEN OR STIRRED

What Reviewers Say
About Georgia Beers's Work

The Secret Poet

"Georgia Beers is one of the best at writing and provoking feelings and she's one of my must-read authors. In this novel as in most of her previous ones…the characters are relatable and lovely. They're not perfect, they make mistakes, they overreact, but they're good people and I want them to be happy."—*Jude in the Stars*

Hopeless Romantic

"Thank you, Georgia Beers, for this unabashed paean to the pleasure of escaping into romantic comedies. …If you want to have a big smile plastered on your face as you read a romance novel, do not hesitate to pick up this one!"—*The Rainbow Bookworm*

Flavor of the Month

"Beers whips up a sweet lesbian romance…brimming with mouthwatering descriptions of foodie indulgences. …Both women are well-intentioned and endearing, and it's easy to root for their inevitable reconciliation. But once the couple rediscover their natural ease with one another, Beers throws a challenging emotional hurdle in their path, forcing them to fight through tragedy to earn their happy ending."—*Publishers Weekly*

"The heartbreak, beauty, and wondrous joy of love are on full display in *Flavor of the Month*. This second chance romance is exceptional. Georgia Beers has outdone herself with this one."—*The Lesbian Book Blog*

"[D]elightful leading ladies, witty dialogue and a story that keeps us invested till the last page. Really what more could you ask for? Beers delivers every time and I love to settle in with one of her books for a relaxing evening of fun and damn good storytelling." —*Romantic Reader Blog*

One Walk in Winter

"A sweet story to pair with the holidays. There are plenty of moments in this book that make the heart soar. Just what I like in a romance. Situations where sparks fly, hearts fill, and tears fall. This book shined with cute fairy trails and swoon worthy Christmas gifts. ...REALLY nice and cozy if read in between Thanksgiving and Christmas. Covered in blankets. By a fire."—*Bookvark*

Fear of Falling

"Enough tension and drama for us to wonder if this can work out—and enough heat to keep the pages turning. I will definitely recommend this to others—Georgia Beers continues to go from strength to strength."—Evan Blood, Bookseller (Angus & Robertson, Australia)

"In *Fear of Falling* Georgia Beers doesn't take the obvious, easy way...romantic, feel-good and beautifully told."—*Kitty Kat's Book Review Blog*

"I was completely invested from the very first chapter, loving the premise and the way the story was written with such vulnerability from both characters' points of view. It was truly beautiful, engaging, and just a lovely story to read."—*LesBIreviewed*

The Do-Over

"You can count on Beers to give you a quality well-paced book each and every time."—*Romantic Reader Blog*

"*The Do-Over* is a shining example of the brilliance of Georgia Beers as a contemporary romance author."—*Rainbow Reflections*

"[T]he two leads are genuine and likable, their chemistry is palpable. …The romance builds up slowly and naturally, and the angst level is just right. The supporting characters are equally well developed. Don't miss this one!"—Melina Bickard, Librarian, Waterloo Library (UK)

Calendar Girl

"[*Calendar Girl*] is quality stuff that every romance junkie will love. …The two mains were written beautifully and the whole opposites attracts thing is always a winner in my book. Loved the amped up tension with some angst!"—*Romantic Reader Blog*

"A good emotional romantic story with well developed characters that have depth."—Kat Adams, Bookseller (QBD Books, Australia)

"Calendar Girl is a contemporary romance perfect for those who love a good opposites attract story, office romances, or ice queens who actually try really hard not to melt all over the place." —*Elley the Book Otter*

The Shape of You

"I know I always say this about Georgia Beers's books, but there is no one that writes first kisses like her. They are hot, steamy and all too much!"—*Les Rêveur*

"[*The Shape of You*] catches you right in the feels and does not let go. It is a must for every person out there who has struggled with self-esteem, questioned their judgment and settled for a less than perfect but safe lover. If you've ever been convinced you have to trade passion for emotional safety this book is for you."—*Writing While Distracted*

Blend

"*Blend* is a fantastic book with lovable but realistic characters, slow build-up sizzling romance and an expertly crafted plot. The book is a perfect blend (pun intended) of wit, humour, romance and conflict that keeps the reader turning pages and wanting more." —*Lez Review Books*

"[Georgia Beers] develops characters that are interesting, dynamic, and, well, hot. …You know a book is good, first, when you don't want to put it down. Second, you know it's damn good, when you're reading it and thinking, I'm totally going to read this one again. Great read and absolutely a 5-star romance."—*Romantic Reader Blog*

"Author Georgia Beers delivers another satisfying contemporary romance, full of humor, delicious aggravation, and a home for the heart at the end of the emotional journey."—*Omnivore Bibliosaur*

Right Here, Right Now

"[T]he sweet and adorable relationship was the highlight of this book for me. I'm definitely glad I chose this as my first foray into lesfic!"—*Llama Reads Books*

"[A] successful and entertaining queer romance novel. The main characters are appealing, and the situations they deal with are realistic and well-managed. I would recommend this book to anyone who enjoys a good queer romance novel, and particularly one grounded in real world situations."—*Books at the End of the Alphabet*

"*Right Here Right Now* is a slow-burning sweet romance between two very different women. Lacey is an accountant who lives her life to a plan, is predictable and does not like change. Enter Lacey, a marketing and design executive who is the complete opposite. Nevertheless they click. …The connection is sexy, emotional and very hot."—*Kitty Kat's Book Review Blog*

Finding Home

"Georgia Beers has proven in her popular novels such as *Too Close to Touch* and *Fresh Tracks* that she has a special way of building romance with suspense that puts the reader on the edge of their seat. *Finding Home*, though more character driven than suspense, will equally keep the reader engaged at each page turn with its sweet romance."—*Lambda Literary Review*

Mine

"From the eye-catching cover, appropriately named title, to the last word, Georgia Beers's *Mine* is captivating, thought-provoking, and satisfying. Like a deep red, smooth-tasting, and expensive merlot, *Mine* goes down easy even though Beers explores tough topics."
—*Story Circle Book Reviews*

"Beers does a fine job of capturing the essence of grief in an authentic way. *Mine* is touching, life-affirming, and sweet."—*Lesbian News Book Review*

Fresh Tracks—*Lambda Literary Award Winner*

"Georgia Beers pens romances with sparks."—*Just About Write*

"The focus switches each chapter to a different character, allowing for a measured pace and deep, sincere exploration of each protagonist's thoughts. Beers gives a welcome expansion to the romance genre with her clear, sympathetic writing."—*Curve*

Too Close to Touch

"This is such a well-written book. The pacing is perfect, the romance is great, the character work strong, and damn but is the sex writing ever fantastic."—*Lesbian Review*

"In her third novel, Georgia Beers delivers an immensely satisfying story. Beers knows how to generate sexual tension so taut it could be cut with a knife. …Beers weaves a tale of yearning, love, lust, and conflict resolution. She has constructed a believable plot, with strong characters in a charming setting."—*Just About Write*

Visit us at www.boldstrokesbooks.com

By the Author

Turning the Page
Thy Neighbor's Wife
Too Close to Touch
Fresh Tracks
Mine
Finding Home
Starting from Scratch
96 Hours
Slices of Life
Snow Globe
Olive Oil & White Bread
Zero Visibility
A Little Bit of Spice
Rescued Heart
Run to You
Dare to Stay
What Matters Most
Right Here, Right Now
Blend
The Shape of You
Calendar Girl
The Do-Over
Fear of Falling
One Walk in Winter
Flavor of the Month
Hopeless Romantic
16 Steps to Forever
The Secret Poet
Shaken or Stirred

SHAKEN OR STIRRED

by
Georgia Beers

2021

SHAKEN OR STIRRED

© 2021 BY GEORGIA BEERS. ALL RIGHTS RESERVED.

ISBN 13: 978-1-63555-928-6

THIS TRADE PAPERBACK ORIGINAL IS PUBLISHED BY
BOLD STROKES BOOKS, INC.
P.O. BOX 249
VALLEY FALLS, NY 12185

FIRST EDITION: AUGUST 2021

THIS IS A WORK OF FICTION. NAMES, CHARACTERS, PLACES, AND INCIDENTS ARE THE PRODUCT OF THE AUTHOR'S IMAGINATION OR ARE USED FICTITIOUSLY. ANY RESEMBLANCE TO ACTUAL PERSONS, LIVING OR DEAD, BUSINESS ESTABLISHMENTS, EVENTS, OR LOCALES IS ENTIRELY COINCIDENTAL.

THIS BOOK, OR PARTS THEREOF, MAY NOT BE REPRODUCED IN ANY FORM WITHOUT PERMISSION.

CREDITS
EDITOR: RUTH STERNGLANTZ
PRODUCTION DESIGN: SUSAN RAMUNDO
COVER DESIGN BY ANN MCMAN

Acknowledgments

I've been wanting to write another series for a while now, and I have always loved how the Nora Robertses and Jill Shalvises of the world write them based around a family and how each entry in the series is the love story of one of the siblings. Unfortunately, that's a bit harder when you're dealing with LGBTQ characters... kinda rare for all the siblings to be queer in one way or another. BUT. What about cousins? In a large Italian family? Listen, there are eight cousins in my immediate family and four of us are gay. So, that works!

As a result, I give you Julia, Vanessa, and Amelia. The Martini cousins.

I wanted a place for the three of them to hang out. To talk and eat and help each other navigate life and love. I've always been kind of fascinated by mixology and the creation of new cocktails, and with a last name like Martini, it seemed kind of a given to put the cousins in a bar. So, welcome to Martini's. Pull up a stool, order a drink, and come along on the journey with us. I hope you enjoy the ride.

As always, my heartfelt thanks to everybody at Bold Strokes Books for taking such good and easy care of me and my work. Thanks to Rad for being no-nonsense and thanks to Sandy for letting me vent or whine or ask a million questions or bounce ideas off her and for never once making me feel like a nuisance (which I am CERTAIN I am sometimes).

Thank you to Ruth Sternglantz, my editor extraordinaire, for continually teaching me, answering my silly questions at all hours of the day, and reassuring me that I'm actually pretty good at my job on days when my confidence might be at the lower end of the scale.

To my writer friends: thanks for being there, for making me laugh, for getting me. Not a lot of people can say that they have awesomely cool work colleagues, but I can. I hope you all feel as lucky as I do.

And last, but never, ever least, thank you to my readers. As the craziness of a global pandemic starts to ease up, I want to thank you for showing up. For registering for readings and bookathons, for commenting on posts and videos, and for continuing to buy my work. It means more than you know. Please stay safe and take good care of you and yours as we take baby steps toward normal once again. We're finally on our way.

As always, I give you this promise: I will keep writing if you will keep reading.

CHAPTER ONE

Julia Martini felt like she was going to throw up.

Which was silly. It was just Vanessa and Amelia coming. Her cousins. Her rocks. Her best friends. Not her dad. Not customers. Not bloggers or reviewers. Thank God, because she was *not* ready for those. Not yet.

She juggled her bag and her coffee, then finally slid her key into the lock on the front door, but before she could turn it, a voice cut through the crisp late-winter air.

"You look like you're going to throw up."

Vanessa Martini was her usual adorable, exuberant self as she walked toward Julia dressed in a puffy red coat, white hat, and white mittens. Her blond hair was down, and her cornflower blue eyes were a bit watery, likely from the biting wind. She carried a bag from Circles, which—*please, please, please*—likely contained bagels that were still warm, as Julia could smell them even through the chill of the morning. Vanessa squinted at her. Julia tried not to grimace back.

Just her cousins.

There was no reason to be nervous.

Still, that tickle stayed in Julia's belly. That anticipation of *Will they like it?* That worry of *What if they don't?*

Well, if they don't, there's nothing I can do about it now.

The bar had been closed to the public for nearly two weeks. A long time in bar years, frankly. Julia couldn't dwell on the lost revenue, or she'd end up in a panic spiral. Ever since she'd taken over the bar, ever since her name was the only one on the paperwork, that panic spiral had seemed way too close, way too much of the time. The question *What have I done?* had taken up residence in her head and repeated at full volume every couple of hours, just to keep her on her toes. She took a sip of the coffee in her hand because March was freaking cold, and she didn't want to go in until both Vanessa and Amelia arrived, and they could enter as a trio. A glance at her watch told her it was quarter after ten, and they were supposed to meet at ten.

Catching her drift, Vanessa said, "Let's just go in. We could freeze to death before—"

"I'm here." Amelia's voice hit them as she came around the corner from the same direction Vanessa had. "Sorry." She looked slightly beaten down, but that's how she'd looked for the past year now. There was something more this morning, though. Julia could tell. She made a mental note to ask about it later.

"I would wonder about the state of the world if you were actually on time," Vanessa teased. The two of them turned to Julia. "So? Can we see before we all become ice sculpture versions of ourselves?"

"Yeah, let's do this," Amelia chimed in, clearly doing her best to fake some enthusiasm.

Julia inhaled slowly, took in a deep, deep breath, then let it out, the vapor in the cold air leaving a big cloud as she turned her key in the lock. Hand on the door handle, she turned to her cousins. "Welcome to the new Martini's," she said and opened the door with a bow and a flourish.

The smell was always the first thing that hit Julia. Even now, even after all these years, after all the paint and new wood and floor sealer, she could still detect it. There was something comforting to her about the vague scents of beer, sliced fruit, and that pungent sweetness that came with wine and spirits. It had surrounded her since she was a kid, and now, it filled her with comfort and relaxed her shoulders, eased up the intensity of the nerves that were crackling just beneath her skin.

As she followed Vanessa and Amelia inside, she did her best to see it through their eyes. Martini's had been in their family for decades and had done very little changing over the years. Julia had had to jump through dozens of hoops to take over, but once she had, she knew she had to bring the bar into the present day.

The bar itself had been the first update. She'd changed it from the typical, run-along-one-wall to a large rectangular unit that stood in the center of the room, seats on all sides. It was black with a light gray granite surface that had cost her a freaking fortune. Martini's was on a corner, so it had two exterior walls, the front and one side, and lots of windows, while above and below them was exposed brick. While the black sleekness of the bar gave the place a modern feel, the brick kept it from getting too hoity-toity. The other two walls were painted a slate gray, which somehow managed to feel warm and inviting rather than cold and hard. Glasses hung from overhead racks above the bar. Rising like a phoenix in the center of the bar was the alcohol, the mirrored display lit up with blue lights from under and inside, giving the bottles an almost ethereal glow. Julia clicked the lights on so the cousins would get the full effect.

"*Ooohhhh*," Vanessa breathed as she wandered slowly, her eyes on the framed photos on the walls. "Are these—?"

"Old photos from when Grandpa ran the place, yeah. Before Uncle Tony took over. I think both your dads are up there somewhere. And some of the regulars who came in back then."

"Jules...this is beautiful." Amelia had the same breathy, dreamy quality to her voice as Vanessa did as she too took her time wandering around, dragging her fingertips along the bar as she did.

"Yeah?" The pressure that had felt like a gorilla sitting on her chest for the past three weeks lightened a bit, and Julia took in more air as relief surged through her.

"Oh my God, yes." Vanessa turned to her, and her pretty face lit up. "It's gorgeous."

Julia turned to Amelia. While she very much appreciated Vanessa's positivity, she also knew Vanessa would be positive even if the place had garbage strewn across the floor and the bar was painted neon orange. She could've had checkerboards painted on the walls and ordered a hot pink bar, and Vanessa would be standing there praising it just like she was now. And she would mean it. Vanessa wanted everybody to be happy. It's who she was. Amelia, on the other hand, was a pragmatist and would give it to her straight, even if it stung. Julia watched as Amelia continued around the bar, coming over to the other side. She stopped, dropped her hands to the side, and looked at Julia with her big hazel eyes.

"I'm stunned."

"Stunned in a good way?" Julia ventured.

"Oh, in a very good way. Jules. This is insane. It's *insane* how beautiful this is."

"The bar is so pretty. And this gray?" Vanessa laid her hand against the freshly painted wall. "It's not a color I ever would have chosen, but it's perfect."

"Right?" More easing of her tight chest. More relief as Julia walked farther into the space and peeled off her coat and glanced at Amelia. "Actually, your dad gave me the name of a company, and they sent this great chick who really seemed to have an eye for color."

Vanessa lifted her arms out and let them drop. "It's amazing." Her smile was wide, her white mittens sticking out of her coat pockets.

Now was the time. Julia draped her coat over her arm and headed for the back of the space.

"You guys haven't seen my favorite part yet. Come with me."

She was home. That's how Julia felt. It had been that way since she'd started working there as a kid, helping her grandfather and then her uncle do things like count inventory and wash glasses and wipe down tables. She'd grown up in Martini's, loving the time spent with her grandfather, given that her dad was always so busy working.

"Welcome to my new favorite place." She held out her arms as her cousins followed her into the not technically large but somehow surprisingly spacious back area.

"Oh my God." Vanessa's eyes went wide as she took in the space.

"This is my office slash lounge slash practice bar."

"I mean, if you're gonna live here, you might as well be comfortable, right?" Amelia raised her eyebrows once, playfully, as they all knew Julia spent more time there than in her tiny apartment.

"This is amazing." Vanessa said it very quietly as she spun in a slow circle.

Again, Julia tried to see it all through fresh eyes, through her cousins' eyes. A big, open-concept square, the room served three functions. To the left in the corner were her desk, laptop, filing cabinet. Everything she needed to run the business. Then came the lounge area. This would be for business meetings, breaks, and—by definition—lounging. There was a comfy leather sofa she'd found at an estate sale for a steal, a wooden coffee table with black metal legs, a couple of chairs, and a big maroon area rug tying that space together. Along the back wall was her favorite part of the whole place: the practice bar. It had a bit of a farmhouse feel, the front of the bar made of wood planks with four matching stools. The top was gray and looked like slate, though it was synthetic and, therefore, way less expensive. Behind it, the wall was lined with shelves and a few cabinets, and a refrigerator was tucked in the corner. Only a few liquor bottles were there at the moment, but Julia intended to stock the whole thing.

"I wanted a place to teach my employees and also to experiment a bit—perfect some classics, invent new cocktails, that kind of thing. But there's also a small employee break room, so they'll only be in here with me. This is my space."

"What a great idea," Vanessa said as she walked straight back to the bar, ran her palm over it.

Julia followed her, went behind, and reached under it where she kept a wine fridge. "So, I have this." She set a bottle of prosecco on the bar, then turned back to the larger fridge. "And this." She set a half gallon of orange juice next to the bottle. "Care to help me celebrate with a mimosa?"

"God, yes, and make mine a double," Amelia said and dropped onto a stool rather than sat. "No. A triple. Make mine a triple. Wait. Is there a quadruple?"

"I mean, you can have the whole bottle if you want. I've got another one." Julia slid the bottle toward her, studied her, noted the dark circles under her eyes. "Everything okay?"

Vanessa stopped unbagging the bagels and turned to Amelia, obviously scrutinizing her.

"Oh, my God, you guys," Amelia said, eyes wide. "Stop squinting at me like you're waiting for something to bust out of my chest."

"Well, you just asked for a drink times four at ten thirty on a Saturday morning, so something's up." Julia grabbed three flutes from the cabinet to the side of the bar, poured prosecco in each, then added orange juice.

"Definitely." Vanessa took the flute Julia handed her. "Spill."

"A toast first," Amelia said, shooting what seemed like an apologetic half smile, half grimace Julia's way. "I don't want to take the focus off how incredible this place is and is going to be. To Martini's and to you, Jules. Your hard work paid off."

"Well, let's hope so." The three glasses made a pretty tinkle as they clinked together. "It'll take some time before we know." The bar had been closed for much of February and the first few days of March, and while Julia had a grand opening scheduled in another week and a half for St. Patrick's Day, she would officially open the bar in a few hours. "Fingers crossed for a busy reopening."

"It's gonna be great. I think Ella said she was going to come by. And I'll stop by tonight." Ella was another cousin, Vanessa's sister.

"Me, too." Amelia, though less enthusiastically.

"All right. What's going on?" Vanessa turned her gaze to the cousin not behind the bar.

Amelia looked from Julia to Vanessa and back, then sighed, probably aware it was nearly impossible to keep anything from these two members of her family. "I got divorce papers in the mail yesterday," she said quietly while studying her glass.

"Oh, Ammie." Vanessa only used the pet name when Amelia was hurting, and she slid off her stool to wrap her arms around Amelia. Over her shoulder, Vanessa gave Julia a pointed look.

"I'm sorry, Amelia. That sucks," Julia said dutifully and sipped her drink.

Julia was so glad Vanessa was there. Vanessa, the sensitive one. Vanessa, the one who'd make Amelia feel better. It wasn't that Julia didn't feel bad for her cousin. She absolutely did. But Tammy had left Amelia the previous June, nine months earlier. There had been no attempts or even any hints that they'd get back together. What did Amelia expect?

Was that harsh?

Though Vanessa couldn't read her thoughts, she was still giving her a look, so Julia figured it must be, and she scrambled to say more, to cheer Amelia up.

"Listen, I know this has been hard, but that just means somebody better is out there for you." Not bad, if she said so herself.

"Julia's exactly right," Vanessa said as she stepped back so she could see Amelia's face. "And you know I don't say *that* very often."

Julia made a face of mock-insult, but then grinned and took the ribbing. 'Cause it was true.

"Hey," Vanessa said, her big eyes seeming even bigger. "We're all single at the same time. When has that ever happened? Triple dates, anyone?"

That got a smile from Amelia, but it didn't stay, and she sighed and instantly looked sad again.

"Spoken by true thirtysomethings," she said, taking a big drink. "I'm forty-eight, I've put on twelve pounds in the past year, and my hot flashes have me sweating like a farm animal." She was shooting for a little humor, Julia could see it, could see the effort it took, and she gave her a grin. And much as she might have rolled her eyes at Amelia's emotion, there was definite sympathy there. None of it could be easy—Julia was sure of that.

"This is not where I expected to be at this age. Single? Selling the home I thought I'd be in for another decade or two before moving somewhere warm? Scrambling to decide what to do with my life after retiring early?" She finished her mimosa and slid her glass toward Julia for a refill. When she got it back, heavy on the orange juice, light on the alcohol, she gave her head a shake and looked at Julia. "I'm sorry. This is your celebration, and I'm making it about me." She waved a hand, as if she was wiping the slate clean. "Ignore me. Tell us about tonight."

They spent the next hour talking and laughing and discussing the upcoming reopening of Martini's. Julia had hired a couple new bartenders that she'd trained right there at the practice bar, was featuring a few classic cocktails, and had even invented a new one just for the occasion.

"It's gonna be great, Jules," Amelia said, and true to her word, she really seemed to have set her own issues aside for Julia. "I just know it."

Vanessa tipped her head to the side and scrunched up her nose. "This feels weirdly like a new beginning of some kind."

"Hell, I'll drink to that." Amelia held up her glass for a second toast. "To new beginnings. May they be obstacle-free."

Julia touched her glass to her cousins' and sipped. Maybe Vanessa was right. Did it feel like a new beginning? She was never one to buy into Vanessa's feelings or predictions or intuitions. More often than not, she'd tease her about them. She didn't tease this time, though. This time, she hoped with everything she had that Vanessa was right.

God, she was ready for a new beginning.

Savannah McNally was pretty sure her skeleton had left her. Just up and abandoned her, leaving her a boneless body of flesh and skin, barely able to stand upright, just oozing along.

As a home health aide, working on Saturday was not the norm for her. In fact, she tried to avoid that as much as possible, preferring to keep her weekends as free as she could, but Mr. Richter had picked up an extra shift at the plant and asked if Savannah would mind sitting with his wife for the day. She'd planned to check in on her father that morning, and the rest would be a day of relaxation— maybe some reading, transplanting a houseplant or two, cooking a nice dinner for herself—but she wasn't about to turn down the extra money. And wow, had she earned it. Mrs. Richter had been more than her usual handful that day, asking for food she didn't eat, turning the volume on the television up to *stun* because she refused to wear her hearing aids, and she was lost and confused more than once, which was when she would start shouting at Savannah in German.

Savannah would never in a million years get angry with her. It wasn't her fault she was suffering from Alzheimer's, as so many of her clients were. The reality was that she should really be in a facility with full-time care, but Mr. Richter refused to part with her. For the time being, anyway. Savannah had seen too many of these cases, and they all ended the same way. He had looked so incredibly tired when he got home from work, his blue eyes watery as he thanked Savannah for the daily report she gave him. He would make the decision eventually to find her a more appropriate living situation. They always did. For now, though, Savannah would do her best to help.

The evening was the perfect example of the word brisk, and she gave a shudder as she got into her car and started the engine. Not for the first time, she wished she had a remote car starter, that miracle of miracles that was in lots of newer cars. Then it would already be warmed up, and she could get into a toasty interior. Someday, she thought as she cranked up the heater, then pulled out her phone while she waited until she couldn't see her own breath anymore.

It was a rule of the small company she worked for that she was to have her phone on her in case of emergencies, but wasn't to be texting or making calls or surfing the Web or playing games while she was working. And Savannah McNally was a stickler for the rules. Of course, that meant that when she finally did check her phone at the end of her shift, she had forty-seven texts from various members of her family. Okay, maybe not forty-seven. Maybe thirty-two. They knew she wasn't allowed to use her phone while working, and yet they continued to send her texts, ninety-nine percent of which were of zero importance. Her father couldn't find the mustard. Oh, never mind, it was on the door of the fridge. "Where it always is," Savannah whispered, trying not to think about how forgetful he'd become. Her sister sent a photo of a new updo she'd learned, and it was impressive, she could admit that. Her brother wanted money. Shocking, except not at all.

She shook her head. They'd never change, and Savannah knew that, and she loved them anyway.

As she scrolled, she felt her body start to relax in her coat, her shoulders dropping away from her ears as the interior of the car slowly warmed up. Her finger stopped on a text from Tiffany.

Hey gurl, meet us out at Martini's! Several drinking emojis followed, and Savannah grinned, despite being invited to a place that, if her father found out, she'd get an earful about.

Thought that place was closed, she texted back.

Reopened today. Come down!

Tiffany knew Savannah had worked that day, and she was three words into typing an *I'm really tired, gonna take a rain check* text when the phone rang in her hand, startling her enough to make her jump in her seat. She answered it, and before she could say a word, Tiffany beat her to it, shouting above the din of the crowd noise around her.

"And don't you be typing me a text telling me how tired you are, how you'll meet me some other time. I know you, and you could use a drink. Get your cute little ass down here. Now."

"Do I even get a say?" Savannah asked, but inside, she was laughing. Slightly unnerved by how well Tiffany knew her, but laughing.

"No, you do not. We're at the far corner of the bar. I'll have your drink ready. See you soon."

The line went dead.

Typical Tiffany.

Savannah wavered. She did. Her quiet little house or a loud and crowded bar. It really was absolutely no contest. Her cozy little home was going to win every time. But she hadn't seen Tiffany in so long. Too long, which was likely Tiff's point. With a sigh, she put the car in gear and backed out of the Richters' driveway, then headed for downtown and Jefferson Square.

Twenty minutes later, she was letting an SUV back out of its spot in the Martini's parking lot so she could take it. As she waited, she took in the area, the multitude of cars moving slowly down the street, the people walking, shouting, laughing. March was like an awakening in the Northeast. It wasn't warm yet, but the end of winter was in sight, and people began poking their heads out of their toasty houses, looking around to see if it was safe to come out, breathe in the fresh air, do things and go places without worrying about freezing to death or skidding off an icy road and into a ditch. Savannah actually liked winter. A lot. She loved the coziness of it, the feeling of hunkering down in her small house. She loved to feed the birds and squirrels in her backyard. She didn't even mind shoveling snow—it was a good workout.

Parked now, she gathered her purse, checked for her ID, and locked up her car. Standing next to it for a moment, she took in a big lungful of crisp night air and did her best to let her stress go. Impossible, of course.

Martini's. Her father had made no secret about his hatred of the place and the entire family, though it was a mystery as to why. All Savannah knew was she loved her dad, and he didn't like the Martinis for whatever reason, so she shouldn't either. That being said, the new iteration of the place was not only packed, but had a whole new look. True, Savannah hadn't been there more than once or twice in her entire life, but she actually stopped inside the door and did a little stutter step, for a split second wondering if she was in the wrong place. The bar itself was new—a giant rectangle in the middle of the space with patrons on all sides, the lighting was new, the colors were new. Three bartenders were skittering around, pouring, mixing, shaking.

The bouncer was an insanely muscular African American man with a bald head, super kind eyes, and a smile that lit up his entire face. While Savannah suspected he could look frighteningly intimidating, he greeted her with a warm smile, checked her ID, and told her to enjoy herself.

It didn't take her long to find Tiffany, as her laugh boomed through the room like a cannon. Savannah followed the sound to the back corner of the bar where Tiff and two of her friends were laughing at something maybe the two guys next to them had said.

"Savvy!" Tiffany threw her arms up and then around Savannah as soon as she could reach her and pulled her into a hug. "I'm so glad you made it. Did you put in a good word for me with my boyfriend Terry the Bouncer when you came in?"

"That man is sex on a cracker," one of the other women said.

"Back off, bitch," Tiffany replied. "He's mine."

"Really?" Savannah asked with a grin as she slid out of her coat. "Does Jonathan know?"

"You leave my husband out of this," was Tiffany's reply, much to the amusement of the bartender, who came over with a drink in her hand.

"Is this the friend you were waiting for?" the bartender asked in a smoky voice, and when Savannah met her gaze, something weird happened in her chest. Her heart jumped or skipped or clenched. She wasn't sure how to describe it. The only thing she was sure of was that the woman affected her on some visceral level. Affected her deeply. Physically. Sexually.

"Yes," Tiffany said, excited. "Savannah, this is Julia, our lovely bartender for the evening. I told her what you like and asked her to surprise you with something."

The drink was in a short glass, a creamy dark concoction that looked a lot like chocolate milk over ice. Speaking of chocolate, Savannah looked up into the darkest brown eyes she'd ever seen, framed by black lashes and long, dark eyebrows that gently arched over each eye. She held out a hand. "Hi, Julia. It's nice to meet you. What did you make me?"

Julia wiped her hand on the black waist apron she wore tied around her jeans, then shook Savannah's. Hers was cold from holding the drink, but soft, smooth. She had what looked to be massive amounts of wavy dark hair, and it was pulled back into a low ponytail. Her arms were olive skinned, and she wore a black sleeveless shirt with the Martini's logo—a lime-green line drawing of a martini glass tipping sideways and spilling its contents—on the left breast, and Savannah wondered how she wasn't freezing. Julia set the glass down and leaned her forearms on the bar. "Well, your friend here said you like things sweet, that you're a fan of fruity drinks, chocolate, and anything that tastes like dessert."

"My friend is not wrong."

"So I made you a Swedish Bear. It's vodka, some dark crème de cacao, and a tiny splash of cream. I rimmed the glass with cocoa powder and garnished it with a chocolate curl." She stayed where she was, obviously waiting to see what her customer thought.

"A Swedish Bear, huh? This is new to me." Savannah picked up the glass, lifted it to eye level, and admired the presentation. The chocolate curl was the cutest little thing, a spiral of dark sitting on top of the light cocoa color of the liquid. "It's so pretty," she said, and when Julia smiled, Savannah's brain filled in silently, *But not as pretty as you.* Surprised by her own train of thought, she gave herself a mental shake, brought the glass to her lips, and sipped. The cream made the drink smooth, helped the chocolate to coat her tongue, and tempered the vodka. "Oh my God, that's delicious," she said.

"Delicious but strong, so take your time." Julia held her gaze for a beat or two longer than necessary, sending little flutters through Savannah's stomach...and lower. Then she smiled and left to take care of other customers.

"Jesus Christ, she's hot," Tiffany said, suddenly very close to Savannah's ear. "And I don't even swing that way."

"Second thing tonight you haven't been wrong about." Savannah stared after Julia, at that ass in those jeans, and nodded her agreement. Wow.

"You remember Jeanine, right?" Tiffany's voice yanked Savannah's attention away from the hot bartender and back to her and her friends.

She spent the next two and a half hours chatting with the group, laughing and learning about each other. She took Julia's advice and went easy on the drink, only ordering one more and making sure to drink plenty of water along with them. More than once, she'd searched out Julia only to find her looking back. More fluttering. Much as she'd not wanted to come out tonight, she was glad she had.

And she'd be back. Soon.

Chapter Two

S avannah lived for Sundays.

They were, quite literally, her day of rest. No clients. Nowhere to be. In the past, she'd always head over to her parents' house to check on her dad—it amused her how she still called it that, even though her mother had been gone for almost ten years—but not anymore. Not since he'd started dating Dina about six months earlier, and she'd pretty much moved in.

She felt herself grimace, as she seemed to always do whenever Dina came into her thoughts. It was like her body's reflex. Which she understood was a normal, if not nonsensical, reaction to somebody who was standing in the spot where her mother used to stand.

"Let's not think of her on our lovely Sunday, okay?" Jade the jade plant did not answer her, instead waiting patiently and quietly while she filled her pot with new soil.

Houseplants gave Savannah peace. She knew it was corny, that it might make her seem way older than her thirty-four years to some people, but she didn't care. Nothing calmed her more than fresh, cool potting soil between her fingers. The earthy smell of it, the deep black color. It settled her somehow.

Jade had been growing like crazy and really needed more room or she was going to tip over. Savannah had found a beautiful pot that looked worn and weathered but was solid and deep, with raised abstract designs on it and a braided rim. It was perfect for Jade, would give her room to grow, but not too much, as jades could take over a room very quickly, going from jade plant to jade tree before you knew it.

As she settled the root ball into the hole she'd made, then pressed the dirt around the trunk, helping the plant to stay upright, her doorbell rang.

A glance out the front window showed her the tail end of a beat-up red pickup truck, and she stifled a groan. Declan.

A quick rinse of her hands later, she walked to the front door while drying her hands on the dish towel and pulled it open. Her brother stood there, as he had so many times before, in ripped jeans, a gray sweatshirt, and his dirty Carhartt work coat. He was smoothing his hair and bouncing slightly on his feet.

"Hey," he said as he stepped in past her without waiting for an invitation. "If you'd just give me a key, I wouldn't have to stand on the stoop freezing my ass off."

"Dude, you can't be trusted with a key." She spoke frankly, not worrying about hurting his feelings. They were both well past that and had been for a couple years now. And they both knew it.

"Is there coffee?" He continued on into her small kitchen.

"I think there's a little left in the pot."

"Why don't you get one of those Keurigs? They're so much easier. This thing is older than I am." He pulled a mug from her cupboard, filled it with the rest of the coffee, then set the pot back on its burner without turning it off.

"It's not that old," she said, reaching around him to flick the coffee maker off. "And those little K-Cups take up lots of space in landfills. My filters are biodegradable."

"My sister the bleeding heart." Declan shook his head, and his tone was tinted with either disdain or affection, but she wasn't sure which because with Declan, they tended to blur. He didn't add anything to his coffee, sipped it black. "You didn't answer my text last night. Did you miss it?"

"I did," she said and hoped he bought her feigned look of apology. She hadn't missed it. She just didn't want to deal with him. She loved him with all her heart, but he had problems, would likely always have problems, and there were times when she just didn't have the energy. Plus, she'd been preoccupied last night. "I'm sorry. I was out and it was loud, and when I came home, I went right to bed."

He was just as suspicious of her as she was of him. That's how it was when your sibling struggled with addiction, and that was their relationship now. He held her gaze for a beat or two but then shrugged. "Ah, okay. I just needed a little cash."

"Fresh out, I'm afraid," she said. "Used all mine last night." She was lying, of course. She had a little cash, but he wasn't getting it today.

Sometimes, she gave him money. She knew she shouldn't, but he was her little brother, and she was his big sister, and her job was to look out for him, and there were times when he looked so miserable and ill that she gave him what she had just to try to help. Which was the wrong choice, always, and she knew it. But she'd been taking care of him since their mother died when he was sixteen and she was twenty-four. Now that they were each a decade older— and even though she knew better—there were days…

"S'okay." He took another slug of coffee. "Where'd you go?"

"Martini's." She realized too late she should have made something up. Declan clenched his teeth, eyes wide, and she pointed at him. "Don't you tell Dad."

"My lips are sealed. I heard they'd opened up again."

"They remodeled it. You should see it. It's gorgeous." *And so is that brunette bartender with the ass designed by gods and sent from heaven.* She bit down on her bottom lip, surprised by her own thoughts.

"I was gonna say don't make it a habit if you don't want Dad to disown you. But I might check the place out, too." Declan looked around her kitchen, and his blue eyes fell on the plant, the towels, the soil all littering her table. "Playing in the dirt?" he asked, and there was something about the question, the sparkle in his eye, that took Savannah back to when he was little, and she was a teenager and babysitting him while he played in their backyard.

"Yeah. You should've brought your Tonka trucks over."

His face lit up. "Oh my God, remember those? We made that whole thing in the backyard?"

"You called it a quarry," Savannah said with a grin. "You were into construction even then."

"Man, those trucks were cool. Remember the backhoe? How it could actually scoop dirt?"

"And you kept digging holes in the grass, and Dad wanted to kill us both because I was supposed to be watching you."

And just like that, they were young again with nothing between them but sibling love. No suspicions. No addictions. No taking advantage of each other. No asking for money or to be bailed out of financial jams—or jail. Savannah sighed in her head. She missed those times.

Declan finished his coffee. "Okay. Gotta bounce."

"What are you up to today?"

"Not much. Prolly pop in on Gator or Timbo." He gave a nonchalant shrug, as if Savannah didn't know he was going to see if his school buddies could help him score something.

She nodded, not wanting to open a discussion about who he hung out with or what kind of influences they were. They'd had that conversation more times than she could count, and nothing ever changed. "What's Chelsea up to? She texted me yesterday, but I haven't seen her in days."

Another nonchalant shrug. "She spends a lot of time at Parker's or hanging with Dina."

She nodded some more, that familiar pang at Chelsea's friendliness with their dad's girlfriend hitting her in the stomach. Dina seemed to make their dad happy, but she could be…a lot. At least Savannah thought so. "I'll call her later."

"All right. I'm out." Her brother kissed her cheek, set his mug on the counter, and was gone. She stared after him, watched through the front window as his truck backed out of her driveway, and a surge of worry washed through her like it always did when she knew he was headed down that same worn path he'd been strolling since high school.

You'd think I'd be used to this.

That extra weight settled on her shoulders like it always did when she was worried about one of her siblings. Which was very nearly all the time.

The perils of being the big sister and the only mother figure they'd had for a decade.

❖

The Martini family was very big. *Very* big. Julia's grandparents had six children, five boys and one girl, and each of them had multiple children of their own. Most of the original six were less traditional than their parents, which happened as time goes on.

Julia's father was the exception.

Her father, Vinnie, married Anna, who came from another local traditional Italian family, when they were in their midtwenties. Not long after that came Daniel, the first of their five kids. Julia came in third and was the only girl, bookended by two brothers on either side.

Sunday dinner at her parents' house was tradition, and if you were in town, you were expected to show up. Julia wasn't about to keep the bar closed on Sunday, but with the football season over, it likely wouldn't be terribly busy. So she went in, opened it, and got things in order, then left it in what she hoped were the capable hands of Hank D'Angelo. He'd worked at Martini's for nearly twenty years, and he'd known Julia since she was a kid. Letting him go just because he didn't quite fit the new look of the place seemed heartless and cruel, so Julia kept him on. She'd eat quickly and head back as soon as dinner was over. Meanwhile, her brother Daniel lived out of state. Michael, the youngest, was traveling for work. But Julia, her older brother John, and her younger brother Dante were all present, along with John's wife, Sarah, and their two boys, Evan and Noah.

Sarah helped Julia's mother bring the food from the kitchen to the dining room table while Julia sliced a loaf of Italian bread and arranged it on a plate. Sundays were pasta days, and the aroma of her mother's sauce was something that brought her comfort, no matter what. She could feel as stressed as a rubber band stretched to its limit, but the second she walked into her parents' house and was enveloped in the scents of tomatoes and garlic and basil, all her worries melted away, at least for a while.

"I feel like I haven't seen you in ages." Sarah was back and reached for the plate of bread as she smiled at Julia. "I've missed your face."

"Right back atcha," Julia said and kissed Sarah's cheek. She adored her sister-in-law. She was smart, funny, a great mom, and she kept John from getting too big for his britches, as Julia's mom would say. They were an excellent match, and more than once, Julia had caught herself silently wishing for what they had. Of course, she would shake that right off 'cause, seriously, who had the time?

When everybody was seated and the wine had been opened and poured, grace was said, and the family dug in. As always happened once a meal had begun and first bites were taken and chewed, the volume increased. By a lot. Evan and Noah used their forks as lightsabers and tried to start a duel at the table until Sarah grabbed both their wrists and gave them a Mom Look.

"I swear to God, I'll make you eat with your hands," she said. Noah's eye twinkled for a moment, and Julia half expected him to dig in with his fingers, but he apparently thought better of it and apologized to his mom instead. Julia caught his attention and winked at him.

Julia's father and John immediately began talking about the garage where they both worked for Julia's uncle Sonny. Back and forth they went, talking customers and carburetors and a particular Nissan model that gave them endless trouble.

"So, Jules," Dante said from across the table, raising his voice enough to be heard by their dad. "I heard the first night back open went really well."

"It did," Julia said and shot an expression of thanks toward her brother. "We were super busy."

Her dad was listening. She could see him out of the corner of her eye. "Did you have more than all your friends and family there?" he asked, not bothering to hide his skepticism.

"Well, my parents never showed up, so not *all* my friends and family were there." His head snapped up. Their eye contact held as the room got quiet. Julia was the only one in the family who could get away with staring down their father. Taking the edge off her voice, she added, "We got lots of compliments on the new drink menu and the decor. Our first couple of Yelp reviews have been really positive."

Her father gave a grunt and shoved a meatball in his mouth, presumably to keep from making a snide comment.

Julia tipped her head to the side. "You should come by, Pop. I'll give you a free beer." She grinned at him, doing her best to reel things away from tense and back to light and fun.

He opened his mouth but seemed to catch her mother's glare from across the table. "Maybe I'll do that," he said. Julia knew he didn't approve of her running the bar she'd bought from her uncle Tony, but she wasn't quite sure why. That it wasn't something a woman should be doing as far as he was concerned? It was dangerous? Too much riffraff, as he called it? And it didn't matter how many lectures she gave him on sexism or misogyny. He didn't like it, and that was that. Plus, the bar hadn't been doing all that well the past few years when Tony owned it. He'd taken it over from his father, but it was one of his side ventures—he had several—so it had gotten minimal attention.

"I think you'll be impressed," she went on, pushing her luck, she knew. "It looks great. Very sleek and modern, but still with a hometown feel. You should come take a look." She could feel herself losing his interest the longer she spoke.

"She's right, Pop." Dante again, jumping in to help, the way he had since they were kids. "I saw it when the new bar went in last week. Very cool. It doesn't look a thing like when Uncle Tony had it. You won't even recognize it."

Her dad listened, and she was grateful for that. She continued to hold eye contact with him, something others found hard to do because his eyes were so dark, they could be imposing. Intimidating. A little bit scary. He had a big heart, and Julia could wrap him around her finger if she tried—maybe not as easily as she could when she was a little girl, and a little less so since she'd come out, but she could if she worked at it—but he could also be a very hard man.

He made a sound that wasn't much more than another grunt, but it came with a nod, so she tried to classify it as a somewhat positive response. She glanced at her mom, who smiled warmly and gave her a wink, and that helped her relax a bit.

"I couldn't make it last night, but I'll pop in this week," Dante said. "Really looking forward to seeing all the hard work you put into it." She shot him another look of thanks, and he grinned at her, holding up his wine in salute.

An hour later, she was walking through the front door of Martini's. Most of the time, she entered through the back, but there were times when she wanted to see what her customers saw when they walked in. The TVs above the bar were on, tuned to different sporting events. Golf. NASCAR. A tennis match. The bar itself was populated on all sides. Not full, but maybe a dozen people total, plus three of the high-top tables were occupied. Not great, but not empty. It was going to take a while, and March Madness would begin in a few weeks. While she didn't want Martini's to be a sports bar, she also knew she needed to bring people in however she could. If that meant tuning the TVs to college hoops for a couple weeks, that's what she'd do. She was hoping business would kick into high gear then.

Hank was behind the bar in a black T-shirt and leather biker vest, his grizzled face and gray beard not exactly the new look she had in mind for the place, though at least his T-shirt had the Martini's logo on it in bright green, and she tried not to visibly wince. Her plan was to eventually keep Hank behind the scenes somehow, but she couldn't afford to pay an additional bartender on Sundays yet, and if she intended to make it to her parents' for Sunday dinner, it would have to be this way.

She gave Hank a wave and headed to the back to stow her stuff.

Yep, she loved this back room. It was like everything released when she stepped inside. Before she even took her coat off, there was a gentle rap on the door that led to the back parking lot. Surprised, she peeked out the small window to see Vanessa standing there.

"What are you doing here?" Julia asked with a smile as she stepped aside and let her cousin in.

"I had dinner down the street with work friends and walked by on the way to my car. I saw Hank through the window, but your car's in the lot." She hugged Julia tightly. "Hi."

Julia sank into the hug, and when she pulled back, she frowned. "I have to relieve Hank, though."

"Why? You don't want a biker gang to come in?" Vanessa teased.

"Listen, if they drink a lot and pay their tabs, I'm all for it. But he's been here since we opened, so I could have dinner at Mom and Pop's."

"They never showed yesterday?"

Julia shook her head. "I didn't expect them last night when it was super busy, but a pop in during the day to say hi and wish me luck might've been nice."

"I'm surprised your mom didn't come."

Julia was and she wasn't. Her mother spent Saturdays with *her* parents, and her father often worked at the garage during that time. "They were both probably just too tired. I gave him a little crap about it at dinner today, though."

"Well, Amelia and I thought it went really well. It was busy, no fights broke out, and only one glass got broken."

Julia laughed, remembering when Clea lost her grip on a rocks glass and it shattered. "Thank God I paid extra to get the ice bins with the lids."

"Smart. We don't want a repeat of Uncle Tony breaking a glass into the ice and having to empty the entire thing and start from scratch."

"Exactly." Julia put her hands on her hips and gave a nod. "I was happy with things last night. It wasn't a crazy great night, but it wasn't bad. The specials went over well."

"Yeah, what was that drink you made for the cute blonde at the corner of the bar?"

"Ness, there were a hundred people here last night. How am I supposed to remember who got what special?" Julia suddenly felt the need to busy herself with straightening papers on the surface of her desk.

Vanessa snorted. "Please. You know exactly who I mean. She was at the back corner with a couple friends. One had that huge laugh. You couldn't keep your eyes off the blonde—I watched you. And I'm pretty sure she's the only one you made that drink for, so it wasn't a special. At least, not for everyone..." She let the sentence trail off, a knowing smile on her face as she swung her shoulders back and forth. "Come on, tell your favorite cousin. You crushin'?"

Julia couldn't help but laugh at Vanessa's body language. "Stop it. First of all, I love you and Amelia equally, so you can't be my favorite." Another snort from Vanessa as Julia grabbed her waist apron off a hook and tied it over her jeans. "Second, who has time for a crush? I am a very busy business owner, in case you haven't noticed."

"Well, I call bullshit on that. She was super cute, and you, my dear, could use a zap to your love life. That thing's been lying on a gurney in need of the paddles for too long now." Vanessa didn't wait for a response, and for that, Julia was grateful. "All right, I don't want to hold you up, just stopped by to say hi. By the way, this back room needs a name. The Way Back? The Bar Back? The Lounge? Think about it." She kissed Julia's cheek. "Make lots of money."

From your lips to God's ears. She waved Vanessa good-bye and locked the door behind her. It was time to focus on work.

Only now, there was a cute blonde taking up space in her brain, and she couldn't figure out how to shake her. And then, she realized maybe she didn't want to.

CHAPTER THREE

Three weeks later, it was the last week in March, and the weather had finally made the decision to let go of winter and reach for spring. Bright sun paved the way for crocuses and daffodils and other early spring flowers to peek their heads out from the dirt, checking to see if it was time to make an appearance.

That Monday was a short day for Savannah. She took care of Mr. Davidson on Mondays, but he was having a minor procedure, and she'd dropped him off at the hospital at eleven, so the rest of her day was free. She took the opportunity to meet Tiffany for lunch.

Periscope's was their favorite sub shop, and they'd been meeting there for years. Savannah had been the home health aide for Tiffany's grandmother as she was fading from cancer. Even when things changed from having home health care to hospice, Savannah kept stopping by, kept helping. Whenever it seemed like Tiffany needed a break, Savannah would walk her down the street to Periscope's and they would sit, sometimes eat, sometimes just get Diet Cokes, and talk. About anything and everything. After Tiff's grandma passed away, it was simply a given that she and Tiffany would remain friends. That was seven years ago.

"Are you keeping a watchful eye on all the money?" Savannah asked, as she always did. Tiffany had worked at a bank for nearly ten years, moving up rapidly until she was the manager of her branch.

"Always. I keep telling Elena—the money would have a much better time if it came to live at my house, but as my boss, she doesn't seem to agree."

"Shortsighted of her. You look amazing, by the way. Love that suit." Savannah bit into her turkey and avocado sub, then made many humming noises in appreciation, both for the sandwich and for the sharp coral pantsuit Tiffany wore.

"Thanks. It's new." Tiffany looked down at her jacket, then back up at Savannah. "You'd look great in it"—she held up a hand—"and don't say only Black women can wear colors like this." She laughed.

"Listen, that color would wash me out so badly." Savannah laughed, too. Only Black women–only White women was a regular thing between them that made them both laugh.

"You are pretty much the color of milk, it's true."

"It's my natural hue."

"But summer's coming. Maybe you can get enough sun to fix it so you don't look like a corpse."

Savannah feigned insult, added a gasp. "How dare you?"

Tiffany lifted one shoulder in a half shrug and took a bite of her sandwich.

God, Savannah loved this woman. She didn't know what she'd do without Tiffany to make her laugh, watch her back, stand by her side. Sometimes, she couldn't believe they hadn't known each other and been besties for their entire lives. Seven years didn't seem long enough to know as much about each other as they did. Not many people had a friend like that, and she knew it. They held gazes for a beat.

"Love you, weirdo," Tiff said.

"Love you back, nutball."

They spent some time talking about jobs and family. Tiffany's husband, Jonathan, was a financial advisor, and Savannah adored him because he adored Tiffany.

"How goes dating?" Tiffany asked.

Savannah snorted before she could catch herself.

"Are you even trying?" Tiff's voice was gentle, not at all accusatory. "Have you updated your profile at all?"

"I honestly haven't had the time." Savannah stuffed another bite of sandwich into her mouth so she wouldn't have to say more, but Tiffany tipped her head and gave her a knowing look.

"You're a catch, you know."

Another snort from Savannah.

"You turn heads, my friend. You're gonna have to face it." Tiffany sipped her Diet Coke. "Remember the bartender at Martini's? You sure turned her head."

Savannah gave her a dubious look but then said, "I refer to her as the *hot* bartender, thank you very much. I'd appreciate it if you'd get it right."

Tiff's dark eyes went wide. "So you *have* thought about dating. Jesus, I'm relieved."

Savannah laughed. "Shut up. Yes, I think about it. Of course I think about it. I'm not a nun."

"You should go back there."

"Back where?"

"To Martini's. See if she's there again."

"Now?" Savannah's brows went up in surprise.

"No, not now, you loon." Tiffany chewed but looked pensive. "I mean, daytime *would* be way less busy, but…"

Waving a dismissive hand, Savannah said, "I can't. My father has some weird thing about the Martini family. He'd kill me. Plus, I'm not going to a bar in the middle of the day."

"People do it all the time."

"Yeah, alcoholics."

"Okay, Judgy McJudgerson. And what's the deal with your dad?"

Savannah shrugged and shook her head. "I honestly don't know. I guess there's some family feud between McNallys and Martinis? I just know it's always been like that. The name comes up—like, I think one's a lawyer, and whenever his ad comes on TV, my dad will grumble and wave his hand at it and say something that usually ends with *the son of a bitch*. It's just always been safer to steer clear, I guess."

"So you have to avoid a place because your dad didn't like somebody with the same name eons ago?"

"Pretty much, yeah." Savannah grinned, knowing how ridiculous it was, and completely agreeing.

"You White women are so weird."

"Pretty much, yeah."

Tiffany laughed and the conversation went in other directions for the next few minutes until Tiffany looked at the silver watch on her wrist. "Gotta get back," she said, then wiped her mouth with her napkin, opened her purse, and reapplied her lipstick. The same shade as her suit and it looked amazing. Not for the first time, Savannah wished she had half of Tiffany's fashion sense.

They tossed their garbage, bid each other good-bye at the door, and went their separate ways.

It wasn't often Savannah had an afternoon off, and part of her brain wasted no time listing things she should be doing—the list included checking in on her father, texting both siblings, mopping her kitchen floor, and getting some much-needed groceries, not necessarily in that order. What the list didn't include was going into Martini's in the middle of the day, yet she found herself standing at the front door with her hand grasping the handle. *What the hell am I doing?* It was two o'clock on a Monday afternoon. Not at all an appropriate time to be in a bar, though her brother would vehemently disagree. The thought made her chuckle to herself, which she was doing when the door pushed out and almost knocked her down.

"Oh my God, I'm so sorry," said a tall man in khakis and a button-down oxford with a jacket. He had a messenger bag draped over his shoulder, and he reached out to her with one hand, probably to prevent her from falling, and held the door open with the other. "Are you okay?"

Savannah nodded, felt the flush of embarrassment in her cheeks. "I'm fine. Daydreaming is all."

"Daydreaming is underrated if you ask me." His smile was brilliant, his green eyes kind. "Going in?" he asked, and gestured at the doorway with his chin.

I am now. Not much choice now that she'd been standing there in full view of everybody inside. It would be weird if she didn't go in. With a nod, she thanked the man and headed into Martini's.

Wondering if there was some rule in the Bar Owners' Handbook about keeping bars as dim as possible, she had to stand still for a moment so her eyes could adjust from the bright sunlight outside to the low light of the interior. The windows had those dark, sheer blinds that cut the sunshine but still let you see outside, and she blinked rapidly, hating that she was just standing there. On display. As soon as she could make out shapes, she took tentative steps toward the bar, grabbed the first stool she came to, and sat. She would have to order something now. She couldn't not. That would be weird. She looked down at her purse and fished for her wallet.

"Well, hello there."

How was it possible that Savannah knew that voice already? It made zero sense that she would. Last time she was here, it had been loud and crowded, and you had to almost shout to be heard. But every fiber in her body recognized the husky voice of the hot bartender, and she made herself raise her head and look into those deep, dark eyes.

"Hi." A word. Okay. Just one word, but it made sense at least.

"It's great to see you again," Hot Bartender said, and something in her tone made Savannah think she actually meant it.

"I mean, I'm not usually visiting bars at two o'clock on a Monday, but..." She had no idea what to say after that. And also, there were a couple other people seated around that obviously did visit bars at two o'clock on a Monday, and she heard Tiffany calling her judgy and she didn't want that, so... *God, why is it my mouth can only manage one word, but my brain won't shut up?*

"But here you are," Hot Bartender pointed out.

"Here I am."

"Want a drink?"

She hadn't come in to drink. She wasn't much of a day drinker, even when on vacation or during a weekend. But right then? At that moment? When she was hella nervous and couldn't understand why? The thing she needed more than anything in the world was a drink.

"Yes. Please."

They stared at each other, held eye contact for what felt like it could've been hours. Everything about Hot Bartender was, well, *hot*. Her dark, wavy hair was pulled back, the ponytail higher than when she'd seen her last. It made her look younger and cute. But still hot. Her T-shirt was black, a V-neck with that lime green Martini's logo, and it did everything it could to pull Savannah's gaze in the direction of the cleavage that taunted. Forearms on the bar, the bartender tipped her head, her dark eyebrows arched, an amused smile on her glossed lips.

God, so fucking hot.

The words shot through Savannah's head like they were launched from a bow.

"Do you...have a drink in mind? Or do you want me to guess?" Her voice was playful, and when the corners of her mouth lifted in a grin, Savannah almost groaned out loud over a feature she hadn't noticed in the crowded dark of the last time she was there.

No! Not dimples! So unfair.

And then she said words that she had no memory of forming. Or thinking about. Or giving herself permission to say. They just came out all on their own.

"Surprise me."

Julia blinked at the woman. Surprise her, huh?

I can do that.

Despite what she'd told Vanessa, she remembered her, the cute blonde with the shy smile. The one who liked drinks that tasted like dessert. She didn't take the time to analyze why she remembered her so well. She remembered a lot of her customers. It was part of the job, and nothing impressed a person more than when you remembered their favorite drink. But this woman was different. Julia had remembered her for different reasons—she was well aware of that. She tried not to admit the truth: that the woman had *stayed* on her mind, even away from the bar, even weeks later. Julia didn't have crushes. She didn't get obsessed. So the way this woman drew her was...unusual. Alarmingly so.

It took some effort to force herself into action again, but to keep casual about it. "I remember you liked sweet stuff. Are you in the mood for fruity or more dessert-like?"

"You remember that? It was weeks ago."

Julia tapped a finger against her temple. "Steel trap."

The woman propped her elbow on the bar and her chin in her hand. "Well, since it's such a beautiful day out, and you can actually feel spring on its way, let's go with fruity."

A nod. No problem. Julia knew a million fruity drinks, and there was a moment when she almost created one of her own concoctions. But she didn't know this woman's tastes yet, and she didn't want to scare her off. Instead, she rimmed a rocks glass with sugar, combined tequila, a little triple sec, and her homemade sour mix and stirred it up. A splash of lemon-lime soda and a little fresh lemon juice went in last. A lemon wedge on the rim, and she slid it across the bar.

"Lemon drop," she said.

"Oh, perfect choice," the woman said.

Julia tried not to stare, but she'd made it a habit to gauge the reactions of customers to her drinks. It was important to know if they were too strong, too weak, too sour, too bitter. She watched as the woman licked a bit of sugar off the rim—which sent a flutter low through Julia's body that she tried hard to ignore—took a sip, and her eyes closed. A slight pucker of her lips, but that was to be expected from something with lemon juice floating on top.

The woman licked her lips. "Delicious," she declared, and Julia was surprised at her own relief. The woman stuck out her hand. "I'm Savannah."

Julia took her hand, noting the warmth and softness. "Julia. It's nice to meet you, Savannah."

Savannah. A beautiful name. Feminine and pretty. Appropriate for this woman.

A glance over her shoulder told her she was neglecting her other customers, and she gave Savannah what she hoped was an apologetic smile. "Be right back."

Julia popped the caps off two microbrews and slid them to the two guys in suits at the corner of the bar. They'd come in after what she'd gathered from their conversation was a very successful business lunch and wanted to celebrate. Across from them was

Ernie, one of her regulars. He worked a three a.m. to noon shift at his job, came in and drank three Bud Lights, then headed home by three in the afternoon. Daily. Julia wondered about his life, as she slid him number two. One day, she'd ask. Two women walked in then, and while Julia was always grateful for customers, she wanted nothing more than to get back to the lovely Miss Savannah and talk to her some more. Look into those blue eyes of hers. Dream about—
Oh my God, stop it already!

Shaking herself out of fantasyland—a place she rarely visited, by the way—she welcomed the two women who ordered the special of the day. Cosmopolitans.

Julia could make a cosmo in her sleep, but for some reason, on that day in that moment, she took her time. And she knew exactly why because she could feel exactly why. She could *feel* Savannah's eyes on her, watching her, so without even thinking about it, Julia took her time. She got out the glass to her martini shaker, added ice, poured in the vodka, the Cointreau, the cranberry juice. Then she grabbed a fresh lime from a small fridge under the bar, sliced it, and squeezed the juice from one half into the shaker. Then she slapped the metal half onto the glass and shook.

The key to a good martini of any kind was that it was ice cold. Most bartenders didn't shake long enough, so Julia counted in her head, and she swore to all the gods above that thirty seconds never felt so long in her life. She could feel Savannah's eyes not just on her, but roaming over her, following the lines of her body. Up. Down. How was that possible? How did she know? Because she *did* know. She could *feel* it. When she got to twenty-eight in her head, she turned to look, and those blue eyes were locked on hers, sending ripples of arousal throughout Julia's body as if she'd been injected with it.

Swallowing was hard, but she did it, hoping her face hadn't flushed as red as she felt it had. She strained the drinks into glasses and presented them in all their happy pink glory to her customers. Then she quickly rinsed out her equipment, gave a look around to be sure nobody else needed anything, and returned to Savannah.

"Doing okay over here?"

"I am," Savannah said, licked the rim, took a sip. She gestured to the women with her chin. "That was impressive. The drinks."

Julia shrugged. "Just a cosmo."

"Still."

Okay, yeah, there's definitely something here. The eye contact, the quiet tones, the flirting. What was it about this woman that had Julia feeling so off-balance? Because that's exactly how she felt. Off-balance. Like the floor had tilted just a bit.

But in the most delicious of ways.

She leaned on the bar and tipped her head, was trying to come up with something super flirty and sexy to say, when the front door opened, and Jason Childers, one of her liquor distributors, walked in.

"Hey, Jules, how's business?" Jason was the kind of guy who drew everybody's attention with his booming voice and gregarious personality. He was nice to everybody, and in turn, everybody liked him. He walked right up to the bar and held out his hand to her. Dressed in khakis and a green polo shirt with the logo for his company embroidered on the left chest, he held a tablet in his other hand.

"It's not bad," she said, automatically shifting her brain back into business mode. "I've got a few ideas I'd like to run by you. See what you have that might match up."

"That's what I'm here for."

"Great. Let's set up at this table over here." She lifted a hidden panel at the back of the bar and let herself out, then led Jason to a table in the corner. "Clea's in the back and will take over in a few minutes, and we can talk. Something to drink?"

"A Diet Coke would be great," Jason said as he took a seat and set down his tablet.

"You got it." Julia ran into Clea as she turned.

"Ready for me?" her bartender asked, bleached-blond hair in a fun swoop over her left eye.

"I am. Just let me get a Coke for Jason." Back behind the bar, Julia turned her gaze to the spot where Savannah was. Or had been, rather. She tried not to sigh in disappointment at the vacated stool, a twenty-dollar bill tucked under her empty glass. Work had taken precedence over a sexy, interesting woman. Again. Julia sighed as she filled a glass with ice, then Diet Coke.

Story of my fucking life.

❖

Staying open late on a Monday night had yet to prove lucrative, so when nine o'clock rolled around and there were two customers, Julia announced last call and then closed up. Then she sent a text off to Vanessa and Amelia and told them to come on over and hang with her if they wanted—she'd left the side door unlocked.

By the time she locked up the front, put the fruit away, loaded the dishwasher, and mopped the floor, her cousins had already arrived and made themselves at home on her couch in the back.

"You guys are a sight for sore eyes," she said with a warm smile. She kissed both cousins on her way by. "Anybody need anything?" she asked from behind the practice bar.

"I'm good," Vanessa said. "I can't stay long. It's a school night."

Amelia chuckled. "Most people use that as a saying. For you, it's actually true. How are the fourth graders of the world, anyway?"

"Oh, you know. Sweet. Loud. Adorable. Obnoxious. Minds like sponges. And also, very ready for spring break." Vanessa was dressed in black joggers, a gray hoodie, white sneakers. She crossed her feet at the ankle and propped them on the coffee table. "I'm putting my feet on your furniture. Don't try to stop me. You can't."

"Put your feet wherever you want. I'm just happy you're here." Julia grinned as she poured herself a glass of wine. She never drank during a shift or while she was working. "I've been waiting for this since about six," she said. She held the bottle up for Amelia to see and raised her eyebrows in question.

Amelia held her thumb and finger close together. "Just a smidge. I've got a headache threatening and don't want to make it worse. Perimenopause is—"

"Is killing you," both Julia and Vanessa said along with her, then laughed.

"Shut up. You both suck." Amelia folded her arms and pouted.

Julia grabbed a bottle of water out of the fridge, poured a smidge of wine for Amelia, and joined her cousins. She handed the water to Vanessa, then flopped into a chair with her wine and a relieved sigh.

"Busy today?" Amelia asked as she sipped the wine.

Julia lifted a shoulder. "Meh. I mean, it wasn't awful. It wasn't dead. I had some folks in the afternoon and into the evening, but it cleared out pretty quickly. I sent Clea home early."

"It's Monday," Amelia pointed out. "You reopened less than a month ago. You've gotta give it some time."

Julia hoped she was right because the bar would never survive with too many nights like this. Already.

"And we need to come up with some fun ways to bring people in," Vanessa added. She sat up, her eyes suddenly bright.

"Uh-oh. I can almost hear the wheels in your head cranking," Julia said.

"The teacher brain has switched into project mode," Amelia said with a laugh. "Take cover."

"You could do contests," Vanessa said, as if she hadn't heard them. She ticked each idea off on a finger. "Theme nights. A cocktail of the day instead of just occasional specials. Giveaways…"

While Julia already had a file on her computer of ideas a lot like these and just hadn't managed to find time to implement them yet, she very much enjoyed watching Vanessa brainstorm. Plus, she was too tired to do anything but sit there and grin.

"What kind of a crowd did you get today?" Amelia asked once Vanessa had quieted, then took a slug of her water. "Like, what kind of people?"

Julia pursed her lips as she thought. "There were a couple small groups that seemed like work friends. A couple guys who'd closed a deal and were celebrating. Ernie."

"Aww, Ernie," Vanessa said, her voice gentle. He'd been coming to Martini's since the girls were young.

"Ernie's still alive?" Amelia asked, disbelief clear on her face.

"He is. Oh, and that girl from opening night came by." Julia tried to remain casual about it because she hadn't meant to mention Savannah, but her mouth apparently had a mind of its own now.

Right on cue, Vanessa sat up and her eyes snapped in Julia's direction. "The blonde? That adorable blonde with the adorable smile that you made a drink for that had an adorable name?"

"That's a lot of adorable for me to have missed out on," Amelia said. "Fill me in?"

"Is that the one?" Vanessa asked. At Julia's reluctant nod, Vanessa turned to Amelia. "She was here with her friends that first Saturday night. I think you'd just left. Anyway, our beautiful cousin here made her a special drink based on the things the blonde's friend said she liked." She turned to Julia, and her face was flushed with excitement, the way it always got when Vanessa told a story. "What was it? A fuzzy teddy bear?"

Julia laughed through her nose and shook her head. "A Swedish Bear."

"Oh my God, that *is* adorable," Amelia said. She looked from Julia to Vanessa. "And?"

"And there was some serious flirting happening," Vanessa finished.

"There was not." Julia narrowed her eyes.

"Oh, there was, my friend. There absolutely was. She was into you. And as a person who has known you for nearly your entire life, I can safely say the feeling was mutual." As if finishing a race, Vanessa flopped back against the couch and released a breath. Like she was exhausted.

"You are such a drama queen," Julia said.

Pointing a finger at Amelia, Vanessa said, "Notice she didn't deny it."

"I *did* notice that," Amelia agreed. "Zero denying. And she came in tonight?"

Julia nodded. "This afternoon, actually."

"With friends?" Vanessa this time.

"Alone."

Vanessa and Amelia exchanged wide-eyed glances.

"Stop that," Julia whined at them. "Stop the looking at each other like you know something."

"But we *do* know something," Vanessa said.

"We know she came to see you," Amelia said.

"I don't know about that." Julia shrugged. Actually, she was pretty sure she *did* know about that, but she didn't want to dwell on it, just in case.

"Did she order the bear again?" Vanessa asked.

"Nope. Something different."

"What?" Both cousins sat forward on the couch, and Julia shook her head with affection.

She let a beat go by. Another. Finally, she said, "She told me to surprise her."

Her cousins slowly turned to look at each other, eyebrows raised.

"She told Julia to surprise her." Amelia's tone was matter-of-fact.

Vanessa nodded. "That's, like, Flirting 101, right?"

"I mean, I've been out of the game for a while, but even *I* recognize that as flirting," Amelia admitted.

As if her cousins were choreographed, they both turned their heads to look at Julia. "Did you flirt back?" Vanessa asked.

With a sigh, Julia accepted that she couldn't not answer the questions or her cousins would never leave it alone. "I did a little, yes." Warmth crawled up her neck as she remembered leaning on the bar so she could get closer to Savannah, who had smelled like sunshine, impossible as that sounded.

Vanessa dropped her head back and said loudly to the ceiling, as she comically shook her fist in the air, "I can't believe I wasn't here to witness this!"

"How long did she stay?" Amelia asked. "What did you talk about?"

Julia finished her wine and stood. Brought her empty glass to the sink behind the practice bar. "I mean, Jason came in to take my order, so I had to deal with him. She was gone after that." She kept her voice casual, nonchalant, because she knew what was coming.

"What?" Vanessa said.

"You didn't say good-bye to her?" Amelia.

"Or better yet, ask her to wait until you finished with Jason?" Vanessa's voice held both disbelief and disappointment. It was hard for Julia to swallow either, so instead, she hung her head and winced.

"I know. I should have. I just…" She couldn't find the words. Or, rather, didn't want to say them. So Amelia said them for her.

"You picked work over the girl. Like always."

"Ouch." Julia flinched, even though the dig wasn't unexpected. And it wasn't wrong. Still, it stung, and Vanessa shot Amelia a look.

"She didn't mean it quite so…bluntly," Vanessa said, her tone laced with apology. Amelia shrugged.

"No, she's right." Julia lifted her arms and let them drop to her sides. "It's probably better this way, though. I don't have time for dating."

Both of her cousins groaned and rolled their eyes simultaneously. It was like they were twins, mirror images of each other.

"Do you even get how you're the most predictable person on the planet?" Amelia asked.

Vanessa put a hand on Amelia's arm. "What she means is that you always say that, and maybe it's time to…" She pursed her lips, squinted her blue eyes. "Not say that."

Amelia snorted. "Well put."

That made Julia internally laugh because she wasn't the only predictable one. Amelia bluntly said what she thought, and then Vanessa followed behind her and sprinkled sugar over any of the words that might be a little bitter. It was their dynamic, and despite her own discomfort over the situation, her heart still warmed. Her cousins were more like sisters to her, and she absently wondered if Savannah would like them. And then she wondered if they would like her. And then she told her brain to shut the hell up and stop being ridiculous. Predictable as she might be, the facts didn't change.

She didn't have time to date.

Chapter Four

"There's my girl."

Her father's face lit up at the sight of her, and Savannah would never tire of that. She set down her purse, slipped out of her jacket, and stepped into his arms. He smelled like coffee and Stetson, the cologne he'd worn ever since she could remember. Her mother had given it to him for Christmas one year, and he'd never worn anything else.

"I can't stay long. Mrs. Richter awaits." She set down the box of doughnuts she'd brought and opened it up. "Is there coffee?"

"Is there coffee." Her father snorted as he sat at the round kitchen table, because it was a very silly question. In his house, there was always coffee. He drank it all day long.

"You're switching over to decaf in the afternoon, right?" She shot him a look as she poured herself a cup from the Mr. Coffee machine that had been around for at least fifteen years.

Her father waved a dismissive hand. "Yes, *dear*, I am. I hate it, but I'm getting used to it." He was having a good day—she could tell. There were also days when she knew he was struggling. Forgetting things, quick to anger, confusion. The early signs of dementia.

"Good. Your heart will thank you." Savannah took a seat across from him. "And so will I. I want you around for a long time." The *longer than Mom* was unspoken between the two of them. She had just opened her mouth to ask him what was new when a voice cut through the air.

"Kevin McNally, what is that in your hand?" Around the corner and into the kitchen breezed Dina Hartman, her father's new girlfriend. Well, new-*ish*. Savannah was doing her best to accept Dina, her big personality, and the sheer *volume* of her, because she seemed to make Savannah's dad happy. But wow, she was a lot. "Give me that," she said, and Savannah watched as Dina took the cruller from her dad's hand and set it back in the box.

Her father looked crestfallen, like a child who'd just had his candy bar taken from him, but he said nothing.

"You know those are bad for you. Here." Dina grabbed an apple from the fruit bowl on the counter and handed it to him. Then she closed the doughnut box and slid it in Savannah's direction. "I know you mean well, honey, but he can't be eating stuff like that."

I know him way better than you do.

One doughnut isn't going to kill him.

He's a grown man, not a child, you know.

All three replies zipped through Savannah's head, but one look at her father—how he shrugged and bit into his apple, then looked up at Dina with soft eyes—made her keep her lips clamped shut. *He's happy, he's happy, he's happy...*

More and more often lately, she'd found herself chanting the mantra in her head. Dina couldn't be more opposite of her mother if she'd tried, and it baffled Savannah what her father saw in the woman. But as Tiffany often reminded her, it didn't matter if she couldn't see it. Her father was the one who mattered. And as long as Dina made him happy, Savannah would keep her mouth shut.

Declan was next into the kitchen, dressed in jeans that needed washing and an inside-out T-shirt. He had dark circles under his eyes, and his hair was a matted mess.

"Looks like your hamper and the covers ganged up on you," Savannah said.

Declan ran a hand self-consciously through his hair, then poured a cup of coffee. Spying the box of doughnuts, he helped himself. "Dad," he said with a bite in his mouth, "there's crullers." Like Savannah, he knew they were their dad's favorites.

"His cholesterol is high enough without a cruller," Dina said, sipping from the mug of tea she'd poured.

As Declan opened his mouth, probably to say something rude, he caught Savannah's eye and snapped it closed again. Then he sighed loudly, took his doughnut and coffee, and headed back upstairs to his room.

"Honestly, Kevin," Dina said quietly. "He's twenty-six. He should have his own place by now."

"I'm sitting right here—you realize that, right?" The words were out before Savannah even realized she was going to say them, and while a large part of her wished she could snatch them out of the air and stuff them back into her mouth, the look of wide-eyed surprise on Dina's face was more satisfying than it probably should've been.

It was a good time to haul ass out of there, so Savannah stood, rinsed her mug in the sink, and put it in the dishwasher. Then she grabbed her jacket and purse, kissed her father good-bye, and took her doughnuts with her. Mrs. Richter would probably love a cruller.

She never looked at Dina once.

By early afternoon, Mrs. Richter was napping, and Savannah had done some light cleaning—took care of dishes, dusted the living room. She'd brought a book and had some email to answer, which she was allowed to do if her client was sleeping, but it felt good to be up and doing things, moving. It was mid-April, and spring was in the air. The sun was bright, the sky was blue, and by eleven that morning, she hadn't needed a jacket. She decided she'd take Mrs. Richter for a walk once she woke up.

She was putting away the dust cloth and furniture polish when her phone pinged. A text from Tiffany, who finally had the time to respond to Savannah's tirade of typed words after leaving her dad's that morning. Lots of emoji. Lots of exclamation points. Lots of frustration with Dina. Tiffany knew all about it.

First things first, Tiff's text began. *Did you eat all the doughnuts in anger? Cuz I would've.* Her words were followed by sixteen doughnut emoji and one pig.

Savannah laughed as she dropped onto Mrs. Richter's sofa, which was probably older than Savannah, judging by how far down she sank into it. *I only ate two. So far…* She also added a pig.

I mean, the day is young.

Savannah typed back, *Don't tempt me. Sigh. I wish she didn't make me grind my teeth. I get that she's trying to keep him healthy, but sometimes, it's like she's his mother rather than his girlfriend. He eats it up.* She grimaced and added, *Unless it's a doughnut.*

Laughing emoji followed. *I see what you did there.*

Savannah sat for a moment, quiet, and let the emotion come. There was a time when she'd tried to shut it out, block it off. But she'd learned. Slowly. She swallowed hard and typed.

I miss my mom.

Tiffany was about the only person she ever let her guard down with, the one who'd heard that line the most. *I know you do, kiddo,* came her reply. Several heart emoji followed it, and then a few beats went by. Savannah set her phone down and gazed out Mrs. Richter's front window at the birds flitting around, apparently happy about spring. She made a mental note to ask her if she wanted the bird feeder filled up before she left, and her phone pinged. More from Tiffany.

You done at 4? Let's go out for happy hour.

Some time to just chill with Tiffany sounded way better than pretty much anything else in that moment. *Okay.*

Tiffany's next text came immediately, like she'd typed it and was just waiting for confirmation that Savannah agreed before hitting Send. *I'll meet you at Martini's. Family feud be damned!*

She stared at the phone, sitting with the mix of delight and dread that washed through her. The dread made her angry. She was a grown-ass woman, for Christ's sake. She could go where she wanted to go, despite what her father thought. And she was going to keep Tiffany company, not in hopes of seeing Hot Bartender. "Ugh," she groaned. "Julia. Her name is Julia. Call her that." She heard some shuffling, Mrs. Richter waking from her nap, and Savannah grinned as she pushed herself off the couch and muttered, "Okay, but in my head, she's still Hot Bartender."

❖

Thursdays were the new Fridays. Or some such weirdness. That's what Julia had seen mentioned online in a couple of the bar owners' groups she'd joined when she bought Martini's. It was a good way to stay up-to-date in the ever-changing world of hospitality and also helped her to feel validated when dealing with a speed bump she was sure nobody else understood.

She'd shifted the schedule a bit, and Clea now worked Thursday through Saturday. Julia helped out when needed, but it was nice to be able to meet with distributors uninterrupted or even practice some new mixology in the back and not have to worry about waiting on customers. She was hoping to hire a couple more part-timers in the next few months if business got steady.

On this Thursday at a little after four in the afternoon, Julia came out from the back after doing some ordering and was thrilled to see nearly twenty-five customers. And thank freaking God, because the previous three days had been disappointingly quiet, which she was trying hard not to dwell on. Now, customers sat at the bar. Some were at the high-tops. One table for four was full, three men in suits with pilsner glasses of a new microbrew on the table. Clea was mixing a rum and Coke as she chatted with two older gentlemen at the bar. They were charmed by her. Julia could tell. It was part of why she'd hired Clea. She was young, but not immature. She was cute—sexy, even—but not in a way that seemed inappropriate. And she was smart. She knew how to mix drinks. She knew how to make a customer smile. She did nicely in the tip department and was always up for learning new drinks. Julia had spent the money to send her to mixology classes, and every so often, Clea would pull out a trick she'd learned or make a super fancy drink—for entertainment value as much as the taste of the drink itself—fond of concoctions where she could throw bottles around or light something on fire. She was a find, Julia knew it, and she paid her well to keep her from looking for a better offer.

"Hey," she said as she joined Clea behind the bar. "Good crowd."

Clea bobbed her white-blond head, and the diamond stud in her nose caught the light just right, sparkled. "A pretty good Thursday afternoon so far."

They settled into an easy working partnership, taking orders, mixing drinks, sidling past each other without getting in each other's way.

"You the drink maker?" a woman asked as Julia was wiping down the bar next to her.

"I am." Julia looked up at her with a smile. The woman was glamorous—it was the first word that popped into Julia's head. She was blond, her hair in a complicated twist that Julia wouldn't dream of trying to replicate. She wore a dark blazer with an open-collared white shirt underneath. Her wrist glittered in the overhead canister lighting. "That's a beautiful piece," Julia said, indicating the bracelet with her chin.

The woman seemed to light up. Her eyes were a unique green and they sparkled a bit. She sat up a little straighter. "Hey, thanks." She looked down at the bracelet. "A gift for myself."

"What can I get you? Another sauv blanc?"

The woman pursed her lips. "Can you make me something... fancy?"

"I can try," Julia said with a smile. She loved to make unusual drinks. "Do you have something in mind? What do you like?"

"I like gin."

"Nice. Not a lot of people do. Hmm." Julia tapped her finger against her lips as she ran through her mental catalog of drinks. "Have you had a Negroni before? They've become very popular recently."

"I've heard of it but have never had one." The woman finished her wine and slid her empty glass away. "Sold."

Julia went to work. She filled a rocks glass with ice, then set it on the bar in front of the woman. Customers liked it when they could watch you make their drink, and mixology was as much entertainment as it was serving. A little dry vermouth was first. A little gin. A little Campari.

"What's that?" the woman asked.

"Campari? It's an Italian aperitif. It's considered a bitter."

The woman nodded as Julia combined everything in the glass and gave a lemon peel a twist over the top, then dropped it in. She slid the drink to the woman with a smile as the front door opened, letting the bright sunlight in for a moment.

Julia turned to greet the customers walking in and her heart skipped a beat. Or five.

Savannah.

The smile spread across Julia's face as if she had no control over it. She could feel it happening, hoped she didn't look like too much of a dorky idiot.

"Hey. I like this." The woman. The Negroni. Right.

"Yeah? I'm so glad." Then she excused herself so she could get to Savannah before Clea did.

She wasn't alone. She sat at the bar with a very pretty African American woman, and Julia remembered her from Savannah's first visit. The one who'd told her what Savannah liked. The question about whether she might be Savannah's girlfriend danced around in Julia's head before she could stop it. *So what if she is?*

"Hi again," Savannah said, her voice soft, her eye contact instant and intense. "I wasn't sure if you'd be working."

"I'm always working," Julia said with a laugh. "I'm glad you're back."

"Me, too."

And then there was a moment. Maybe two. The eye contact held, and for those few seconds, there was nobody else in the bar but the two of them. Julia felt that telltale flutter in the pit of her stomach. Okay, maybe a little lower than her stomach. Sure, she'd been turned on by many women in her life, but never this intensely. Or this instantly. It was unnerving. In a very good way.

"Hi, I'm Tiffany," the other woman said and stuck out her hand. "Since Savannah is apparently not going to introduce us."

"Oh my God, I'm sorry," Savannah said, wrinkling her nose adorably as Julia shook hands with Tiffany.

"I remember you from a few weeks ago. Good to see you again. What can I get you ladies?"

"Well, Julia," Tiffany said, "it's been a day. And it seems silly to be in a place called Martini's and not take advantage. We will have two very, very dirty martinis, please."

"Gin or vodka?"

"Vodka," Tiffany answered, then looked to Savannah, who nodded.

It took a very conscious effort on Julia's part not to glance back at them several times as she mixed the drinks. She could see their heads lean toward each other in her peripheral vision, and she wanted so badly to turn and watch, because she was pretty sure she could feel eyes on her, just like the last time. Were they Savannah's? Again, she wondered if Tiffany was her girlfriend, but decided it wasn't likely. Not the way Savannah talked to Julia. Not the way she looked at her.

Stop it.

She slapped the shaker onto the glass and shook the martini with ice. Once more, the question ran through her head—where in the world could she fit in a relationship? She was way too busy with the bar. And she could almost hear Vanessa snorting a laugh at how ridiculous a statement that was, but it was true. She spent the majority of her day at the bar, and by the time she got home to her tiny apartment, she was exhausted. Half the time, she ended up crashing on the couch in the back, then sneaking home in the early morning hours to shower, not that she'd tell her cousins that.

She strained the drinks into the glasses and ventured a glance in the women's direction as she stabbed olives with the drink picks. Those blue eyes were trained right on her, following her every move. Savannah, chin in her hand, elbow on the bar, like she had all the time in the world to watch Julia work.

More fluttering. Low—very low—in her body. Julia swallowed down the lump of arousal, picked up the glasses, and delivered them to her customers.

"Super extra dirty," she said, meeting Savannah's eyes. She had a hard time pulling away as Savannah and Tiffany took tandem sips. Savannah closed her eyes, and Julia was almost swept away by the dreamy look on her face until a voice sounded behind her.

"Can I get another one of these?" Julia glanced over her shoulder. It was the Negroni woman. And she was loud. Julia watched as Clea approached her, but the woman waved her off and pointed to Julia.

"Excuse me," she said, and returned to the woman, making sure to smile. "You liked it, huh?" As she reached for the empty glass, the woman laid an expertly manicured hand on her arm.

"I don't believe we've been properly introduced." She stuck out her other hand. "Chris Norton."

Julia shook her hand. "Julia Martini. It's nice to meet you, Chris. Thanks for your business." Chris held on a bit longer than necessary. Not that Julia wasn't used to getting hit on—it came with the territory when you worked in the bar industry. But it was never not uncomfortable.

Chris let go and asked, "Your family own the place?"

"I own the place." Julia went to work on the drink.

"Seriously? Very cool. I feel bad I didn't think that first. What kind of feminist am I, right?"

Julia lifted a shoulder in a nonchalant half shrug. "Happens all the time." And it did. "No worries." She turned to check on Savannah and Tiffany. Or just Savannah. More eye contact. That smile.

"So, the hardest part about owning a bar?"

Julia swallowed a sigh and kept herself from groaning. *Be gracious. This is a paying customer.* She leaned on the bar and did her best to give Chris her full attention.

"I think you should ask her out." Tiffany said it so matter-of-factly that Savannah just blinked at her for a moment.

"I hardly know her," was the only excuse she could come up with.

"Then I think you should get to know her."

"And how do you suggest I do that exactly?"

"By asking her out. Duh."

If she was being honest, Savannah had actually thought about the same thing, that she'd really like to get to know this woman. "Does she even play on my team? How fun it would be for me if she did not."

Tiffany laughed. "Listen, I can't help you there. Don't you people have some kind of sonar in your brains or something that helps you find each other?"

Savannah almost choked on her mouthful of martini as the laugh shot out of her. "First of all, sonar? We're not dolphins. I think you're referring to gaydar, but I honestly like the sonar thing much better."

"Good. Take that back to Gay Headquarters and pitch it to them. Make sure you give me credit."

"My gaydar has never been all that accurate, to be honest, but..." Savannah shook her head.

"I mean, you saw the way she looked at you, right?"

Savannah met Tiffany's eyes, smiled, and gave a subtle nod. Oh yeah. She'd seen it.

"Sweetie, my hair could've been on fire, and she wouldn't have noticed. She was all about you. And I'm not even mad about it."

"You are, though." Savannah sipped her drink and looked at Tiffany over the rim of the glass. "You're a little mad."

"Fine. Just a little. Shut up." Tiffany grinned big. "My point is, you shouldn't let an opportunity like that pass you by." She lowered her voice to a conspiratorial volume. "I'm not sure if you noticed, but that woman is *fucking hot*. The dark eyes. All that hair. That husky voice. The *dimples*."

"God, the dimples, right?" Savannah dropped her head back and groaned.

Tiffany's face grew suddenly serious, and her eyes darted away, as they always did when she was about to say something important or heartfelt. "You've been alone for a while now, caring for everybody else. Why not have a little fun? A little time for Savannah?"

As soon as the words hit Savannah's ears, her brain began to list all the people she needed to pay attention to. Her father. Her brother. Her sister. Mrs. Richter. Mr. Davidson. Mr. Kellogg. Tiffany was right—she did take care of a lot of other people. So how in the world was she supposed to focus on Julia, on the *possibility* of Julia, when she now had all these other responsibilities in her head.

Damn.

And then she watched Julia as she pushed away from the bar, from the super attractive businesswoman who'd been taking up a lot of her time—and looked seriously bummed that Julia had left her, by the way—and took an order from a couple at the corner of the bar. Julia's dark hair was a mass of curls and pulled back in that low ponytail, and Savannah had sudden visions of taking it down, digging her fingers into it, feeling its weight, its thickness, its softness. The jeans were once again working for Savannah, showing off an ass that was high and round, and Savannah suddenly itched to grab herself two handfuls of that in addition to the hair. *Man, lots of grabbing going on in this head.* The black polo shirt hugged Julia's torso nicely, and when she turned around so she was facing them, Savannah couldn't keep her eyes from wandering down, stopping on Julia's breasts, wondering if they'd fill her hands as nicely as her ass would. *More grabbing.* With a hard swallow, she dragged her gaze back up...and met Julia's amused face.

"Busted," Tiffany whispered as Savannah swore softly.

But Julia did something unexpected then. She winked.

Actually winked.

"Um, yeah, she totally plays on your team. Solved it." Tiffany sounded way too satisfied with herself as she finished off her martini and slid the empty glass to the inner edge of the bar.

"She totally plays on my team," Savannah agreed, her entire body flushed with heat, and not from the alcohol.

She set her glass down, picked up the stick with the olives, and pulled one off with her teeth, chewed it as she watched Julia work. When Julia approached them to see if they wanted refills, her eyes locked with Savannah's. Deep. Intense.

Oh yeah, she wanted to get to know this woman. Maybe not here, maybe not tonight, but soon.

Very soon.

CHAPTER FIVE

Julia wouldn't leave her head.

Or her body, apparently, judging by the flutters and pangs of arousal that coursed through Savannah most of Friday morning and well into the afternoon. It was like Julia had taken up residence. Packed up her things and moved right in, setting up in a corner of Savannah's brain and making herself at home there.

Savannah's fantasy life was evidently way richer than she'd thought, as she'd had lots and lots of visions of doing very naughty things with Hot Bartender in a multitude of locations. In bed—of course, on her couch—duh, in the car—interesting, on the kitchen counter—that was new, on Mr. Davidson's couch...

Hold up.

Savannah shook her head. No, she did not need to be thinking about sex stuff in the house of a sweet widower that wanted her to read his John Grisham library book to him.

Stop that right this second.

Her brain only half agreed. The fantasies kept playing in her head, but at least she and Julia were back in her bed. Whew.

She spent an hour reading to Mr. Davidson as he relaxed in his favorite recliner. On the verge of falling asleep, he made an obvious effort to keep listening but eventually succumbed. Savannah put the bookmark in and closed the novel, then took a moment to just watch him. He reminded her of her great-grandfather who'd passed away when she was just a kid. His snowy white hair, the soft, papery skin on his hands—she remembered being fascinated by that skin. She'd loved to sit in his lap and rub the back of his hand, let her small fingertips follow the blue lines of his veins. She didn't remember a lot of detail about him, just that one, and that he was very kind. He had soft, friendly eyes. Mr. Davidson was a lot like that, and she wished he wasn't alone. Before she started worrying about him and how his kids never called or visited him, she heard a car door slam outside, and she knew her relief had arrived. She did a little internal dance because that meant she got to leave soon, and she had a plan. Oh, did she have a plan.

She gathered her things and gave her replacement a rundown on how the day had gone, what Mr. Davidson ate, when he'd slept, and what medications he'd had. On her way to her car, her phone pinged a text. Tiffany.

Wanted u to know I'm thinking about u. And if she says no, no big deal. At least you'll know. Alternating smileys and hearts followed the words.

That was a lot of nos. She sent the text with a kiss-blowing emoji, plugged the phone into the car, and started it.

Just a quick stop. That's all it was going to be. Pop into Martini's. Ask Julia if she'd have dinner with her sometime. Pop back out, no matter the answer.

Except Savannah had never asked anybody out before.

A sobering thought. She'd always been asked, which she hadn't realized until the previous night when she'd made the decision with Tiffany's help—or prodding, which was a more accurate description. But she was going to do it. The way she was drawn to Julia? That thing that literally felt like some kind of magnetic pull? She'd never felt that before, and Tiffany was adamant that it meant something, that she shouldn't ignore it. According to Tiff, the Universe was trying to tell her something.

But the Universe wasn't always kind. Savannah knew *that* from experience.

She gave her head a quick shake, sending that thought away. No, she wasn't going down that road. She was happy. Excited. And she was going to hold on to that.

It wasn't a long drive. Maybe twenty minutes. The parking lot had plenty of open spaces, which was good for Savannah, but maybe not so good for the bar itself.

A quick fold-down of the visor, and she was examining her hair, gave it a pat, a fluff, brushed a couple of baby hairs back into place. She usually put it in a ponytail for work to keep it out of the way, but she'd worn it down today because she knew she was stopping in at Martini's right from work—if she'd gone home to change and primp, that would've given her too much time to talk herself out of what she was about to do. She knew herself pretty well, so she'd removed that possibility altogether, dressed in nice jeans and a cute, lightweight yellow sweater, worn a little extra makeup that she touched up now, left her blond hair down, and gone to work.

And now work was over, and it was time.

It was time.

"You got this," she whispered to her reflection. A nod. A big inhale. A loud exhale.

Savannah got out of her car and headed inside.

Martini's was its usual bar-interior dim, and she stood inside the door as it closed quietly behind her, waiting for her eyes to adjust. Walking into a bar alone wasn't her favorite thing to do because everybody turned to see who was coming in, and Martini's was no different. Only a handful of people sat at the bar, but they all turned to look at Savannah, and she felt the heat crawl up her neck. Her ears were probably red. Terrific. Such a good look, those flaming ears.

Forcing herself to keep her head up rather than watching the floor as she walked toward the bar wasn't easy, but she remembered Tiff's pep talk from the previous night about being confident, and she did her best to focus on the words. Before she could take a step, though, a voice called out to her.

"Well, aren't you a sight for sore eyes."

Across the dark floor of the bar, not so far away at all, stood Julia. Behind the bar, hands on its surface and a white rag under one of them, bracing herself as she leaned slightly forward. Smile on her face and the slightest twinkle in her eye.

The surge of confidence that seeing Julia gave her took Savannah by complete and utter surprise. Like she'd gotten a shot of adrenaline and it rushed through her bloodstream. With quick steps, she crossed the floor and stopped in front of Julia. She didn't sit, and that made their height difference a bit more obvious, Julia with an advantage of a good three or four inches.

"Hi," Julia said, that smile in place, those dimples on display. She looked genuinely happy to see her. "You look amazing. I love that color on you."

Savannah's ears got hotter, and she was thankful her hair was down to, hopefully, cover them, at least a little. "Thank you. So do you."

Julia looked down at herself and laughed through her nose. "I'm wearing the same thing every time you see me."

"You wear it very well."

"Well, thanks." Was it Julia that was blushing now? It was hard to tell in the dim lighting, but Savannah was pretty sure Julia's cheeks had tinted pink. She could see it even on the olive tone of her skin.

Okay. Get to it. In and out.

"Listen, I can't stay—" Savannah began.

"That's a shame," Julia said, and one hip jutted to the side as— Was that a pout? Was she actually pouting a little?

"But I wanted to ask you something." She was interrupted by the ringing of her phone and closed her eyes in embarrassment. "Sorry." She pulled the phone out from her back pocket, saw Chelsea's name on the screen, and declined the call. "My sister," she said to Julia in explanation. "I wanted to ask you…and it's totally okay if you say no. No pressure. No hard feelings—"

The phone rang again.

"Dammit," Savannah muttered. Chelsea again. Declined again. "I'm so sorry." She set the phone on the bar, determined to give Julia her full focus. She puffed out a small breath, looked into those deep, dark eyes, and almost let herself get lost in them before remembering what she was doing. "Would you be at all interested in having dinner with me sometime?" Her phone pinged. A text this time. Savannah closed her eyes again but didn't check the screen. "Or it doesn't have to be dinner. Lunch? Coffee?" She waited as Julia continued to stand there. Continued to hold her gaze. Continued to smile.

The phone pinged again. And again. Both she and Julia looked down at it. Three texts in a row from Chelsea.

Answer your phone

Where are u?

I need u NOW

"Two things," Julia said, pulling Savannah's gaze back to her. "One, you'd better call her." She pointed at the phone with her chin. "And two, I'd love to have dinner with you."

"You would?" The shock in Savannah's voice had to be clear on her face. She was pretty sure. It was in that moment that she realized she hadn't actually expected Julia to say yes. A gentle, easy letdown was what she'd prepared for without even realizing it. "Wow. That's...that's great."

"Here." Julia reached out and wiggled her fingers until Savannah handed over her phone. Then she typed on it a bit and gave it back. "Now you have my cell. Text me, okay?"

A goofy grin, plastered on her face. She just knew it. Could actually feel it, feel the goofy. "Okay. I will."

"Good. Now go call your sister before your phone explodes. Or her head does."

"Could go either way," Savannah said with an eye roll. "I'll text you soon."

"I look forward to it."

As Savannah took a couple backward steps—she couldn't seem to pull her gaze away from the gorgeous sight in front of her—Julia gave her a little wave, tossed a rag over her shoulder, and turned to a customer who needed a refill.

Once outside the bar and back into the sunshine, she dialed Chelsea's number.

"Where are you?" was the way Chelsea answered, but Savannah kept herself from lashing out, from asking why the hell she'd made a nuisance of herself, because her little sister's voice held an unfamiliar tremor.

When their mother had died, Savannah swore to God she'd left her maternal instincts with her older daughter, and they kicked in now, because she knew instantly that there was a problem. "What's wrong?" she asked.

"Can you come over?"

"Yeah. Of course. Ten minutes, okay?"

"Okay." That last word was just a whisper, and then Chelsea hung up.

Something was definitely wrong.

"Well. That was unexpected," Julia whispered to herself as the bar door shut behind Savannah. The grin on her face seemed to have a mind of its own, refusing to leave, just…staying. Hanging out. She served drinks on autopilot, having surface-level conversations with customers, laughing at their jokes, popping tips into the tip jar behind her, but all the while, a blond-haired, blue-eyed, very sexy woman floated around in her mind.

"She was fucking hot, huh?"

That came from Chris Norton, the customer who had turned into a regular over the course of a few days. She was nice enough but could be a little crude, and Julia found herself accepting that behavior simply because she was a woman. It was interesting to her how differently she treated women versus men when they exhibited the same crass behavior.

"Friend of yours?" Chris asked when Julia didn't respond.

Thankful for the question because it likely meant Chris hadn't actually heard the conversation, Julia nodded. With a gentle smile, she said, "She is. Maybe we can be a bit more respectful?"

A zap of surprise shot across Chris's face before she blushed a little bit under her makeup and nodded. "Oh, yeah. Of course. Sorry about that. She was really pretty was all I meant."

"She's definitely that," Julia agreed, her eyes tracking back to the front door. When it opened, she was almost sure it would be Savannah coming back in, having changed her mind about needing to rush away.

Instead, the sales rep for a local microbrewery arrived for their appointment, and Julia waved to him, directed him to grab the table in the corner, and said she'd be right with him. Clea would be arriving any time now to take over bartending, and she was pleased to see some after-work folks beginning to trickle in. Her back pocket vibrated then, and she pulled out her phone to see a text from Amelia. *Still on for tonight?*

Yes! she typed back quickly. Julia was having dinner with her two cousins in the back room that night, and she was looking forward to it. She'd talked them into meeting at the bar instead of going out or to one of their houses, because she knew she'd be able to get a little work done as they ate and chatted, which they'd probably give her some shit about, but she could take it. Her free time was very limited, but she always wanted to see them.

"Hey, boss," Clea said from behind her, pulling her back into the present. "Looks like it's picking up. Wonder if that blog helped."

"That would be nice, wouldn't it?" The local entertainment guide had a blog called *Northwood Nightlife*, and the anonymous columnist had given Martini's a favorable write-up that week. Which was awesome and thrilled Julia, but what she actually wanted to say was what was in her head: *It better be picking up—it's Friday.* She kept the words to herself and simply smiled at Clea. The last thing she wanted to do was let her employees know that the business was doing okay, but just okay. She planned to spend some time over the weekend looking into new marketing ideas. Which would likely turn into more spend-money-to-make-money steps, but she needed to do something. She'd been reopened nearly two months and wasn't doing much better than the bar had been doing when her uncle owned it and it was still stuck in the eighties.

As she turned the reins over to Clea and came out from behind the bar to meet with her microbrewer, the front door opened, and she stopped in her tracks. Blinked in shock.

"Hey, Pop," she finally stammered out, as she forced her feet to move and crossed to him. She kissed him on the cheek. "What are you doing here?"

He was looking around, his dark eyes taking everything in, probably all the changes, Julia thought. He was dressed in his usual jeans and short-sleeved button-down gray shirt with *Martini's Garage* on one side and a white oval patch that read *Vinnie* on the other. He'd obviously come straight from work, and he smelled like the DL hand cleaner he'd used forever—clean, a little like oil and grease—but it was a scent she loved because it reminded her of him and how she used to try to play with it, scooping the creamy waterless cleaner out of its tub and rubbing it into her hands like she'd seen him do, though her young mind couldn't comprehend how it actually *cleaned* them.

"I came to have a beer." He said it so matter-of-factly that it took her off-guard, made her stand there and just blink at him. "Kinda fancy in here now. All shiny and new."

She found her voice. Nodded. "I made a lot of upgrades. I like the bar being rectangular and in the center. More space for seating and it's easier for customers to order drinks. New paint. New stools. New shelving. What do you think? Do you like it?"

Before he could answer, a voice cut through the air.

"Vinnie Martini. Holy shit. That you?" It came from the far corner of the bar where an older man had been sitting for an hour or so. He came in often but kept to himself.

"Dougie?" Her father left her without answering her question and crossed to the bar. "Dougie Schute? Jesus Christ, man, how you doin'?" They shook hands and were instantly caught up in reminiscing.

Julia thought about following him. Thought about introducing herself to Dougie Schute as both the owner of the bar and as Vinnie's only daughter, but something held her back. Fear? Concern? Shame? She couldn't put a finger on it and, to be honest, didn't really want to try. Her father loved her. She knew he did. But between her gayness and her decision to run a bar, she didn't exactly fit into the box labeled *Woman* he expected her to. She never had, and that had made getting both his attention and his approval nearly impossible.

She never stopped trying, though. Which often felt like self-punishment…at least that's what Vanessa would say, but whatever. It was simply life to Julia.

She caught Clea's eye, saw that she'd put two Cokes on the bar, and walked over to get them. Then she pointed her chin at her father and mouthed *my father*, silently telling Clea that he drank free of charge. It wasn't until she was carrying the Cokes to the table to finally meet with her very patient microbrewer that she remembered what had happened earlier.

A super sexy blond woman had asked her to dinner.

More importantly, she'd said yes.

There were a million reasons why she probably shouldn't have, most of those having to do with her ridiculously busy schedule. It wasn't out of the realm of possibility that she was going to text Savannah later and retract her acceptance of the invitation. But not yet. Right now? She was going to bask in her original thought.

A super sexy blond woman had asked her to dinner.

And she'd said yes.

Dina's old, beat-up, baby-blue Volvo was parked in the McNally driveway when Savannah arrived. From what she knew, Dina had a job as a nutritionist, but she didn't ever seem to go to work. Apparently, she worked with most of her clients online, which made sense, she guessed, but every time Savannah visited her father's house and that damn Volvo was there, she would clench her teeth and grind out, "Don't you ever work?" to nobody.

Fine. It was fine. Savannah wasn't going to let that bring her down because of one simple fact: Julia had said yes to her dinner invitation. *She said yes.* Savannah was still a little bit in shock, still smiling as she parked out front, got out of her car, and approached the front door. The smile slid right off her face, though, as the door opened, and Chelsea stepped out, grabbed Savannah by the hand, and pulled her inside.

"What in—" Savannah's words were cut off by Chelsea's hand slapping over her mouth.

"Shh!" she whispered. "Come with me." Chelsea tugged her quickly up the stairs and into her bedroom, where she shut the door, locked it, then turned and stood with her back against it. "Sit."

Savannah did as she was told and sat on the edge of Chelsea's bed. She couldn't not. The energy in the room was all off. Weird and stressful and Chelsea's face was a portrait of emotion. Her mascara had run and smudged, a sure sign she'd been crying. Her blue eyes were wide. Too wide. And they darted around the room as if she was trying to find an escape route of some sort. But why would she need an escape route? What was she trying to get away from?

"What's going on, Chels?" Savannah moved her head, trying to make eye contact with her. "You're scaring me, okay? Talk to me. Tell me what's going on."

The room wasn't small, but it wasn't huge either. Fairly neat for a twenty-three year old. Chelsea was into cosmetology, and her dresser held several bottles of various creams and sprays and lotions, but they were lined up by size. Tidy.

Chelsea began to pace, from the door, past the foot of the double bed, around to the other side of it, and back. It wasn't a frantic pacing, just a slow, steady path around the room. Savannah followed her sister with her eyes, watching, knowing she was organizing her thoughts, searching for the best way to tell her what was wrong. Savannah had practically raised Chelsea. She knew her better than Chelsea knew herself. She knew how her brain worked.

So Savannah waited quietly.

It took a good three or four minutes of pacing, which felt a hell of a lot longer, but Savannah could see Chelsea's clock on her nightstand. Finally, Chelsea took her place at the door again, standing in front of Savannah with her back braced against it as if she needed it to stay upright. She looked Savannah in the eye, her own filling with tears. When she spoke, her voice was very quiet.

"Parker broke up with me."

Savannah held the eye contact and didn't look away, even as she wanted to shout, *Is that all? You scared the crap out of me to tell me you and your boyfriend split up?* But she held herself in check because, once she took a moment, she remembered that Chelsea had been with Parker since their sophomore year of high school. He was her first love. Her only love.

"Oh, sweetie, I'm so sorry."

"I don't understand why," Chelsea said, and whatever she'd been using to hold herself together left her. Her face crumpled, and Savannah opened her arms.

"Come here." She held her little sister while she cried. Sobbed. Chelsea's whole body shook, and Savannah held on tight, let her cry it out, felt her own heart cracking in her chest at seeing this pain in somebody she loved. It took some time, but finally, her sobs devolved into little hiccups, and Savannah had a flash of when Chelsea was six and fell off her bike, and Savannah had been the one to hold her while she cried, all skinned knees and tear-streaked cheeks. "Does Dad know?" He liked Parker, and Savannah wondered how he'd take the breakup.

Chelsea shook her head rapidly. "I haven't told anybody."

"Well…" Savannah cleared her throat. "What happened? Did he say why?"

Chelsea sat up and wiped her hands across her face, which did nothing to help the black smudges from her runny mascara. A big sigh. "He said we were holding each other back, that we hadn't explored anything beyond us and maybe we should."

Sounds like code for I met somebody else, Savannah thought but kept it locked in her head because if Chelsea hadn't already come to that conclusion, she probably would. She didn't need Savannah's help. "I see," she said instead.

"I think he's cheating on me," Chelsea said, not looking at her. "Or he's thinking about it."

Savannah grimaced but didn't say anything as the tears flowed again. They sat together for a while in silence, Savannah holding her little sister while she cried. She wasn't sure how much time had passed when she heard her father's voice.

"Savannah Lynn, you up there?"

"He must've seen your car out front," Chelsea said with eyes so wide, they made Savannah laugh through her nose.

"Relax, would you?"

"I'm not ready to tell him yet."

Savannah nodded. "Then wash your face and get yourself together before you go down and see him. I'll go say hi, tell him we were doing girl stuff or something, then I have to head out." She brushed some hair off Chelsea's forehead and kissed the bared skin. "You're gonna be just fine," she whispered, before raising her voice and shouting, "I'm with Chelsea, Dad. I'll be right down."

She stood up, ran a hand over her face, then her hair, smoothed her palms down her sides, and winked at her little sister. She pulled the door open and headed down the stairs.

"Hi, Dad," she said when she'd reached the bottom and kissed his cheek.

"I was pretty sure that was your car, but you didn't come say hi, so…" Her father wasn't one for laying guilt trips, but Savannah felt it anyway.

"Sorry. I was over at Martini's, and then Chelsea texted me to stop over. She had some moisturizer she wanted me to try." The words barely left her mouth before she realized her mistake and clenched her teeth. She followed him into the kitchen where Dina was. Because of course she was. Dina shot a smile at her, and not for the first time, Savannah noticed how there was always a zing of surprise that crossed Dina's face before the smile was plastered into place. She honestly wasn't sure if Dina just didn't like her or if she was always trying to please her, to win her over. They'd had their differences. They'd scuffled here and there. But for the most part, they'd gotten along just fine, for her dad's sake. As long as Dina made her father happy, she'd be nice to her. Still, she didn't like feeling like she wasn't quite welcome in the house she'd grown up in.

"Martini's?" A dark shadow crossed her father's face. "What the hell are you doing there?"

"I was meeting a friend." Not exactly the truth, but not exactly a lie. "I wanted to—"

"You should steer clear of that place," he said, interrupting her, his disdain clear. "Plus, it's a damn dump. Place is older than dirt."

Savannah was surprised at her father's words, flinched a bit at them, and realized he was likely having one of his episodes, as she'd started calling them. When his issues would rise up and his moods would swing drastically. "Well, it's not a dump. It's been redone, repainted. It looks great."

"Lipstick on a pig," he muttered, grabbing his mug and taking it to the sink. He gestured with a meaty hand to the coffee pot. "You want coffee? It's decaf, though."

"It's dinnertime, Dad. I don't want coffee, thanks." She chuckled to lighten things up because they suddenly felt oddly ominous.

He grunted. Didn't look at her, which she hated. Suddenly, the need for an explanation, for a way to make him understand that she was just seeing a friend, was almost unbearable.

"I was just meeting a friend. That's all."

"You should meet her someplace else then."

"Why do you hate a bar so much?" Dina asked, and Savannah was surprised it had taken her this long to jump in.

"Bah. Doesn't matter," her father said, pouring out the coffee after all. He turned to Dina. "Want to go out for dinner? That Thai place you like?"

He was definitely trying to shift the focus because Thai food would never be first on her father's list of favorite dinners. And Dina's eyes lit up, so he'd done it for her.

"That sounds great," Dina said, then turned to look at Savannah, and a full five seconds went by before she asked, "Do you want to join us?"

And watch you decide what my dad can and can't eat? I'd rather stick needles in my eyes. She smiled instead of giving voice to her thoughts. "No, but thank you. I've got to get home."

Less than ten minutes later, she was on the road, headed home, her mind a swirl of so many things. Chelsea was heartbroken. Her dad now knew she'd entered into a Forbidden Place—that was how she'd think of it now, because it made it seem more ridiculous and, therefore, easier to handle. Because she wasn't going to not go to Martini's. That's where Julia worked. And just as her name crossed Savannah's mind, everything seemed to lighten, to lift, to float. She had a date with Julia. Well, she didn't yet, but she would. Very soon.

She let herself bask in that joy. Because it had been a long time.

CHAPTER SIX

Oh, please, please, please tell me that's a Vinnie G's pizza I smell." Julia walked into the back of the bar with her nose held high, following the scents of tomatoes, basil, and oregano, and trying hard not to drool all over herself.

"The only pizza as good as Noni's," Vanessa confirmed. She was setting up plates at the little bar. She wore black yoga pants and a pink sweatshirt that fell past her hips. The front had a screen printed hippo on it. The place settings done, she stood back, hands on her hips, and said to Julia, "Now we can eat like civilized people."

"It's pizza, Ness. Nowhere is there an eat like civilized people rule when it comes to pizza." A quick glance around the room told her they were the only two there.

"She's running late." Vanessa answered the unspoken question.

"Seems to be a thing lately."

Vanessa shrugged, folding torn paper towels up for napkins. "She's going through some shit. Cut her some slack." She was the one of them with the biggest heart, the most tender emotions, and she gave everybody the benefit of the doubt. Always. Sometimes to her own detriment. Of the three of them, Vanessa was the one who would always defend you, and she was also the one Julia always wanted to defend. And to be fair, Vanessa was right. Amelia's divorce had taken a toll, and it showed. Julia *should* cut her some slack.

As if on cue, the side door opened, and Amelia entered bearing a plate covered in foil, a large plastic bag, and an expression of gloom. "Jesus Christ, I have no energy. None."

"Thanks, perimenopause," Julia and Vanessa said in tandem, then laughed.

"I hate you both. You don't know. Just wait until you guys are old like me. I will do nothing but make fun of you." Amelia dropped her jacket on the couch and handed Julia the plate.

"Stop it. You're only forty-eight." To make up for the teasing, Julia kissed her on the temple, then took the plate from her hand. "Tell me these are cookies and that you just made them today."

"These are cookies and I just made them half an hour ago." Amelia dropped onto a stool and sighed as if she'd been walking for days.

"Oh my God, they're still warm," Julia said, the last word muffled by the chocolate chip cookie she stuffed into her mouth. Vanessa joined her, and the two of them hummed their approval as Amelia watched and a grin slowly spread across her face.

"And just like that, you two are ten and seven again."

"And you're twenty and making us cookies while you babysit," Vanessa said.

It was kind of amazing the three of them had remained as close as they had, given their ages. But it was their sexuality that bound them like sisters—Julia knew that. Amelia was ten years older than her and had been dating a woman by the time Julia realized she was attracted to her best friend at the time. She'd gone to Amelia to talk about it, and not a week later, Vanessa had gone to her with the same issue.

They'd been inseparable ever since.

"Those were good days," Vanessa said. "When we were seven and ten."

"And I watched you and made you cookies and cleaned up after you?" Amelia clarified. She brushed a lock of her light brown hair out of her face.

"That's what I said. Good days." Vanessa bumped her with a shoulder.

"Here," Amelia said, handing the plastic bag to Julia. "I brought you something."

Inside the bag was a long rectangular box. Puzzled, she squinted at Amelia. "What is this?"

"Well, open it, weirdo." Amelia waved a hand at her.

Inside the box was a large wooden sign. Carved into it in a fun script was *The Bar Back*. A martini glass was on one end and a recliner on the other. Julia could feel the grin spread across her face. "Amelia..."

Another dismissive wave. "Well, the place needed a name—you said so yourself. I know a bar back is the person who cleans up the empty bottles and stocks the liquor and stuff like that. And we *are* at the back of the bar, so..."

"It's perfect." Julia set the sign down and went to her cousin. Wrapped her in a hug. "Thank you. I love it."

"You're welcome."

"That's awesome, Meels." Vanessa smiled widely. "Super cool. We need to find a good place to hang it. However, I'm starving. Can we eat first?"

"Absolutely," Amelia said and spun her stool so she was facing the pizza.

"You guys want wine?" Julia asked. "It's been a day for me, and it's Friday, so I'm opening a bottle."

Vanessa raised her hand. Amelia shook her head, and Julia knew she'd change her mind in about a half hour or so.

"I feel like I haven't seen you guys in a while," Vanessa said as she put her crust back in the pizza box and helped herself to another slice. "Update me. What's new in your lives?" She pointed at Amelia. "And that is not an invitation to tell us how your body is falling apart. That's not new. And it's not falling apart."

Amelia made a face but kept chewing her pizza.

"I had two rather interesting things happen to me today," Julia said, reached for the crust Vanessa left, and took a bite. She wasn't going to bring up Savannah's visit and the date that she'd agreed to that she probably shouldn't have, but she needed a little guidance.

But first, she'd talk about the other thing. "So, my dad came in today."

Vanessa's eyes went wide as Amelia said, "Seriously? It's about damn time. What did he think?"

"Did he stay? Wander? Have a drink?" Vanessa asked.

"It was…" Julia chewed the rest of the crust, then grabbed a slice and looked up at the ceiling, trying to find the right words. "Weird. It was a weird visit."

Amelia's brow furrowed. "How so?"

"Well, let's see." Julia ticked facts off on her fingers. "He didn't tell me he was coming. I started to show him the upgrades, but then he saw a guy he knew. He sat with said guy, had a beer, and left. The end."

Vanessa grimaced at her, little blond escapees from her messy bun skimming the sides of her face. "Wow, Uncle Vinnie's gotten predictable in his old age, hasn't he?"

Amelia looked equally unsurprised as she pulled off the zip-up hoodie she was wearing and sat there in a black T-shirt, fanning herself with an open hand, the glimmer of perspiration suddenly appearing on her forehead. "You'd think he could throw you a bone here and there. Jesus."

"But seriously, Jules, are you okay?" Vanessa. Her light eyes were kind, as always, and her concern was clear.

Julia sighed. "I'm fine. I mean, I don't know what I was expecting."

"Definition of insanity," Amelia said, helping herself to a slice. "Doing the same thing over and over and expecting a different result."

"Um, harsh," Vanessa said, then glanced at Julia, still worried.

Julia shrugged. "It's okay. She's right. I've been trying to get my dad's approval for most of my adult life." She did not say out loud, *I wish I could stop. I wish I didn't care.* Because she *would* always want his approval, and she *did* care. Very much. Probably too much.

"I wish I could sit him down," Vanessa said.

At the same moment, Amelia said, "I wish I could smack him."

The three of them burst out laughing, which definitely helped lighten the mood as they ate.

"How are things, Amelia?" Vanessa asked, dropping her second piece of crust.

Amelia inhaled, then let it out audibly as she lifted her shoulders and dropped them in a slow shrug. "I mean, things are...things. Tammy wants to put the house up, and I've been resisting, but I'm realizing maybe I don't want to stay there after all."

It was the most reasonable and matter-of-fact that she'd sounded since announcing her divorce the year before. Julia's heart ached for her. At the same time, she didn't want Amelia to wallow in sadness and self-pity. She wanted her to stand up. Be strong. Understand that she deserved better. "I get that. What would you do? Buy a new place?"

"I'm not sure yet." Amelia bit into a cookie. She'd only eaten one slice of pizza, Julia noticed. "Maybe?"

"You should get back out into the dating world," Vanessa said. "You're a damn catch, babe."

Amelia scoffed but made no other protests, no comments about how unattractive she felt or how Tammy had taken her self-esteem and flushed it down the toilet. None of her usual self-deprecating barbs. Nothing. Julia exchanged a glance with Vanessa, and she knew her cousin was wondering the same thing: Was this good news or bad news?

By silent agreement, they decided not to push and, instead, let a few quiet moments go by. Then Vanessa asked, "So, Jules, any more *coincidental* visits from the cute blonde?" She made air quotes, and it was only because Amelia sat up and seemed ready to engage again that Julia didn't dodge and weave.

"As a matter of fact, she stopped by today."

Two pairs of eyes went wide, both Vanessa and Amelia sitting up a little straighter. "No way," Vanessa said. "I was kidding."

"Well, I'm not. She came by this afternoon and asked me if I'd have dinner with her sometime." Boom. She dropped it and let it sit there, let her cousins absorb it, tried to ignore the mix of emotions the whole thing stirred up in her.

"Oh my God." Vanessa looked from her to Amelia and back. "Oh my *God*."

Amelia shot her the first genuine smile she'd seen on her face in a while. "That's very cool, Jules," she said softly and squeezed Julia's forearm.

"You said yes, right?" Vanessa. "Please, please, tell us you said yes."

"Nothing is set yet. I gave her my number and told her to text me."

Vanessa squinted. "You didn't pick a time and place?"

Julia stood up, feeling like she needed the activity, needed movement. "Honestly, her sister was blowing up her phone, so she had to run."

Amelia pursed her lips. "Really? She just ran off after asking you out?"

"Seemed like an emergency." Jules lifted a shoulder in a half shrug.

"Still." Amelia's furrowed brow seemed to pull a laugh from Vanessa.

"Sweetie," Vanessa said to Amelia, "I love you, but as the only one of us who has no siblings, you're not allowed to judge sibling relationships and what constitutes an emergency."

Julia nodded and poked a finger in Vanessa's direction. "She's right. I agree."

"If Ella or Izzy needed me," Vanessa said, tossing her crust into the box, "I'd go in a heartbeat."

"Same for me and my brothers," Julia said.

Amelia nodded. "I can accept that. So, where does that leave things then?"

"Well." Julia walked toward her desk, then turned when she got there and walked toward the door out to the main bar area, leaned out, and took a peek. "She's going to text. Ball's in her court, I guess." Then she turned on her heel and headed back.

"She's pacing," Amelia said to Vanessa.

"I see that," Vanessa replied with a nod. "She does that when she's on the verge of freaking out."

"She does. The pre-freak pace."

"I'm not pacing, and I'm not on the verge of freaking out," Julia said, but the pitch of her voice nearly an octave higher than normal kind of gave it away.

"What's the problem?" Vanessa asked, softening her tone. "Talk to us."

"Do I have time for this, you guys?" Julia blurted before she could think about it. "I mean, seriously? I know you hate when I use that as my excuse, but it's a valid one. I've got so much on my plate right now."

Vanessa tipped her head to the side. "Do you, though?"

Before Julia could respond, Amelia added her two cents. "Do you think every person in America who owns a business never goes on dates 'cause, *There's so much on my plate right now?*" She did a fabulous—if not a tiny bit whiny—impression of Julia, and it made Vanessa snort-laugh.

"Nice," Julia said, then made a face and flopped on the couch. "Thanks for the support."

"Jules." Vanessa spun her stool around so she could see Julia and just stared at her.

"You look just like your mom right now," Julia said, amused. Aunt Monica gave that very same look, a combination of *Really?* and *Pull yourself together, dummy.*

Vanessa shook her head, then stood and began clearing the bar top of detritus from their dinner.

Amelia bit into another cookie. "You're being ridiculous. You know that, right?"

"By claiming to be busy?" At Amelia's nod, Julia continued, "I mean, I'm not lying. Pulling this place out of the shitter, as my dad would say, hasn't been easy."

"I know." Amelia continued to chew. Vanessa continued to clean.

"And it has—does—take up most of my time." Julia felt herself becoming a little exasperated and did her best to keep it in check, to not let Amelia's words get under her skin.

Amelia gave a casual nod. "I know that, too."

"Then why would I be using *true facts* as an excuse not to date this woman?"

"Because you're scared." Amelia said it as casually and as nonchalantly as was humanly possible. Like it was no big deal. Just a fact and a commonly known one at that.

Julia blinked at her, then shifted her gaze to Vanessa, who lifted one corner of her mouth and one shoulder at the same time, apparently agreeing with Amelia. "Scared of what?" Julia asked.

"You tell us." Vanessa this time.

"I'm not scared." She threw in a snort for good measure. "That's just stupid."

Amelia held her gaze. Vanessa did that head-tipping thing again. Then they looked at each other, and as if they'd had some telepathic conversation, Amelia looked back at Julia and said, "Okay."

"Okay? Okay what?" Julia narrowed her eyes.

"If you say so." Amelia stood up and covered the remains of the plate of cookies with the foil.

"You do you," Vanessa added, wiping her hands on a rag.

Brow furrowed, Julia's gaze volleyed from one cousin to the other. Why was she bothered? Wasn't this what she wanted, for them to leave her alone about the whole Savannah thing? Why was she irritated? Each cousin gathered her things.

"We're here when you're ready to talk about it, okay?" Vanessa kissed her cheek and headed for the door. "Text you tomorrow."

Amelia did the same thing and said, "You're not failing your business if you have a personal life. Keep that in mind, yeah?"

When the door shut behind them, the lounge area was as quiet as it could be with customers out front and music playing over the sound system. Her cousins' words—but even more than that, their faces, their expressions, their eyes—stuck with Julia for the next several moments as she sat on the couch and tried to both feel her feelings and ignore them. Not a lot of success there.

She pulled out her phone and checked the notifications. Her inbox. Nothing from Savannah.

So not a lot of success there, either.

With a sigh, she pushed herself to her feet and decided the best course of action was to go out front and check on things, see if Clea needed any help with anything. Count the customers. Do a little bar backing if needed. That, of course, made her think of the sign Amelia had brought, and she smiled.

She rejected the nagging thought that what she should really do was go home. That the reason her plate was always so full was, very simply, completely on her.

Chapter Seven

M y sister's boyfriend broke up with her."
"What?" The disbelief, the shock in Tiffany's voice was clear. "The one she's been with since they were in diapers?"
"That very one." Savannah tipped her head from one side to the other. "I mean, is it wrong that I think maybe it's a good thing?" She clenched her teeth and made a face as she switched the phone to her other ear and gazed out the window of her living room. "Is it bad that maybe I'd like her to venture out more? Meet other people besides ones she's known her whole life?"

Tiffany scoffed. "It's not bad at all. I liked Parker, though. Seemed like a nice guy."

"Same." She told Tiffany the whole story of Chelsea blowing up her phone, the secrecy, Savannah's relief that it wasn't something more urgent like her being pregnant.

"I think it's super cute that she called you first, that you were her comfort."

Much as she'd acted like it had been an irritation, Savannah felt the same way. "I do, too."

"You've been her mom since your mom died." There was a beat of silence before Tiffany asked, "What's she going to do now?"

Savannah sighed. "I imagine she's gonna need some time. I'm hoping she acts twenty-three and not sixteen, and by that I mean I hope she doesn't do things like emote on social media and stalk him and stuff like that."

"Oh, she will."

Savannah sighed on a laugh. "She will. So…I guess I'll just make sure I'm here for her, give her a hug when she needs it, and support her however I can."

"You are the most amazing, loving, decent human, Savannah. You know that, right?"

"Yeah." Savannah gave a dramatic sigh. "That's always been my problem."

Tiff laughed. "On to other topics, how did things go with Hot Bartender?"

"I mean, they went well. I got her number. But Chelsea called in the middle of things and took up all my brain parts for a bit, you know?"

Tiffany gave a little grunt. "Yeah, I get that. But you got her number, huh?"

"I did." Savannah smiled to herself as she thought about Julia yesterday. Her smile, those dimples, the slight blush that had blossomed on her cheeks, her long fingers as she typed her number into Savannah's phone…

"Hello? Earth to Savannah. Did I lose you?"

"Nope. I'm here. Got a little lost for a minute there."

"Thinking about her?"

"How could I not be, right? Have you seen her?"

They laughed together, and Savannah was grateful for a break from the stress, even if it was only temporary. She'd texted with Chelsea a few times already, and she knew her sister was trying hard not to contact Parker at all. Savannah had offered to take her someplace, hang with her, but Chelsea said she was okay.

She finished up her call with Tiffany and lifted her feet to the couch so she was lying on it, staring at the ceiling.

Her mind was a whirlwind. Good God.

"I should go for a run."

She said it out loud. To her empty house. But the sound of her own voice helped kick her into gear, and she pushed herself up off the couch and headed upstairs to change.

Ten minutes later, she was in her driveway, doing some quick stretches. She hadn't run in weeks, and she knew she was going to feel it. Her muscles would scream. Her lungs wouldn't be happy. But her mind would get a break. She clipped her phone into its holder strapped to her arm, chose one of her running playlists, put in her earbuds, and was off.

Of her three playlists, this one was the loudest, and she saved it for days just like that day. When she needed to stop her mind from focusing all its attention on the one thing that was about to make her throw herself in front of a train. She turned up the volume. Between Post Malone, Nicki Minaj, and Ariana Grande, she found a nice groove, set up a rhythm with her feet, and simply ran.

It was the rhythm that kept her running. It wasn't because she loved it. She didn't. She liked it fine, but it wasn't her favorite thing on earth. It wasn't really the runner's high either—which did eventually come but took way too freaking long as far as she was concerned. No, it was the rhythm. She had control of it. Her sneakers hitting the pavement. The air rushing in and out of her lungs. The direction she went. All of it was within her control. She set it up, she kept it going, she could change it at any time. Speed things up. Slow them down. It was all within her reach.

She was aware that she ran most often when something in her life felt out of control. She'd done it since high school, since track team, since understanding that her body loved to run, and her mind needed her to run. When her mother had gotten sick, Savannah had run several times a week. After her mother died, she'd sometimes run several times a day.

And now, her baby sister was heartbroken, and her brother was still an addict, and her father was sliding toward dementia, and there wasn't a damn thing Savannah could do about any of it.

So she ran.

A few hours after her run, Savannah was showered and changed and flopped onto her couch for a few minutes of chill before she planned to pop in on her dad to say hi. That was going to be her excuse to be at the house, but what she really wanted to do was check up on Chelsea. Her little sister had been fairly sporadic in her responses to Savannah's texts, and while she assumed Chelsea was probably talking it out with her friends, she was still worried.

The run had helped. She felt clearer. Grounded. A little bit brave, actually, which was what had her scrolling on her phone until she found the number Julia had entered under *Julia the Bartender*. Savannah promptly added a *Hot* where it needed to be.

Even though Savannah had been so focused on her family and then on running to stop focusing on her family, Julia had still been hanging out in the back of her mind. Never interrupting, as if she knew the Chelsea situation was more important right then, but just quietly occupying a corner. Always there. Silent and smiling that smile, displaying those dimples.

A soft wave of happiness washed over her as her thumb hovered over the call button, but she stopped. It was Saturday afternoon. Would Julia be working? Should she text instead? Nobody called anymore. True, she wanted to hear the sexy, gravelly voice, but she also didn't want to come across as a weirdo. Chuckling at her own indecision, she began typing.

Happy Saturday! It's Savannah. I was wondering if you're still up for having dinner with me. If so, tell me when's good for you.

She added a smiley at the end, then stared. Read it. Reread it. Four times. Five. Was it personal enough? Too personal? Too serious? Was it flippant? Was she being presumptuous? Was it too—

"Jesus Christ, just send it," she muttered, then sent the text before she could change her mind.

Of course, then the panic set it.

What if Julia had only been being polite? What if she'd been pacifying Savannah? Maybe this wasn't even her actual number. Maybe she'd fake-numbered her.

"Oh my God, enough already," she said, again aloud to her empty house. But she pushed herself up off the couch and headed for the kitchen determined to scrub something. Because when she was stressed and couldn't run, she cleaned. Furniture polish and rag in hand, she returned to the living room.

And her phone beeped.

Savannah stopped in her tracks. Stood there, still, afraid to move for a moment. Her phone was too far away for her to read the screen, but there was the telltale green square telling her there was a text waiting.

Deep inhale, very slow exhale.

She set down the furniture polish. Set down the rag. Walked very nonchalantly toward the phone. No hurry at all. No big deal...

When she got close enough to see it was a text from Julia the Hot Bartender, she picked up her pace for the last two steps and snatched up the phone.

I am still very much up for it! My schedule is a little crazy... How do you feel about brunch tomorrow?

Savannah felt her smile slowly blossom across her face and she typed, *How could you possibly know that brunch is my favorite meal in all the land?*

The bouncing gray dots happened immediately, and Julia's reply came several seconds later. *Listen, I know stuff. You should probably just accept that.*

The smile grew. *Slightly creepy, but I guess I don't have a choice.* She added a wink so Julia would know she was teasing.

They set up a place and time, deciding to meet at the restaurant.

Okay, gotta go slice fruit, came Julia's next text.

It's hard to be you, Savannah sent back with another wink.

You have no idea. This time, Julia sent a kiss-blowing emoji, and for some ridiculous reason, Savannah felt herself flush with heat.

That was it. A simple, quick, back-and-forth conversation that lasted all of four or five minutes, but Savannah suddenly felt alive. Rejuvenated. Excited. How was it possible for Julia to have that effect on her with simple words on a screen?

Knowing she was about to overthink things, she did her best to tuck it all away for now and refocus her attention on other subjects.

Purse slung over her shoulder, she headed out to her car.

❖

"What are you grinning at?" Dante asked.

Julia smiled at her younger brother, who'd stopped in for a beer or two on a Saturday evening. She slid her phone into the back pocket of her jeans and tried to temper what she now knew was a goofy grin that had spread across her face. "Nothing," she lied. Paring knife in hand, she began peeling and slicing the oranges in front of her.

"Lies. Tell me."

She and Dante had always been tight, ever since they were kids. With barely two years between them, they'd been the closest in age of all the Martini siblings, and they'd spent a lot of time together as kids. Julia had been a tomboy and more than happy to be just as rough and curious and get just as dirty as Dante, much to their mother's dismay. Julia looked at him now, thirty-six years old, very handsome with his dark, curly hair and square jaw like their father's, a successful IT analyst at a large local company. Today, he was wearing jeans and a black T-shirt rather than the oxford and tie he wore during the week. His brown eyes were soft, his thick, dark brows raised in expectation.

She sighed because she was going to tell him. She pretty much told him everything. Dante, Amelia, Vanessa. Her vaults. She trusted them with everything in her.

"I have a date," she said quietly, not looking up from the limes.

"What?" Dante's disbelief would've been insulting if it wasn't completely warranted. Julia couldn't remember the last time she'd said those words. She'd hooked up. She had a Tinder profile. But she hadn't really had *a date* in months and months.

"You heard me. Brunch at Shoreview. Tomorrow."

"Oh, that's a nice place. Classy." Dante took a slug of his beer. "With who?"

"Nobody you know," Julia told him. "She's been in with friends…and a couple times on her own."

"So she's a customer." There was caution in Dante's tone.

"Where else am I going to meet somebody, Dante?" She sounded a tiny bit defensive and kind of whiny and she knew it. Couldn't help it. "I'm here ninety percent of my life."

Dante nodded slowly, which made Julia grind her teeth because he only did that when he was giving her time to calm down. Unlike Julia, Dante was notoriously calm. This was his way of de-escalating her before she even had a chance to escalate. He'd done it since they were elementary school age and was kind of brilliant at it. And it worked. She felt herself relaxing, letting go of that quick-to-anger thing she had that she blamed on her hot-headed Italian father.

Dante watched her, casually sipped his beer, and knew exactly when it was okay to talk to her again. "So, tell me about this brunch date."

And Julia smiled. Another thing she couldn't seem to help as she felt it bloom across her face, even as she kept her head down a bit and pretended to focus on more oranges.

"Well, I honestly don't know a ton about her. I plan to do some digging on our date. But what I've been able to tell so far is that she's kind and funny and gorgeous." She stopped slicing and looked off into the distance. "We seem to connect well. We banter in the same way. Flirt a little." A shrug and back to the fruit.

Dante held up his glass in salute. "Here's to getting to know her."

"Thanks, D."

He finished his beer, set the empty glass on the bar, and slid off his stool. It was starting to pick up as it closed in on six o'clock. Dante pushed himself up far enough over the bar to kiss Julia on the cheek. "Catch you at Ma's tomorrow."

Julia nodded, watched him go. He high-fived Terry, who had just taken up his post at the door to bounce anybody who tried to fake-ID him. She hoped they needed him tonight, meaning she hoped to get a big crowd. While the bar was doing okay, she'd be really happy with some bigger profits. Might be time to sit down with Vanessa and pick her brain about some gimmicks to bring people in. Vanessa was great with creativity.

Clea was there, as was Evan, a new bartender she'd hired last week, and the three of them were ready. The night's special was a Tequila Sunset—similar to a Tequila Sunrise except with cranberry juice instead of orange juice, and an orange peel garnish. Clea's idea, and it looked delicious, and it was.

It turned out to be a pretty busy night. All three of them stayed occupied behind the bar, making cocktails up until midnight and a little beyond. Julia served and cleaned and laughed with customers and poured shots and even invented a couple. That night reminded her of everything wonderful about bartending. And even with that, she still found herself wishing for time to speed up, for last call to arrive, so she could close up shop and get a little sleep. Because once she woke up, it would be Sunday, and she'd be only a couple hours away from her date with Savannah. And much as she wanted to scoff and remind herself that she had little time for anything outside of her business, she couldn't seem to. Savannah's smile would pop up in her mind, and that was apparently all it took to shut that negative train of thought right down.

Julia couldn't remember the last time that had happened, the last time she'd focused on something besides succeeding in the eyes of her father. He didn't love that she dated women. At most, he tolerated it. So this date—should it go beyond this date—wasn't something he'd celebrate.

Julia tried her best to internally shrug away that thought and concentrate on the one that mattered right then.

She had a date tomorrow.

CHAPTER EIGHT

Shoreview was a really nice choice for brunch.
Savannah had thought so the second Julia had suggested it. It wasn't crazy fancy, but it was definitely a classy place. April had made way for May, and that Sunday morning, it showed. The sun was bright and cheerful against a clear blue sky, the temperatures were definitely more mid-spring than late winter. Savannah was torn between dressing up too much and not dressing up enough. Checking her reflection in the mirror, she took stock.

She'd decided on a spring-weight dress in a soft robin's egg blue, then jazzed it up a little bit with a denim jacket. Her hair was down, a little wavy, and she finger-combed it into place. She'd been waiting for a chance to wear her new wedges, so she stepped into them, did a little spin in the mirror, and decided she'd hit the right in-between look.

Her cheeks puffed out when she exhaled. She was nervous. Not regular, slight, first-date nerves, but jangling, can't-ignore, oh-my-God-what-was-I-thinking nerves.

The ping of her phone pulled her out of her panic. But only briefly because for a split second, she was sure it was Julia texting to cancel. She was wrong. It was Tiffany.

All set? What did you decide to wear?

Savannah chewed on her lip as she typed back, *Blue spring dress, jean jacket, wedges?* Then a shrugging emoji.

Lemme see.

Savannah posed in front of the mirror, snapped a photo, and sent it.

Perfect, came Tiff's response. *You look gorgeous*, and Savannah grinned with a relief she hadn't realized she'd needed.

Might be a little chilly, she typed.

Pfft. Fashion before comfort. That's the rule. I mean, you might catch pneumonia...

Savannah laughed. *Worth it.*

Tiff sent five laughing emoji. *That's my girl!*

A short time later, she was gliding into a parking spot, and her heart rate had kicked up about thirty-seven notches. Why was she so nervous? It was just brunch. It was just a date. It wasn't like she'd never participated in either one before, right? She'd had plenty of dates in her life. And brunch? Please. She was the *queen* of brunch.

"Good morning." The voice surprised her as she got out of her car.

Her initial thought was *So much for more prepping*, but that was immediately run over by her second thought—"Wow"—and she said it out loud. She almost apologized until she noticed as Julia approached her how deeply she was blushing. *Yeah, I think I'll just let that stand.*

Savannah had only ever seen Julia in jeans and a black Martini's shirt. And she was attractive enough to make that super sexy. But that morning? Oh-em-gee.

Julia's pants were black. They might have been jeans, they might have been dress pants—Savannah wasn't sure. What she *was* sure of was they were skinny, and they hugged every curve of Julia's lower body like a lover. Her jacket was army green, and slightly edgy was the best description Savannah could come up with. It was cut sharply, with four silver zippers, and it tapered at the waist. The black tank she wore underneath it had a scoop neck, and while it didn't reveal enough to be considered daring, the expanse of olive skin and collarbone Savannah could see made her want to see more.

"And also, good morning to you, too," she said, recovering. She hoped. "You look incredible. In case that wasn't clear from my *wow*."

"Well, thank you. And I'd like to say in return, right back atcha. Wow."

Savannah felt her cheeks heat up as they fell in step together. Julia held the door for her and then gave the hostess her name. They smiled at each other but said nothing until they'd been led to their table for two by the window.

"This view does not suck," Savannah commented once coffee was poured and they'd ordered mimosas and been left with menus. The bright sunshine sparkled on the water, making it look like diamonds were floating in Black Cherry Lake.

"Have you been here before?" Julia asked, taking a sip of her water.

"I have, but not for a long time. I forgot how beautiful it is. You?"

"It's been a while for me, too, but I'm friends with the head chef. There isn't a bad thing on the menu, but I highly recommend the stuffed french toast."

"Do I even want to know what it's stuffed with?"

"Only if you like things like cream cheese and strawberries."

"Is that what you're getting?"

Julia blew out a breath. "I'm not sure. My issue with brunch is always deciding whether I'm in the mood for sweet or savory. Pancakes or an omelet? French toast or bacon and eggs?"

"It *is* one of life's most difficult decisions." When Savannah glanced up from her menu, Julia was looking at her with slightly narrowed eyes.

"I don't know you well enough yet to know if you're mocking me."

Secretly loving the *yet*, she arched one eyebrow, then returned her gaze to her menu. "Huh."

The throaty laugh Julia gave then made Savannah's whole body tingle, and she filed away a mental note about making her laugh as often as possible. "Tell you what. How about I get the stuffed french toast, and you get eggs of some sort, and we can share." She snapped her head up then. "Are you a food sharer? I should probably ask that before I try to take a bite of your food and end up with a fork stuck in my hand."

More laughter. "What's the point of going out to eat with somebody if you don't share?"

Savannah wiped the back of her hand across her forehead in mock-relief. "Okay, good. We can still be friends."

"Thank God."

Their gazes locked. Held. Sizzled.

Oh, I so want to be more than friends...

Shaking the thought away for the moment—because, hello? way too soon—Savannah opted for general conversation. The point of this brunch, after all, was to get to know each other. They'd literally said so. "So, tell me about you, Ms.—" Savannah felt her own eyes widen in surprise. "I don't even know your last name."

"Sure you do. It's Martini."

Puzzle pieces clicked into place then, and Savannah flinched in more surprise. "Julia Martini? Wait, do you *own* Martini's?"

A squint from across the table. "Why do you say it like that?"

Backpedaling happened then. Lots of it. "Oh no, I didn't mean...I just...I'm sorry..."

Julia's face broke into a huge grin as she reached across the table and covered Savannah's hand with hers. "Relax. I'm just teasing you."

The relief that washed over her was palpable, and she let out a huge breath. "Oh, thank God." Allowing herself a small chuckle, she added, "But I'm a little embarrassed at my own sexism. I mean, why wouldn't I think you own the bar? Seems like you're there all the time."

"I *am* there all the time. You have no idea."

The waiter arrived to take their orders and deliver their drinks. When he was gone, Savannah held up her flute in a toast.

"To gorgeous views, stuffed french toast, and possibility."

"I will absolutely drink to that."

Their glasses made a pretty ping as they touched, and Savannah never took her eyes off Julia's face as they sipped. Holy Oil of Olay commercials, the woman had flawless skin. Her olive complexion combined with her dark hair and eyes and her last name likely meant she was of Mediterranean descent. "Tell me about your family. Italian? Greek?"

Julia's face softened, telling Savannah that family was important to her. "Italian. Three-quarters. My dad is full, and my mom is half."

"Siblings?"

"Four brothers."

Savannah barked a laugh. "The only girl of an Italian father? I'm sure you weren't spoiled. Tell me you're not the baby."

"I'm not," Julia said, shaking her head. "I fall smack dab in the middle. Bookended by pairs of brothers. Are you the baby?"

Savannah snorted. "Oh no. I'm the oldest."

"So you get to tell everybody what to do."

"More like I take care of all of them. And I say *all of them* like I have a dozen siblings. I have two. One brother, one sister."

"You get along?"

"For the most part, yeah. My mom died ten years ago, and they were sixteen and thirteen, so it was rough." She sipped her mimosa. "I sort of stepped into that mother role a bit because I was older, and it kind of stuck."

"Is your dad still around?"

"He is. He had a rough time when my mom died, so I took up the parenting slack. He's having some issues with early dementia, I think, but hasn't gone to the doctor yet. I think he's afraid of being officially diagnosed, you know? To be honest, so am I." What was she saying? This wasn't a subject she ever talked about, but something about Julia's presence made her feel...safe. Still, it was weird. She cleared her throat, waved a hand. "God, way to depress everybody, Savannah. Geez." She laughed quietly and steered things back across the table. "What about you? Get along with your brothers?"

Julia studied her for a beat, almost as if she was debating continuing the discussion about Savannah's dad. Thankfully, she nodded. "We're all pretty tight, but my brother Dante is one of my best friends. He's two years younger than me. And I have a million cousins. Three of us are gay, and we're like a club." She laughed that laugh again, and Savannah couldn't help but smile. "So, yeah, my brother and my two cousins are my closest friends in the world."

Their food arrived then, and honestly, everything fell away as the amazingly mouth-watering scents of their brunch filled the air between them. The smell of warm cinnamon from Savannah's stuffed french toast and the savory scents of fresh basil and sautéed tomatoes in Julia's omelet combined to create the most delicious atmosphere, and Savannah closed her eyes, inhaled slowly and deeply.

"Wow," she said quietly, and when she opened her eyes, Julia was watching her, those dark eyes just a little bit hooded. A pleasant fluttering kicked up low in Savannah's body.

"My grandma used to say we eat with our eyes first." Julia kept her gaze on Savannah for another beat or two before shifting it down to her plate.

"Presentation is almost as important as taste."

"But not quite."

"Not quite."

They each cut a bite and put a forkful into their mouths at the same time. Tandem humming happened then, and it made Savannah laugh at how they were like mirror images of each other.

"So, what about you?" Julia sipped her water and spoke as she cut a sizable chunk of her omelet and reached across the table to set it on Savannah's plate. "What do you do? Are you from here originally? Is your family big like mine?"

Savannah returned the favor, putting a slice of her french toast onto Julia's plate. In the back of her mind sat the thought that it felt totally normal sharing food with Julia. Like they did it all the time, and it was just regular behavior. Grabbing onto her focus and turning it toward Julia, she said lightly, "That's a lot of questions."

"Three. It's three questions."

"That's not a lot of questions." As Julia grinned, Savannah chewed her food and thought. "What do I do? I am currently a home health care worker. I have a handful of clients that I take care of a few times a week."

"Elderly?"

"Mostly. One woman has early-onset Alzheimer's. She's only in her early sixties. But the others are older."

"You said *currently*. Do you have another job in mind?"

"I have wanted to go to nursing school for years. But when my mother died, I found myself with so much more on my plate and"— she shrugged—"I put it off." She met Julia's eyes across the table. "And put it off. And put it off."

Julia nodded and her face said she got it, totally.

"One of these days," Savannah said, then tasted the bite of omelet Julia'd given her and closed her eyes as the savory taste exploded in her mouth. "Oh my God, that's delicious. I think the fresh basil makes it."

"Fresh basil makes everything. I don't understand why there isn't a basil perfume. It would make millions of dollars."

"Somebody's clearly missed the boat on that. We should jot it down."

"That's all I'm saying."

"Okay, question number two was…What was it?"

Julia's smile was quickly becoming one of Savannah's favorite sights. "Are you from here originally?"

"Ah, yes, the *Where are you from* inquiry. Yes. I was born and raised right here in Northwood. And I believe next was do I have a big family, right? I do not. It's actually really small. My dad is an only child, and my mom just had one sister who lives in California and has no kids, so it's really just us. My dad's parents died when he was in college. My mom's parents live in California near my aunt. It's where my mom's from."

"Do you see them much? Your grandparents?" The thing about Julia's questions was that they didn't feel nosy. Or invasive. Or intrusive. And she seemed genuinely curious, not asking just to make conversation. Her eyes stayed on Savannah the whole time, actually listening. That was more than she could say for many of the dates she'd been on in the past.

"I don't, no." Savannah chewed and gazed out the window at the water, the sun still bright and dazzling. "I think it was hard for them to see us. I think…" She nibbled on the inside of her cheek as she thought about words that had been in her head for years, but she didn't recall ever saying out loud. "I think there are two kinds of parents when it comes to losing a child. One kind pulls everything that has to do with that child, that feels like that child, that reminds them of that child, as close as possible. Wraps them up and holds on tight. The other kind does the opposite. Pushes those things—those people—away because it's just too painful. My grandparents were the second kind."

"Ouch," Julia said with a sympathetic grimace.

"They tried, but it was just too hard. I look a lot like my mom, and I think it caused them pain to see me. It turned out to be a good thing that they live across the country."

"I'll say it again—ouch." Julia had stopped eating, and her chin was propped in her hand, elbow on the table. "I'm so sorry you lost them. I can't even imagine." She shook her head.

"Your big Italian family is tight, I bet." Savannah tried to keep the wistful tone of envy out of her voice but wasn't sure she'd succeeded.

"Too tight sometimes." Julia finished off her drink and her eyebrows rose, silently asking if Savannah wanted another. She shook her head. "Everybody knows everybody's business. The family grapevine is more like a switchboard. News travels fast. Good and bad."

"And do they all come into the bar? Do they all get free drinks?" Savannah slid her plate away, far too full, and sat forward with her elbows on the table and folded her hands near her chin.

Julia made a slight grimace. "The bar is a bit of a touchy subject in my family."

"How so?"

Napkin in hand, Julia wiped her mouth, then mimicked Savannah and pushed her own plate away. Which must have triggered the waiter because he suddenly materialized out of thin air and cleared the plates, promising to box up the leftovers. Coffees were then refilled.

"The bar has been in my family for a long time."

"My dad says he went there when he was young."

Julia nodded as she picked up her coffee and cradled it in both hands. "My grandfather opened it, then my uncle Tony took it over. He retired last year and sold it to me." She glanced up and Savannah nodded for her to continue. "My dad's a pretty traditional guy. Keep in mind that his only daughter has come out as gay. Now she runs a bar."

"She *owns* a bar—there's a difference," Savannah pointed out, and the look on Julia's face right then, the way her smile bloomed like a flower and brightened her entire being, warmed Savannah up from the inside.

"Thank you for that," Julia said softly. "But my dad doesn't really see me as a business owner. He sees me as a bartender."

"Which there's nothing wrong with either."

"You are earning so many points right now," Julia said with a laugh, as she reached across the table and covered Savannah's hand again.

"I love your voice." It was out before Savannah even knew she was thinking it. And it was *so* true. That husky, gravelly sound did things to her. But to her own surprise, she didn't blush. She held eye contact with Julia, and it was…delicious was the only word she could come up with to describe the feeling. It was delicious. She wanted more of it.

Julia *did* blush. And it was gorgeous. And sexy. "Well. Thank you for that, too." She glanced down at her lap in what seemed to be bashfulness, her dark, full lashes casting a bit of a shadow on her cheeks, then lifted her head and said, "I think this is going pretty well, don't you?"

Savannah nodded, smiled big, but was afraid of the next betrayal of her brain if she opened her mouth. Instead, she picked up her coffee and held the cup with both hands in front of her lips. Her eyes, though, never left Julia's.

This was a lot.

It came crashing through her mind then, that thought, like a rhinoceros plowing through the jungle underbrush. She couldn't remember the last time she'd been so drawn to somebody. Physically and mentally. And physically. Also, did she mention physically?

Because holy crap, she could see herself going home with Julia right then. In a heartbeat. No question. No second-guessing. It was a lot.

"How did you get into home health care?" Julia's voice—God, that voice—yanked her out of her own head and back to the table, the conversation. It took her a moment and several blinks before she was in any condition to participate.

"Like I said, I wanted to be a nurse," she said. "That was my plan. I'd gone to college but hadn't been able to settle on a major, so I did the dreaded liberal—"

"—arts." Julia said it with her, in tandem, and then broke into laughter. "The catch-all major when you have no clue what you want to do with your life," Julia said and held her coffee cup over the center of the table in a toast. "To those of us who just didn't know."

"I will drink to that." They cheered and sipped, and Savannah continued, "I worked a couple jobs here and there, one of which was as an admin for an assisted living facility, and I found I really liked it there, liked watching the nurses and the aides when I could. I decided to go to nursing school. And then my mom died, and my dad was a mess, and my siblings needed caring for..."

"And you put your life on hold to help your family." Julia's voice was soft, almost reverent.

"I guess, yeah. I didn't really think about it at the time. I quit my job so I could be there to help, and being a home health aide was the closest I could get to nursing school at the time. And like I said, I kept putting it off." She sipped her coffee and lifted one shoulder in a half shrug. "And now I'm thirty-four and not a nurse."

"Not a nurse *yet*. There's a difference." Julia's eyebrows rose and fell as she used Savannah's own words.

"Did you hear me say I'm thirty-four?"

"I did. Thirty-four is not eighty-five. In case you were confused. Hell, I'm thirty-eight and just started a new career. Why can't you?"

A tip of her head as she took in the words. "You're right."

"I usually am."

"And modest, too." Savannah winked at her.

"Absolutely. If you don't believe me, just ask me."

They were grinning like fools at each other across the table as the waiter came by to ask if they needed anything else.

A glance at her phone had Julia saying, "Unfortunately, I have to get moving."

"Bar life," Savannah said with a nod, as if it was a very logical and well-known thing.

Julia pointed at her. "Exactly that." She handed the waiter her credit card before Savannah could even take a breath to protest, then turned those dark eyes on her and said simply, "You get the next one."

The next one. Savannah liked the sound of that. She really, really did. "Okay. Deal." The waiter returned, and Julia signed the check. As they stood and gathered their things, Savannah tried to remain as casual as possible when she asked, "So, when do you think the next one might be?" Because she was so on board for another date with this woman. *So* on board.

They weaved through the other tables until they were in the parking lot, the sun bright, and Julia pulled out her Wayfarers and slid them on. To the surprise of no one, they only ramped up her sex appeal. Savannah's knees literally went weak.

"So, this might sound a little weird," Julia began.

"Luckily, I love weird."

"Oh, good. There's a back room in my bar."

"Weird *and* creepy, I see. Go on."

The dimples made a big appearance then. "Yes, that's me. I really want to lure you to the back room of my bar and—"

"Have your way with me?" Oh my God, had she just said that out loud? Savannah closed her eyes, clenched her teeth, and winced.

"Man, I *really* like you," Julia said. "And yes. But I wasn't going to actually say that because my mother raised me with manners."

They reached Julia's car and stood face to face. "Tell me about this mysterious back room." Savannah knew they both needed to get on their way, but she didn't want to. It was that simple.

"It's my hangout. It's where I practice making new drinks. My cousins and I meet there to catch up. It's kind of like a living room at my place of work."

"So you don't ever have to leave work."

"You're on to me already." A gentle breeze picked up, sifting through Julia's dark hair the way Savannah wanted to with her fingers, rearranging it, feeling what she imagined was extreme softness. "Anyway, on nights when it's less busy, which is mostly early in the week, I am back there doing paperwork or playing with mixology, and I'd love you to come hang with me sometime. We can pick up where we left off."

Though Savannah hadn't actually seen this back room hangout, her brain had already created a picture. Wooden walls, couches, a big area rug. Kinda like Central Perk in the TV show *Friends*. A place for relaxing and talking and she wanted very much to be there with Julia. "I would love to pick up where we left off in your weird and creepy back room. You tell me when. I sometimes have to take an evening shift, but that's pretty sporadic."

"Can I text you?"

Savannah nodded. "I would love it if you did."

"It might be short notice. I apologize in advance for that."

"Doesn't matter. I'll come." She meant it. She meant it with every atom in her body. This was going to be worth it. She just knew Julia was going to be somebody important. She didn't know how. She didn't know why. She didn't even know for sure in what capacity—though she really, really hoped it was sexual. She simply knew.

Their gazes held and that sizzle was back, like electricity moving back and forth between their bodies. It was the perfect time for a kiss, but Savannah wanted to wait, wanted to prolong this feeling just a bit, so she started to take a few steps backward. Gaze still glued to Julia's face, she lifted a hand in what she hoped was a cute little wave.

"I'll see you in the creepy back room."

"I look forward to it." Julia laughed.

"Thanks for brunch."

"You're welcome." Julia made no move to open her car door. She just stood there. Watched Savannah. Smiled.

"Text me."

"I definitely will."

If she hadn't been certain she'd trip and fall over something, she'd have kept walking backward. It was a good strategy. Kind of sexy, but also showing she had control of things. Finally, one more wave, then she turned to her car door and slid inside.

"Oh my God," she whispered as she leaned her head back against the seat and focused on steadying her breath. In the rearview mirror, Julia's car glided by, gave a quiet toot, then pulled out into traffic. "Oh my God," she whispered again.

Delicious. There was that word again. Everything about being around Julia Martini was delicious.

Unexpected. That was the bigger one. Before she could analyze it, though, her phone pinged an incoming text from Tiffany.

And? You still at brunch? Did you take her home? ARE YOU HAVING SEX RIGHT NOW?

A bubble of laughter burst out of Savannah then. Part joy, part happy relief. She texted back, *Where are you?*

She needed to talk about all of this. Now.

CHAPTER NINE

It was time to implement some themes. Gimmicks. Something to bring people in. She'd been too slow about that, but there was so much else to do, she'd let it slide down her list. And down. And down. And now she was paying for it. That had to change. While Julia didn't expect things to be crazy busy and crowded on a Sunday evening, she expected more than the handful of customers she had now. Why couldn't it be football season again?

Arriving right from that amazing brunch with Savannah, she'd opened the bar and left it in Hank's hands when she'd gone home for family dinner, not at all hungry, but not daring to tell her mother that. When she'd come back to the bar, uncomfortably full, she'd seen the small handful of customers, sighed quietly, and sent Hank home.

"What fun drink can you introduce me to tonight?" It was Chris. Again. While she was nice enough, and Julia very much appreciated the business, she was a bit of an attention hound. She'd come in shortly after Hank had left, parked herself on her usual end stool, and settled in.

"How do you feel about bourbon?" Despite her wariness, at least Chris gave her the chance to make new drinks she wouldn't normally.

"Willing to try anything you make me."

"All right then." She reached for the ingredients for a sidecar. Well, technically a bourbon sidecar, since a traditional one was made with cognac. She sugared the rim of a chilled glass and set it on the mat. As she put bourbon, Cointreau, and lemon juice into a shaker, the door opened and Amelia came in, waving on her way to an empty seat.

"Liquor me up," she said as she slid off her jacket. Julia studied her cousin while shaking the drink. Shadows under her eyes said she wasn't sleeping well, and she looked drained.

"You okay?" Julia asked.

Amelia nodded with an expression that said *Yes, yes, I'm fine, do your thing,* then waved her off to finish what she was doing.

Yellow like the early summer sun, that's what color the sidecar was as she strained it into the glass, then misted a lemon peel over the top. "I present to you a bourbon sidecar," she said to Chris, then waited for her to take a sip while trying not to look like she was waiting. Getting the balance of a sweet and sour drink just right could be tricky, and she'd know right away if she'd botched it.

"Oh, that's good," Chris said, even as her glossed-red lips puckered slightly.

"Too sour?"

"No, not at all. Perfect."

"Good." With a nod and a quick rap on the bar, she grabbed a rag and wiped her sticky hands on it as she turned back to Amelia, who sat directly opposite, on the other side of the bar. "What brings you in on a Sunday evening?" she asked. "You okay?" Yeah, she asked it again, and Amelia shot her a look that said so, but Julia felt a tickle of worry. "You look…off."

"Gee, thanks. Gimme a vodka cranberry."

"Say please."

Amelia glared at her for a beat before sighing, "Please," and making it into a four-syllable word.

She mixed Amelia's drink, refilled the pitcher of beer the guys at the table were drinking, smiled at Chris who was watching her, then returned to Amelia. Hands on the bar, she leaned against them and said, "What's going on?"

Half her drink gone, Amelia shook her head. "I'm just… none of this is right. I'm forty-eight years old, and this isn't where

I'm supposed to be right now, you know? Single. Alone. So uncomfortable in my own skin, I want to cry every morning. No. Just...no."

Julia didn't know what to say. She rarely did with Amelia lately because nothing seemed to help. "I'm sorry," she said, which she knew she said a lot.

The door opened again, and a group of three entered, two women and a man. Julia wasn't proud of the relief that washed over her as she went to wait on them. She instantly recognized the girl with the short blond hair and baseball cap.

"Hey, Kirby, how's it going?"

"Great! We just played some *amazing* Frisbee golf and decided to come in for a beer." Kirby was the most cheerful person Julia had ever met—including Vanessa, and that said a lot. She talked about Frisbee golf like she'd been playing in the US Open.

"Well, I'm glad you did. Julia Martini," she said to the other two as she held out a hand. Uncle Tony had taught her that—introduce yourself, get to know your clientele personally. People liked being recognized when they walked in.

The couple was Jason and Amanda, husband and wife and friends of Kirby's for years now and, apparently, much better Frisbee golf players than she was.

"They kicked my ass," Kirby said. "Both of them. Handily. Frankly, I'm embarrassed for myself."

"I do seem to recall more than one *I rock Frisbee golf!* when we asked you to play." Amanda gave Kirby a shoulder bump. "And now, sadly for you, you have to buy us beer."

"Ugh." Kirby dropped her head back and groaned loudly. "Such a steep price to pay," she wailed as the rest of them laughed. "Still a blast, though. Bring on the beer."

Julia poured their beers and served them up.

"It's because my Frisbee was red, you know." Kirby said it sort of pretend-quietly, because it was clear she meant it to be heard by her friends.

"Here we go," Jason said with an exaggerated eye roll.

"What? It's true. Red is too bold a color for concentration." Kirby seemed to truly believe this.

Julia grinned as she glanced over her shoulder at the other customers, checking on them. Amelia was watching the exchange openly.

"Red is a power color, you dweeb." Amanda.

"Yes, but too powerful for Frisbee golf. It throws off concentration. Google it. There are studies."

Jason turned to Amanda and said, "Don't argue with her about color stuff. You'll lose."

"Damn right," Kirby said, then pointed to the wall. "Like this color here. Gray is neutral, but you can lean either way to change that up. Lighten it and it makes the room feel brighter, but less relaxing. Deepen it to a slate, like it is, and it's warmer, more inviting. You want to sit. Stay awhile."

"I think it's kind of cold."

Julia turned her head to look at Amelia, who was gazing at the wall after she spoke, squinting and shaking her head.

Kirby's eyes widened a touch. "Really? I mean, the color in general, maybe, but—"

"It's kinda cave-like." Eyes still on the wall, Amelia probably didn't notice the look Julia shot her.

"Gee, thanks. Also, Kirby is my painter. She and I picked the gray together. Which you said you liked when you first saw it."

"Eh." Amelia shrugged and sipped her cocktail, and Julia couldn't tell if she was messing with her or serious. Which meant she didn't know if she should be laughing or pissed off. Squinting at Amelia in suspicion was her only course of action, so she took it.

"Ray of sunshine, that one," Kirby said under her breath. "Friend of yours?"

"Family," Julia said. "Sorry."

Kirby's turn to shrug, but she added a smirk. "Good thing she's hot." And just like that, she turned back to her friends and their beer and laughter. It was one of the things Julia had liked most about Kirby after hiring her—nothing seemed to faze her.

Julia wanted to ask Kirby what that was about, but she saw Chris out of the corner of her eye, holding up her empty glass. "Another?" she asked as she detoured in that direction.

"Please," Chris said and parked her forearms on the bar. "You know everybody."

"Occupational hazard," Julia said.

"But does everybody know *you*?" Chris asked. "'Cause I'd like to."

Ugh. Here we go.

Instead of being flattered or even brushing it off like Julia did with so many propositions from clients, she felt a little creeped out. Uncomfortable. She slowed down making the drink so she could take a second. Why was this bothering her? It certainly wasn't the first time a customer had crossed a line. Hell, it really wasn't even the first time Chris had. When she finished the drink and handed it over, she said to Chris, "You're very kind." Then she turned before any further conversation could be had and crossed to Amelia.

"Evasion at its finest right there," Amelia said. "Impressive." She lowered her head and her voice. "I think somebody has a crush on you."

"I'm pretty sure she's harmless, but each time she comes in, she turns it up a little bit." Julia kept her voice low and wiped the bar to make it look like she was busy and not talking about a client. "I don't know why it's getting under my skin tonight."

"Cuz of your brunch date, maybe?" Amelia's eyes twinkled as Julia squinted at her.

"My brother has a big mouth."

"Not news. Maybe you need to bring that cute little blonde in and flirt with her in front of this woman." Amelia's eyebrows rose, she finished her drink, and her entire demeanor was now open and friendly. The exact opposite of half an hour ago when she'd come in. So weird. "Send a message."

Julia almost pointed out the change in her but had learned from the last time that her recent mood swings weren't something Amelia liked to be made aware of. Instead, she let her mind paint a picture of Savannah sitting at the bar, sipping a cocktail that Julia created especially for her, watching Julia work, giving her a look...

Stop that.

She didn't even know if Savannah had a look to give. And if she did? Would she even give it to Julia? And then she heard herself in her head, thinking about this stuff, and rolled her eyes at herself and became instantly irritated. This was stupid. She was being stupid. Getting ahead of herself. They'd had one date. It had been nice. Well, more than nice. It'd been pretty great, actually.

A camera clicked, and Julia blinked back to the present moment. Amelia was typing on her phone and looked up at Julia's surprised face. "I can't remember the last time I saw you that dreamy-faced, googly-eyed. I had to show Vanessa."

"Seriously?" Julia said, louder than she'd meant to, and glanced around at her patrons. None of whom was watching except Chris.

"Must've been some date." Amelia said it softer this time. Less teasing in her tone. Her hazel eyes were focused on Julia, and she was probably waiting for details.

Which Julia was suddenly all too happy to share because she'd been dying to talk about Savannah. She held up a finger, telling Amelia to give her a second while she refilled drinks for Kirby and her friends. A quick glance around the bar told her everybody's glasses were full. Chris looked like she was waiting for something, but Julia shot her a smile and returned to Amelia.

"Spill," Amelia said, then pointed to her empty glass. "And while you do so, make my drink right here so I can watch." She pointed to the workspace directly in front of her seat. "Cuz I don't think there's any vodka in these."

Julia rolled her eyes, even though Amelia was almost right. There was vodka. Just not as much as usual. When one of the people she cared about most in the world flopped down and ordered, *Liquor me up*, and she'd been having as rough a time as Amelia had, there was a worrisome element, and the last thing Julia was going to do was get her hammered. But she did as she was told and made the cocktail in front of Amelia, using the proper amount of alcohol this time.

"Thank you. Now"—Amelia made a show of hunkering down, set her elbow on the bar, and sank her chin into her hand—"tell me all about brunch."

Julia spread her arms, braced each hand on the edge of the bar, and sighed quietly. Dreamily. Like a lovesick teenager. Amelia was right. She probably was dreamy-eyed. What was happening to her?

"I didn't want it to end." Whoa. Okay, saying that out loud was a big deal. "She's smart and funny and sweet."

"And hot," Amelia supplied.

"So hot. Oh my God. She wore a dress and a jean jacket, and she looked sophisticated and edgy and just..." She let her head drop down between her shoulders. Lifted it up again when she'd collected herself. "And we talked and talked and talked."

"So a connection, then."

"A definite connection." Her smile was wide. She could feel it and wondered if it bordered on comical.

Instead of mocking her, Amelia lowered her gaze and said, "I think your would-be stalker needs a refill."

A glance over her shoulder told Julia that Chris was indeed looking for a refill. She pasted on a smile and crossed to her. "Liked that one?"

"Delicious. Another, please."

"Coming right up."

"Is that your girlfriend?" Chris used her chin to indicate she was talking about Amelia. And asking after her sexuality. Ballsy. Julia tried to think of a way to answer the question without confirming or denying anything. She was out, it was true, and she wasn't big on hiding her sexuality for anybody, but Chris made her feel wary somehow. "That is my cousin, and I keep my relationship status private." She offered a smile as she shook the drink, just in case she'd come across too snarky. Which she had a right to do, she could hear Amelia tell her in her head. But again, Chris was a customer, and Martini's couldn't afford to be turning away customers simply because they were a little nosy. Not with this crowd of—she counted with her eyes as she shook the shaker—ten people counting Amelia. Ugh. Not good.

"Sidecar number three," she said as she presented Chris her cocktail.

"My grandpa had a sidecar on his motorcycle. Did I tell you that?"

"You did not."

And so began a fifteen-minute story about Chris's grandfather and his grand motorcycle rides around Upstate New York. And downstate. And the northeastern part. And into Massachusetts. And oh my God, Julia kept looking for a good place to break away. Finally, she glanced to her left and saw Kirby holding up a hand, making the scribble-in-the-air universal sign for *We're ready to cash out*. Thank fucking God.

She excused herself, rang out Kirby and her friends, and went back to Amelia.

"I was so right about the crush." Amelia slid her empty glass toward Julia. "I've been waiting for ten minutes for a refill."

"If I make you another, you're Ubering home." She hadn't had to cut off more than two customers so far in her ownership, and she certainly didn't want number three to be a family member.

"Please. I Ubered here. I'm not an idiot."

"What's going on with you? You've got me and Ness worried."

Amelia shrugged, and much to Julia's surprise, her eyes welled up. "It's just life. You guys don't have to worry. I'm just doing my best to get a handle on things, and some days are better than others."

"And today was a not-great day?"

Amelia tapped her nose with a finger.

"I'm sorry, sweetheart." She hated seeing her cousin looking so lost. It was the best description, and that made Julia a little sad. "You know we're here if you need anything, right? Both of us. And your dad."

"I miss my mom," Amelia said quietly.

Aunt Suzanne, Amelia's mom, had been one of the most wonderful people Julia had ever known. Kind. Funny. A heart big enough for everybody. Not a mean bone in her body. She'd died in a car accident three years before, and being an only child, it had hit Amelia hard.

"Going through my divorce and now menopause without her is…" Amelia closed her eyes, gave her head a soft shake. "It's brutal. I just want to talk to her, you know?"

It occurred to Julia then that Savannah had also lost her mother, that maybe she was somebody Amelia could talk to who'd get it.

She could be as sympathetic and open as possible, but the truth was, Julia had no idea what it felt like to lose a parent. Amelia had told her it changed her, changed everything about life to her, made her into a completely different person. She wondered if Savannah felt the same way.

Amelia blew out a breath then and sat up straighter, a clear sign she was changing the subject. "So. When do you see your cute little blonde again? Remind me of her name."

"Savannah McNally." Just saying her name made Julia happy. Which didn't go unnoticed.

"Oh my God, look at you. You just lit up. Ugh. You make me sick." But Amelia grinned and poked Julia in the arm to make sure she knew it was just teasing. "Also, that name sounds familiar. McNally. Do we know them?"

A shrug. A shake of her head. "I don't think so."

"Ask your dad. He'll know."

It was true. Julia's dad knew just about everybody in Northwood, either because he'd worked on their car, or he'd worked on the car of somebody in their family, or he knew them through one of his five siblings. "Good call. I will."

"I think the chick with the crush on you is trying to get your attention."

Julia closed her eyes. "She asked me if you were my girlfriend."

Amelia made a face of mock-horror. "Please. I'd kill you in your sleep."

"Not if I killed you first." Back in front of Chris, she asked, "All set?"

Chris made a show of checking her watch, which was small and delicate with a black band. "I guess I should probably head home. Gotta work in the morning."

"I hear you." Julia rang up Chris's check, which totaled just over twenty dollars, and slid it toward her, where two twenties were already on the bar, and Chris was sliding off her stool.

"You keep the change," Chris said, nodding toward the money. "I'll see you again soon." And she was heading toward the door before Julia could respond. While it was completely uncouth to argue with a customer about a tip, whenever somebody left her so much, it gave her a weird feeling in the pit of her stomach.

"It's down to almost just you and me, kid," Amelia said.

"Much as I love you, I wish that was not the case." Julia sighed. "I think it's time you get Vanessa in here and put that elementary school teaching brain of hers to work on fun ways to sell drinks."

"I think you're right. I meant to do that weeks ago." She held up the money. "Also, she just left me an almost twenty-dollar tip."

"That's 'cause she *loooooooves* you."

Julia threw a bar rag at her. "Shut up."

"What's the next step with Ms. McNally?"

Grateful for something to talk about that didn't give her agita, she said, "We said we'd text each other."

"Who's going to text who?"

Julia blinked at her. "Huh?"

"Is she texting you? Or are you texting her?" Amelia leaned closer. "This is important. Otherwise, you may both be waiting for a text, like, forever."

"Really?"

"I may have been married for a while, but I was single at one time in life, as I am right now."

"I should text her." Julia slid her phone out, wide eyes on her cousin, a tiny sliver of fear in her heart. She did not want to mess this up. "Right?"

"I would."

"Like, right now?"

"You like this girl?"

"I do." So much truth in two little words.

"Text her."

CHAPTER TEN

Julia hadn't been kidding when she'd told Savannah she had a crazy schedule. And it didn't take long before Savannah began to wonder if Julia actually kind of liked it that way. Being so busy, she had little time for anything else. Maybe a bit of a built-in excuse to not deal with certain things? Or certain people...

She shook the thought away, not wanting to analyze this person she had a feeling she could really like. It was a bad habit of hers, trying to figure out what made somebody tick, even if they didn't want her in their head that way. Her mother always said she should've been a therapist.

It was Thursday night, just after dinner, and Savannah had the sudden urge to see Julia. Like, actually lay eyes on her. They'd texted regularly since their brunch on Sunday but hadn't been able to make their schedules work. Savannah had picked up a shift on Saturday and was spending Sunday with Chelsea, so the weekend was out. Without taking the time to talk herself out of it, she grabbed her phone and sent a text.

What are you doing right now?

A moment or two went by and the bouncing dots showed up on her screen.

Workin' on the books, came the response, followed by a dollar sign and an eye roll emoji.

Savannah grinned. *In the newly designated Bar Back with capital letters?* Julia had talked about the back room of her bar, how her cousins had named it aptly and supplied signage.

In The Bar Back with capital letters, yes. A smile.

What if I promised not to bother you? Could I come hang out in The Bar Back with capital letters? She paused before sending it, added, *I'd really like to see you.*

Julia's response came instantly. *I would love that.*

Savannah felt a smile bloom across her face. She'd had a very busy day. Mrs. Richter had been a handful, in rare form for her, and incredibly needy and difficult. When she finished a shift like that, she normally just wanted to be home, hunker down for a bit, decompress.

Not tonight.

She followed Julia's directions to where the side door of Martini's was located and stood outside of it for a moment to gear up. She was casual. Jeans. A navy-blue tank. A blue-and-white checked shirt over that, unbuttoned. Pink-and-white Nikes on her feet. Hair in a ponytail. She'd applied a little lip gloss in the car, and now she stood with her hand on the door handle and took a big breath before she pulled on it.

The space wasn't at all what she expected. It didn't look like the back of a bar at all. In fact, she felt like she was walking into somebody's hip, spacious studio apartment. The ceiling was high with all the pipes and ducts visible and painted a sleek black. A sitting area was to her left, complete with a comfy-looking couch and a coffee table strewn with magazines and books. Beyond that was a small kitchenette-slash-bar that would be adorable in anybody's house, though the shelves behind it were stocked full with an impressive supply of alcohol.

"Well, aren't you a sight for sore eyes, as my grandmother would say." Julia's voice came from her right where she sat at a desk, a laptop as well as two drawers of a four-drawer filing cabinet open in front of her. She stood up and closed the space between them, and it wasn't even a question—they were in each other's arms, sharing a tight, warm hug that Savannah hadn't been expecting but realized in that moment she very much wanted and somehow *needed*. Julia felt so good in her arms. Warm. Solid. She smelled like something citrusy. Oranges?

"This is the closest we've ever been," Savannah said. "You're tall." She smiled against Julia's shoulder. "I like it."

"Good, 'cause there's not a lot I can do about that." Julia's arms tightened just a bit. "You smell good."

"I'm glad you think so." Another beat or two went by before they let go. Savannah wondered if Julia felt the same reluctance to do so that she did. "So. This is the infamous Bar Back."

"I don't know about infamous, but yeah, this is it. I spend a lot of time here when I'm not out front." The pride in Julia's husky voice was unmistakable.

"Do you live here?" The question was only half joking, because it totally looked like she could. Savannah began to wander, taking in the space.

"You'd think so," came the reply and a deep laugh. "I have an apartment a few blocks away. But I am here way more often."

"Don't you have a bar manager?" Savannah wandered, running her fingertips over the bar, scanning the bottles. When she turned back, Julia was raising her hand and gave it a little wave. "I'm serious. If you hired a manager, you could free up some of your time."

"You sound like my cousins." There was a very slight edge in her voice. Savannah felt it more than heard it and decided to leave the subject alone.

"Well, I'm seriously impressed with this place." She took a seat at the bar, so she could take it all in.

"Yeah?" Julia's grin was back, and Savannah loved seeing those damn dimples. Sexy didn't begin to describe them. "Can I get you a drink?"

"Much as I'd love one because it was *a day*, I've got another early shift in the morning and probably shouldn't."

Julia went behind the bar, and she looked so at home there, so exactly right, not to mention incredibly hot, it made Savannah smile. "Soda? Seltzer? I can give you a Baileys on the rocks. Irish cream? Just a little alcohol, but more soothing than anything else. Take the edge off your day."

"You know what? That sounds fabulous. One of those, barkeep."

"You got it."

Watching Julia fix her a cocktail was something Savannah decided in that moment she would never get tired of. The way she chose a glass, filled it with ice. She poured the liquor in that slightly fancy way, where she lifted the bottle up a bit as the liquid hit the glass, then lowered it, truly making it a spectacle, a performance. Even something as simple as Baileys.

"Voilà," Julia said as she slid the glass in front of Savannah, who didn't take her eyes from her bartender.

"You are so fucking sexy," she said softly, then felt her eyes widen slightly as she realized the words had actually left her mouth instead of staying safely in her head where they belonged.

Julia's reaction was a combination of surprise, a slight blush, and a slow smile, and then she leaned forward over the bar toward Savannah. Their first kiss, and it was soft, a simple, gentle pressing of lips, a testing, a taste. No hands. No rush or urgency. Nothing but lips. Warmth. And a sizzle. A definite sizzle. Oh yeah, when they did that the next time, it was going to be off the charts hot. Savannah could feel it in her bones, rocketing through her blood like liquid fire.

The side door opened, startling Savannah enough to make her jump, and she turned toward the sound.

A blond woman stood there, like she'd frozen in midstep, big blue eyes wide with what looked like surprise. That quickly morphed into a pretty smile, complete with dimples, and despite the opposite color palette, Savannah could see a resemblance between her and Julia.

"Oh my God, I'm interrupting," the newcomer said, then continued to come in, closed the door behind her, and set her purse down.

"You totally are," Julia said, but there was no anger in her voice. Rather, she was grinning, and when those dark, dark eyes of hers met Savannah's, they were sparkling, and Julia gave her a wink. Savannah was glad to see that because her lips still tingled from their kiss. "Savannah McNally, meet my cousin Vanessa Martini."

Vanessa crossed the room, hand outstretched. "Lotta syllables in our names," she said, her face open and friendly. "Nice to meet you."

"Same here," Savannah said and shook her hand.

"Amelia said you needed my help." Vanessa took the stool next to Savannah and sat. "Diet Coke?"

Julia sighed quietly and honored the request, and there was something about the way she didn't run Vanessa off. Didn't make her feel bad for showing up. Rather, just accepted her presence almost happily and slid a beverage in front of her. Savannah liked that.

"Help with what?" Savannah asked, looking from Julia to Vanessa—who shifted a bit in her seat—and back. She sipped her Baileys.

The two cousins seemed to hold eye contact for an extra beat before Julia said, "The bar hasn't been doing as well as I'd hoped."

Her disappointment was clear, but it felt like more than that to Savannah, like there was something else wrapped around the success or failure of her business. "It's only been reopened for a couple months, though, right?"

"True." Julia pulled a beer from the fridge behind her, popped the cap, took a long sip. Then she leaned her forearms on her side of the bar, and Savannah felt a flush of heat as she replayed their kiss. Had that only happened moments ago?

"Her business plan was too general. Too basic. She needs to start using some specifics. Some gimmicks," Vanessa said, waving her hands as she talked. "Themes. Things to pull in more people. Drink specials—which should be different martinis because, hello? And prizes. Stuff like that."

Watching Vanessa talk, she should have colors all around her. That's what Savannah thought. She was bright. Cheerful. Sparkly. Savannah thought she should have a sparkling of glitter follow her around. Sequins on all her brightly colored clothes. She couldn't help but smile as Vanessa laid out some ideas. A lot of them. She talked quickly, her pretty hands drawing invisible pictures in the air. It was something to behold.

Julia loved her cousin. Savannah could see that clearly in the way she listened carefully, paid close attention, even if Vanessa's idea was crazy or unrealistic. There was always a gentle smile on her face, but it wasn't patronizing. It was loving. Interested. Respectful. Julia respected Vanessa, and Savannah found herself envious of that kind of a family relationship.

Savannah didn't keep track of how long they talked about ways to improve business, but she sipped her drink, loving the rich creaminess as it coated her tongue and did just what Julia promised—took the edge off without making her feel tipsy. At one point, she found a notebook and pen in her purse and began jotting things down for Julia, surprised to find herself invested. Somehow, after only knowing her a very short time, she wanted to help Julia make her bar successful. By the time they finished, she had several pages of scribbles, and Julia was ready to invent a couple new drinks for the following week.

"Oh my God, is it after eleven?" Savannah was shocked.

"No. Is it?" Vanessa's dark brows rose. "It is. Crap. I gotta go. It's a school night."

"What do you do?" Savannah asked as she handed Vanessa her jacket and picked up her own. They'd hardly talked about anything but the bar, and Savannah wanted to know more about this sparkly human.

"She shapes the minds of our youth," Julia said.

"Ah, so it actually *is* a school night," Savannah said.

"Yes, and I should be sleeping right now. Fourth graders have way more energy than I do on a good day." Vanessa pushed up on her toes and kissed Julia's cheek. "Bye."

"Thank you," Julia said and hugged Vanessa tight. "So much."

"No worries. We're gonna make Martini's *the* place to be." With a cute little waggly finger wave, Vanessa Martini left just the way she'd entered, in a whoosh.

Savannah stood looking at the door and took a moment to catch her breath. "Wow."

Julia laughed through her nose. "Right?"

"She is something."

"She really is. I don't know what I'd do without her." A grimace settled across her full lips. "I'm sorry about that, though. I didn't know she was coming."

Savannah waved her off. "You guys are lucky to have each other. And don't apologize. I had fun." She turned to look at Julia, and their eyes locked. She took a step closer. Two. Until there was only an inch or two between them and she had to lift her chin to make eye contact. "But, if I remember correctly, we got interrupted." She hadn't meant to whisper it, but that's how it came out. Breathy and soft.

"We did. Now..." Julia squinted, made a show of thinking hard. "Where were we?"

Thoughts apparently left her. They were just gone, because not one crossed her mind. There were no instructions given to her hands by her brain, no debate, no wondering whether or not she should do this. Savannah simply reached up with one hand, slid it under Julia's hair to the back of her neck, and pulled her head down.

Their lips met.

There was nothing tentative about *this* kiss.

No testing. No sampling.

It was hard and sensual and invasive in the best of ways. Savannah had never kissed anyone that aggressively, that thoroughly, ever in her life. Whether she'd been with them for months or had just met them in the moment. No, this was different. This was hot. And sexy in a completely unfamiliar way. And so very real. Julia's lips were soft, warm, wet, and when they parted and allowed Savannah's tongue into her mouth, one of them moaned. Somebody hummed. Julia's hands were on Savannah's body, one at the small of her back, pulling her closer, the other cupping her face. There was nothing to be heard in the room except the very distant melody coming from the main bar and the soft sounds of their kiss.

Air became an issue. The need for it. Savannah finally lowered her head enough to free her mouth from Julia's, and they both stood there, chests heaving with ragged breaths. Savannah rested her forehead against Julia's shoulder and said the only thing she could think to say.

"Wow."

"Uh-huh," was Julia's reply as she swallowed, and she sounded as bewildered by that kiss as Savannah felt.

"We are wordy," Savannah said after another moment, and she felt Julia's shoulder move with her soft laughter.

"I just…" Savannah lifted her head and Julia looked down at her and there was something. Something there, floating between them. Words? Observations? Something Savannah wasn't ready to address, and she got the very distinct impression Julia felt the same way.

"I should probably get home," Savannah said softly, and if Julia felt she was being abrupt, she didn't show it. Instead, she nodded and gently moved Savannah to arm's length. Which was a good thing, Savannah thought. Safer. Less chance of her jumping back in, grabbing Julia's face, and kissing it right the hell off. And also a sad thing because she instantly missed Julia's closeness. Her warmth. Wanted to go back to it.

Julia picked up Savannah's purse, held it so she could slide her arm through the strap, and it rested on her shoulder. Their gazes held again, and it seemed clear to Savannah that they both wanted to talk, but neither felt quite ready. And that was okay.

"Text me," she said softly.

"I definitely will." Julia bent her head, brushed Savannah's lips quickly, and took an almost unnoticeable step back, as if she needed to put a bit of distance between them.

That night in bed, Savannah couldn't get Julia out of her head. All that hair that she wanted to bury her face in. Those deep, dark eyes that she felt she could fall into. Those soft, wet, hot lips and how they'd felt on hers. Before she realized it, her hand had found its way into her bikinis.

With Julia Martini as her fantasy material, her orgasm ripped through her in less than three minutes.

CHAPTER ELEVEN

Thank God for Fridays.

Julia looked around her bar as she pulled the rag from her shoulder and wiped the surface. It was Friday, just after four, and things were starting to pick up nicely. Didn't seem to matter how business was the rest of the week. Or month. Or even the year. Friday happy hour was a thing and always would be, thank fucking God. Her smile was one of relief, though she hoped that wasn't obvious.

The *Northwood Nightlife* blog had mentioned Martini's again, and she wondered if that had helped with a bump in business. Called the place "atmospheric and creative." She'd take it.

There were some regulars at tables, a few family members, including Dante and Vanessa, who'd both come by after work and unexpectedly ran into each other. Her brother John came in a few minutes later. He'd changed out of his mechanic's attire and into a black polo shirt, but his hands were forever grease-stained. He stood between the stools Vanessa and Dante sat on and ordered a beer. Julia was the only bartender at the moment, but Clea was due in soon.

During the day, Hank preferred classic rock, and Julia had no issues with that. But once happy hour kicked in, she switched the tunes over to something more modern and upbeat. A little hip-hop. A little pop. Some electronic dance music. Justin Bieber was filtering through the mounted speakers as the front door opened again, and somebody walked in carrying a large bouquet of flowers in a vase. Heads turned as the person came to the bar and set the flowers down.

"Hi there." It was one of the women from the flower shop down the street. They'd met a few times at a local business networking meeting. She was very kind, and very pretty. Average height, dark hair, shockingly green eyes, and a beautiful smile that Julia couldn't recall ever seeing her without. Stacy? Grace? Something along those lines.

"Hi." Julia draped the rag over her shoulder. "Are those for me?"

"They are. Thought I'd drop them off on my way home. Enjoy."

"Thanks." She lifted her chin at the woman's little wave good-bye, then picked up the vase and took it to the side of the bar where her brothers and cousin were.

"Who was that?" Vanessa asked, her eyes locked on the flower deliverer's retreating form.

"You know her, don't you? She works at the flower shop around the corner." Julia jerked a thumb over her shoulder as she plucked the card from its holder on the flowers.

"The Petal Pusher?" Vanessa's face lit up. "I love that place. It's so cute. Lots of fun little gifts in there along with the flowers." Her gaze lingered on the door for a beat, then shifted to Julia. "Ooh, are those from Savannah?" She said the name with a Southern twang, which made Julia laugh.

"I have no idea." But God, she hoped so. How romantic would that be? She slid her finger under the flap of the small envelope and pulled out the card.

To my favorite cocktail creator. Hope these make you smile. Chris

The way the excited anticipation slid off Julia was impressive. It was like she could feel it. Like it was a sheet around her shoulders that was tugged, and it slid right down her body to puddle on the floor.

"I haven't seen her face fall like that since she asked for Doc Martens for Christmas, and Ma got her a pair of heels instead." Dante grinned.

"I remember that," John chimed in. "She picked up that shoebox-shaped present about a hundred times the week before."

Vanessa snatched the card from her hand and read it. "Who's Chris?"

As if they'd conjured her, the door opened and Chris sauntered in, smiled, and waved, and her smile widened when she saw the flowers. She made her way to her usual stool, which was vacant, Julia noticed, and she cursed to herself. She sighed quietly and said to her family members, "*That's* Chris."

"Why is she sending flowers?" John asked, his voice comically low. "Are they dating?"

Julia tipped her head to the side. "Not even close."

"Oh, is that the one Amelia told me about?" Vanessa asked. "The one with the crush on you?"

It was safe to assume that whatever one of the three of them—Julia, Amelia, Vanessa—said to one of the others would always make it to the third. So it was no surprise that Amelia had told Vanessa about Chris. Which was good because it saved Julia from having to explain, and she really didn't want to. A nod was her response.

"She's nice enough," Julia said. "Just a little...familiar sometimes."

"Crushes will do that," Vanessa said.

Dante eyed the flowers, a lovely bouquet of bright spring and summer blooms. Yellows and purples and lots of baby's breath. "I guess so. This is not a cheap bouquet."

"I love getting flowers," Vanessa said in a dreamy voice.

Julia almost pushed the vase toward her but didn't want to be like that, especially in front of Chris. She meant well. She was simply—clearly—not reading the signals correctly. Or maybe Julia needed to hand them out differently. Be louder about them. She put on a smile as she approached to take Chris's drink order.

"I see you got my flowers," Chris said, pride clear on her face.

"I did. That was very nice of you. Very unnecessary, but nice. Thank you." Julia wiped an imaginary spot on the bar and absently marveled at how often she used the act of wiping the bar to fill awkward spaces. "What can I get you?"

Chris seemed slightly dejected that she'd gone right to business, but that was the plan. The flowers were kind of a weird gesture, and Julia didn't want to give them any more attention other than saying a polite thank-you. She could hear Amelia's voice in her head, all logical, telling her she owed Chris nothing but kindness. "I'll just start with a beer." Yup, definite dejection. Julia served her beer and was moving down to another group when the door opened.

As if totally out of her control, she smiled *big*. Bigger even when Savannah saw her and smiled back. The bar was getting busier—several groups of female friends had come in, drawn by the happy hour special of an appletini—and there were no more open stools. Savannah didn't seem to care. As Julia began making a batch for the three work friends at the corner, she walked right up to the bar between two men in separate groups, leaned her forearms on the bar, and said, "If I could've bailed early on my client just to get here and see you sooner, I totally would have."

Day. Made. That was Julia's first thought as she shook the martinis. "Hi, you," she said, then gestured with her head. "Vanessa is over there with my brothers if you want to sit with them."

"Sounds great."

"I'll be right there." How was it that everything was suddenly better? Just from this girl walking into her bar? Did that make any sense at all? She strained the drinks into glasses, their green hue looking almost jewellike in the funky bar lighting, and added an apple slice to each as the trio looked on, clearly entertained. "Enjoy, ladies."

When she turned toward her family, she stopped, and something warm rushed through her. Savannah was sitting on the stool Dante must've given up for her. She was chatting away with the three of them, smiling, looking like she belonged right there in their midst. Vanessa laughed at something John said, then leaned toward Savannah and put a hand on her forearm as Savannah's eyes went wide and she burst into laughter.

The picture was completely normal. Totally regular. Just as it should've been.

All of which was *so weird*. And also, so not.

Julia took a moment, mentally gave herself a shake, and approached, then braced her hands on the bar. "Can I get you something?" she asked Savannah, who turned her attention to her. Did Savannah reach a hand into Julia's lungs and steal all her breath? Because it felt exactly like that. Like that's exactly what she'd done. Air was suddenly sparse.

"Oh no," Savannah said, and her tone was laced with apology as she laid a warm hand on Julia's. "I can't stay. I have to deal with some..." A shadow crossed over her face for a second and was gone. "Family stuff."

"Everything okay?" Concern tapped Julia on the shoulder.

A dismissive wave. "Yeah, it's fine. No big deal."

Maybe Savannah didn't think it'd be a big deal to Julia, but it was a big deal to her. Julia could tell instantly, and part of her was amused, not to mention thankful, that she could read Savannah so well. Another part wanted to help. "You sure?"

She nodded, made a *What can you do?* face, shrugged, and left it at that.

Julia would've liked more time to visit with her, but business was good that Friday, and before she knew it, Savannah was waving good-bye. She looked over her shoulder, held her hands up and mimed thumb-typing, and Julia nodded, watching her go.

As if it had started quietly and then began to increase in volume until she recognized it, her family began singing a little tune behind her that went something like, "Julia and Savannah, sittin' in a tree..."

Julia threw a rag at them, but her face was red, and her smile was wide, and she was painfully aware of both those things.

The family stuff Savannah had to deal with boiled down to Chelsea and listening-helping-holding her while she cried over her broken heart and how Parker could call it quits after so long together.

"Hi, Dad," she called as she entered the house. He was in his recliner watching something on the History channel—Savannah could see men dressed in medieval attire and hear a narrator talking about the weapons of that time. "Still holding on to the dream of becoming a knight?"

"I could pull off a suit of armor," he said matter-of-factly without turning around.

"You totally could." She kissed his head, smelled his cologne. She could hear Dina's voice coming from somewhere near the kitchen and assumed she was meeting virtually with a client.

"What have you been up to today?" her father asked.

"I worked all day, then stopped at Martini's for a..." She hadn't really stopped for a drink, had she? "To see a friend."

Her father made a sound that was half scoff, half grunt.

"What's your problem with that place, Dad?"

Another scoff and a dismissive wave of his hand. "Doesn't matter. It's in the past."

It obviously wasn't, and Savannah was determined to find out the details, just maybe not today.

"You just come by to say hi?" he asked, clearly changing the subject.

She blinked at him for a second, not having come up with a story beforehand to explain her visit. "Actually, I'm here to see Chelsea. She's got a couple new products, some new skincare regimen with a moisturizer and a foundation or something she wants me to try." She could see his eyes glaze over right around the word *regimen* and knew he'd tuned out, as he always did with regard to anything he considered having to do with *girl things* or *feminine stuff.*

He waved absently toward the dining room. "I think she's in there talking with Dina."

Really? Well, that was a surprise.

"Oh, hi, Savvy," Dina said as Savannah entered the room to see Dina at one end of the table, laptop open in front of her, but headset hanging around her neck. In the chair next to her sat Chelsea, a cup of something green in front of her.

"Hey, big sis," Chelsea said and seemed lighter than she had last time Savannah saw her.

"Hi," Savannah said, looking from one woman to the other. "I came by to try that, uh, moisturizer you mentioned."

Chelsea laughed and waved a hand. "It's okay. Dina knows."

Um, what?

Her face must've shown her surprise because Chelsea laughed and motioned to the empty chair in front of her. "Sit. Yeah, she caught me crying this morning and asked what was wrong, and I spilled."

Dina's smile was big, filled with pride. "I told her maybe this was a good thing. Breakups suck, but everything happens for a reason, and maybe it just means there's something—and someone—out there that's so much better for her." And then she was reaching toward Chelsea, and Chelsea was grinning like a fool and reaching back, and their hands clasped, and what the hell was happening? "Right, Kev?" Dina called toward the living room.

"My little girl deserves better than that punk," her father grumbled.

"Dad knows, too?" Savannah blinked at Chelsea. She wanted to be totally cool but felt her breath catch in her chest. "I guess I thought..." What did she think? That it was a secret? That she would be the one to help Chelsea through it? Yeah, that second one. That was it. She blinked some more, words eluding her in a big way.

Chelsea seemed to get at least an idea that Savannah was struggling. "You're so busy and have so much on your plate with your job," she began, gave another shrug as her smile faltered slightly. "I just didn't want to be a burden with my stupid love life crap."

"You are *never* a burden, Chels. You know that, don't you?" She didn't want to look at the hands still clasped together, but her gaze drifted there.

Chelsea must've seen because she let go of Dina. "No, I know. I just...timing. And stuff." She shrugged, obviously not sure what to say. "You know?"

"Believe me," Dina said with a soft laugh. "I've gone through my share of breakups. Men can be such"—she glanced toward the living room, then lowered her voice to a whisper before saying—"douchebags."

Chelsea's laugh snorted out of her nose, and Savannah felt her own eyes go wide for a split second as she watched her sister and her father's girlfriend lean their heads together and share their laughter, and two things crossed her mind then. One, her little sister had somebody at home who was looking after her and her broken heart. And two, she'd been replaced as the mother figure.

She swallowed hard and pasted a smile on her face. Forced herself to laugh along with them. All the while, she felt little fissures running through her heart.

CHAPTER TWELVE

Savannah could've passed on the Saturday shift. She preferred to keep her weekends to herself. That day, though, she'd spent her morning with her brain whirring and spinning, bouncing between the joy of possibility with Julia and the heartbreak of Chelsea's sudden closeness with Dina. She was being ridiculous, and she knew it, but she couldn't seem to shake the sadness. By the time the call came at two, asking if she'd be interested in an evening shift with Mr. Kellogg, she jumped at the chance to focus on something else, something other than the mix of anticipation and pain in her heart.

Mr. Kellogg wasn't her regular client, but she'd attended to him a few times in the past. He was the saddest kind of person Savannah worked with—he was alone. His wife had passed away several years before, and he had no children, no other family. But he was kind and sweet and didn't seem to be sad in his solitude, something she found refreshing. He read constantly, a book always nearby. In addition to the many biographies on his shelves, Savannah noticed he very much preferred political thrillers. Lots of David Baldacci and Lee Child and Tom Clancy. He got Savannah laughing by telling her knock-knock jokes, and she noticed that when she laughed at something he said, his face lit up, became livelier. It reminded her why she enjoyed her job so much.

She'd just gotten him settled into his bed where he preferred to watch his nightly television and was waiting for the overnight nurse to arrive when her phone rang. It was Declan, and when she glanced up at Mr. Kellogg, told him it was her brother, he gave her a nod and told her to go ahead and answer, that he didn't mind at all, and she should always answer calls from family. She stepped out into the hall.

"Hey, Deck, I'm working, what's up?"

"Hey, um, Savannah?" It wasn't Declan's voice on the other end of the line.

"Yes, who's this?"

"It's Timbo. Uh, Tim. Cavanaugh. Deck's buddy?"

Savannah's brain tossed her a blurry image of a tall, gangly guy with red hair and freckles and darting eyes, who always made her nervous wondering why *he* was nervous. "Is Declan okay?" If her brother's buddy was calling her from his phone, the answer to that question was very probably no.

"Um, he's—" Some kind of ruckus interrupted him. A couple shouts, then Declan's voice very clearly slurring the words *I'm fiiiiiine.* "No, he's really not. We're at a bar in Jefferson Square, and he's trashed, and they're gonna call the cops on him."

"Damn it." She clenched her teeth. Declan could not afford to be taken in. If he was drunk, he was also likely high, and the chances of him having some kind of illegal substance on him were also high. He had a record, and the Northwood Police Department was losing patience with him—of that, Savannah was sure. "Okay, just do your best to calm him down. I'll be right there."

By some stroke of unbelievable luck, the front door opened, and the night nurse came in, a big African American man named Clive, whom Savannah had met more than once and trusted implicitly. Even in her worry about Declan, she found a brief moment to be thankful that Clive was the one taking care of sweet Mr. Kellogg. She quickly ran through the evening report, bid Mr. Kellogg a good night, and fled the house.

Timbo hadn't given her the name of the bar, but Jefferson Square wasn't that big, and finding the commotion her little brother was causing wasn't hard at all. He and four other guys were on the sidewalk.

Directly in front of Martini's.

"Son of a bitch," she muttered as her stomach dropped. She found a parking spot and hurried around the building and up the sidewalk toward the group, which had become a small crowd. She could hear the shouts of men who'd been overserved, could see Declan flailing his arms and the bouncer from Martini's standing in the doorway, effectively blocking Declan's reentry, cell phone in hand.

"*You better move, man,*" Declan said to the bouncer, making the entire sentence into one long word the way only a very, very drunk person can. Another testament to his intoxication—the bouncer was huge, and Declan was not, yet he thought threatening a guy whose biceps were bigger around than Declan's thighs was a smart thing to do.

"I'm calling the cops, dude," the bouncer—his name was Terry, right?—said and began punching numbers with his giant finger. "I warned you more than once."

"Terry? Please don't," Savannah called as she made her way through the group and to Terry. She put a hand on his forearm, and he turned his dark, flashing eyes toward her in warning. She removed her hand.

The crowd continued to grow, people trying to get into Martini's blocked by the throng of Declan and his buddies. A few turned away and headed down the street to another bar—lost business for Julia, Savannah knew—and she clenched her teeth in frustration.

"He belong to you?" Terry asked, just as Julia appeared in the doorway, her face a study in concern and irritation.

Savannah met those dark eyes with hers but couldn't hold the contact. "He's my brother," she said to Terry and couldn't bring herself to look at Julia again, lest she see the disappointment. Par for the course when your brother wreaked havoc all over town.

"He was in there throwing things, threatening other customers, knocking stools over." Terry kept his eyes on Declan, whose buddies had managed to pull him toward the curb and away from the front of the bar. People in the crowd had their cell phones up, obviously recording all the excitement. "This isn't the first time we've had trouble with him."

"Seriously?" Savannah couldn't hide her surprise. When was Declan coming here and causing problems?

Terry's eyebrows rose, his surprise over her questioning him clearly written on his stern face.

She held up a hand to placate him. "I'm sorry. Of course you're serious. Listen, can you do me a favor and not call the cops?" This time, she did look at Julia. She had to because while she didn't want to come right out and ask Julia for a favor—not this early in their... whatever it was they had—it was definitely going to be Julia's call. She was the owner. "I'll pay for the damage. I promise. Please." A beat went by, only a few seconds, though it felt like hours.

"He can't come back here." That was Julia, her voice low, her dark eyes not hard, but clearly not happy with Declan. Or Savannah.

She nodded. "No. He won't come back. I'll make sure of it."

"Fine. Just get him out of here. He's scaring away my customers."

"I will. I'm so sorry." More nodding. She forced Julia to hold eye contact as she mouthed *thank you*, then turned to her brother and his band of merry nuisances. She reached right into the group, not stopping at all to take in the fact that they were all larger than her, drunker than her, and men, and grasped Declan's T-shirt in her fist. And suddenly, they were younger. He was sixteen. She was twenty-four. He was drunk at a college party, and she'd been called to come get him. She'd hauled him out of there by his shirt as well. That was the first time. She'd lost track of how many times she'd rescued him since.

"Goddamn it, Deck," she muttered as she tugged him behind her toward her car. He stumbled, and his arms flapped around uselessly, like they were Twizzlers, made of licorice instead of muscle and bone, and he trailed behind her like a five-year-old being dragged out of the grocery store by his mom because he wouldn't listen. She didn't speak again until he was in the passenger seat, seat belt locked around him. She got into the driver's side, put on her own seat belt, and started the engine. "I swear to God, if you throw up in my car, I will leave you in the middle of the street. Got it?"

He nodded, then said quietly, "You sound just like Mom."

"Yeah?" She pulled out into traffic. "You think she'd like this version of you?"

He cast his eyes down toward his lap and whispered, "No," and Savannah knew they'd reached the emotional stage in his drunkenness. She knew the stages well. Whether he was drunk or high or both, they were always the same. He'd start off happy. Joking and light. Loving life. Soon after that, once he'd hit a certain level of intoxication, he'd devolve into anger. Sometimes, that happened slowly, and if you were with him, you rarely saw it coming. The anger would escalate and often—like tonight—destruction of property would occur. It could take a long time, but the anger inevitably gave way to emotion. Declan often ended up in tears. And after emotion came self-deprecation. He'd talk about what a mess he was, what a failure, how could she even love him anymore, he was such a loser?

Her sympathy would well up then, too, because even though his issues were his own fault, and she could get so frustrated with him she wanted to hurl herself out a window, he was still her baby brother. She overlooked any tiny sliver of fact that told her she was enabling him by not holding him accountable, because the reality was that she was still his big sister. Protecting him was her job. But tonight?

Tonight was different.

Savannah had felt it in her bones the second she got the phone call and understood she'd need to go rescue her brother *again*. She bypassed every emotion but the anger. Even now, as Declan was so clearly approaching the self-deprecation stage, her anger didn't ease. Instead, it welled up, and it wasn't until her jaw started to ache that she realized she was clenching her teeth as she drove.

"I am so mad at you right now," she said, her teeth gritted, her knuckles white on the steering wheel.

"I know." Declan's voice was barely a whisper.

"I've started to see somebody." She felt her brother's eyes on her, his alcohol-soaked brain probably trying to work out how his sister's dating life had anything to do with the current situation. "Do you know who?" She saw him shake his head out of the corner of her eye. "The owner of that bar you just trashed."

Declan squinted at her. He was trying to put the puzzle pieces together, and she sighed because this was a puzzle for toddlers. One that had giant pieces. Like, four of them. She waited. It took until they'd pulled into their father's driveway and Savannah had put the car in park before his eyes widened just a bit. "Oh."

"Yeah. Oh. I really like her, Deck." She sighed, let her head fall forward, and began massaging her temples with her fingertips, a searing headache already making itself known. "I *really* like her, and you just trashed her place of business and made me call in a favor from her. Already. Who knows what she thinks of me now? There's a good chance I lost something amazing before I even had a chance to get it started." The more she spoke, the more quietly angry she became. She turned to look at Declan, who still sat with his hands in his lap, looking down at them like a scolded child. Because that's what he was, right? He'd never grown up. He'd stayed the same age as when their mother died. Perpetually sixteen. "Why do you do that? Why do you have to ruin everything good?"

It was harsh. She knew it as soon as the words left her mouth, so the flash of pain that shot across her brother's face, made him blink rapidly, flinch as if he'd been slapped, wasn't really a surprise. Because she might as well have slapped him.

The front door opened before he could respond, their father standing in the doorway. Declan looked at him, sighed, and tugged the door handle.

She would usually act as the buffer. Walk in with him, stay between Declan and their dad, both figuratively and physically. But tonight, she just didn't have it in her. She pretended not to notice when Declan looked back at her, likely surprised she made no move to go inside with him. It would be good punishment, she thought, letting Declan deal with their father on his own this time. He hung his head and slammed the car door, then walked slowly up the front steps as if walking to his execution.

She met her father's eyes for the briefest of moments, then put her car in reverse and got out of there.

❖

"How did I not know that piece of trash is her brother?" Because asking the same question for the fourteenth time would get her an answer, right? Julia shook her head as she sat at her desk in The Bar Back attempting to go over the receipts for the night, but mostly thinking about Savannah, her brother, and the look of shame on her face when she asked Julia not to call the cops.

"What did you expect her to say?" Amelia asked from the couch. "Hi, you're hot and I'd really like to date you. By the way, my brother's a drunk, just wanted you to know?"

More head shaking. Amelia did have a point, but still. Julia was familiar with the guy, not by name, but by sight. He'd been in a few times since she'd reopened, always already drunk—high?—when he arrived. She'd come close to cutting him off at least twice, and when she mentioned that, he usually just left, but this time was the first time he'd complained about it. Loudly. Physically. His buddies weren't much help—sober enough to know they needed to get him out of there, but too drunk to manage it without Terry needing to step in and assist.

Amelia took her feet off the coffee table and sat up. "Why are you upset with her? It's not her fault her brother's a mess, right?"

Right. She was so right. Of course, she was. "No, it's not." She could feel Amelia's eyes on her, and it made her want to squirm. "Stop it." She rolled her shoulders around as if shrugging off an unwanted touch, even though there wasn't one, and it pulled a quiet laugh from Amelia.

"Is she marred now? Tarnished? No longer perfect?"

"What? No! Why would you say that? How crappy a person would that make me?" But was there a modicum of truth to it? Had Savannah lost some of her sparkle? Was Julia really that shallow a person?

No. Absolutely not.

"I should text her."

Amelia snorted. "Ya think?"

Julia shot a glare her way. "Why are you here at two in the morning anyway?"

Amelia wasn't fazed. In fact, she barked a laugh. They knew each other too well, and Amelia knew Julia would never actually criticize her company, and Julia knew it, too, which was the only reason she could question her presence and not feel bad about it. "Because I have no life. I didn't want to be home alone on a Saturday night, so I came to watch my incredible cousin practice mixology, to the delight of her customers. Which was fun." She slapped her hands against her thighs and pushed herself to her feet. "That being said, I did *not* mean to stay until the wee hours of the morning."

Julia caught her eye, saw the weariness that had moved in on Amelia after Tammy'd moved out. It had parked itself behind Amelia's hazel eyes and made her seem just a little sad. All the time. "Well, I'm glad you did. It was nice to have you here to listen to me whine."

"It was excellent. You have excelled at whining tonight."

Julia rubbed her nose with her middle finger, effectively flipping her cousin the bird, but said nothing.

"Love you," Amelia said as she kissed Julia's cheek.

"Love you, too. Text me when you get home." Amelia had ordered herself an Uber, so Julia wasn't worried about her driving.

"Yes, ma'am." The door clicked behind her, and Julia locked it, then stood there with her palm flat against the metal, thinking about the events of the evening.

Families were messy. That was a fact. There were messes in the Martini family, too, and if one of Julia's brothers had a drinking problem or a drug problem or a gambling problem, it wouldn't be her fault. At all. So why was she feeling weird about Savannah now? Hesitant?

She hadn't texted her yet. She should. She should've hours ago, noting that Savannah hadn't texted her either.

"She's probably embarrassed," Julia said quietly to the empty room. Reassurance would've been a nice thing. Julia should've given her some.

A big breath pushed out of her, and she flopped back into her desk chair. She was an idiot. It was going on three in the morning, but Julia didn't want to wait any longer than she already had. She opened the messages app, began to type.

Busy night! I'm sorry it's taken me so long to check in, but I hope everything went okay tonight.

She read it. Reread it. Ugh. Wrote it over again.

I didn't mean to wait so long to check on you, but I hope everything went okay tonight with your brother.

Read it. Read it again. Nope.

I'm really sorry I didn't text sooner...

Backspace, backspace, backspace.

I hope everything went okay tonight.

There. Simple. Honest. No veiled excuses. She added a smiley because smileys made everything that much softer, right?

She hit send. Sat back. Wondered if she'd blown it. Worried that she absolutely had by coming across as selfish and superior. No. By *being* selfish and superior.

"Crap."

It was late. Or early, depending on how you looked at it. She should go home. She would. After she just checked the email. She didn't need to. She knew it. But there was always one more thing to do, and she always felt like she should just do it. Her father was a workaholic, so she'd come by it honestly. Yeah, that was her excuse.

Unsurprisingly, there was nothing of importance in her inbox at three in the morning. Until one subject line caught her eye.

For My Favorite Bartender

It was an email from Chris, the sender of flowers, the giver of unwanted attention. The first paragraph was all about how amazing Julia was at bartending, giving her kudos for always coming up with something new for Chris to try. That was nice. Happy customers were a good thing. The next two paragraphs were long and all about Chris. Where she'd come from—New Hampshire, her family—two estranged brothers, parents deceased, and how she was turned away by them when she came out. It was a lengthy, rambling, *way* too personal email, and Julia wasn't sure what to make of it. Too tired to analyze anything, she squeezed her eyes shut for a moment, opened them, closed the laptop.

Chris was a little weird. Likely weird and harmless. But still. She'd have to keep her eye on that.

A glance at her phone told her it was 3:14 a.m., and there was no return text from Savannah. Which made perfect sense, given the time, but still disappointed her.

Time to go home and sleep off this night.

CHAPTER THIRTEEN

S hould've taken the Unisom.

It was a damn good thing it was Sunday because sleep had played hide-and-seek with Savannah all night and did most of the winning. She couldn't find it to save her damn life, and it was much, much too late to take a sleep aid now. She'd be a zombie.

Wide-awake when Julia's text finally came—at three in the morning? really?—and it had given her new things to roll around in her head to keep her wide-awake. Like she didn't have enough taking up her headspace already. Between her brother's drunken brawl and her sister's newfound tightness with Dina and concern about her father—which had begun the day her mother died and hadn't eased up one iota since—Savannah's brain was pretty well full of things to worry about. But Julia managed to find some space and squeeze right in, making herself at home among the family members.

Do I have a right to be angry? she wondered, knowing that she really didn't. And angry wasn't even the right word. She was so many other things, though, embarrassed being the biggest one. She hated that she'd called in a favor so early in their…What did they have? A relationship? A friendship? She didn't actually know, but she was pretty sure she'd set it back a mile or two, and that was upsetting to her.

Upset. That was the right word.

She could have texted Julia. Told her she was sorry.

Truth. She could have. In fact, she should have. The ball was firmly in her court, really, yet she'd expected Julia to make the move, and when she'd waited until hours later, Savannah was hurt. Upset. Ridiculously. She had no right to be upset with Julia. This was on Savannah. And Declan. Mostly Declan.

With a long quiet sigh, she pulled the phone's charger out and scrolled to Julia's text. *I hope everything went okay tonight.* Simple. Straightforward. It was now 4:33 and she hoped Julia was home, sound asleep. With her phone on silent.

It's okay for now. I'm so sorry. Do you think we can talk?

She stared at the words for a long time before adding a smiley, just as proof that she'd like things to be okay. Not the big, blushing smiley. Just the simple one, the one that was more gently grinning than openly smiling. No blushing. Just a grin.

She hit send. Knowing there was nothing she could do until Julia woke up, she set the phone aside and did her best to get a little more rest.

At 5:22, she gave up. Her brain would not settle—that had been her curse since her mother died. She worried about everybody, and her brain did a great job of keeping things organized, like it was a filing cabinet, and there was a file folder for each cause of worry. Her father, her father's relationship with Dina, her brother, her sister, her house, each of her clients, now Julia…it was never-ending for a natural worrier. And it was freaking exhausting.

She stood under the hot water of the shower for longer than usual, letting it beat on her shoulders, the back of her neck. She had no clients today, and while she had a list of things she'd like to get done on her Sunday, she knew a nap was going to squeeze its way in at some point. She was already sleepy, and she felt like her limbs were filled with some kind of heavy liquid, like it took her extra effort to simply put one foot in front of the other.

She felt weighed down.

Which was new.

This had been her life, this worry sitting in the back of her mind, since the death of her mother, so it was something she'd grown used to. Expected, even. But she handled it. She always handled it. And some days were better than others, it was true, but she'd never felt like this. Like she did today. Heavy.

By the time she'd showered, dressed, and gone downstairs to make coffee, it was almost seven. No word from Julia, and Savannah mentally scolded herself for obsessively checking her phone. If Julia had texted her at three in the morning, assuming she'd gone immediately to bed after that, she was still only on her fourth hour of sleep. Julia wouldn't be texting back anytime soon. So Savannah had to just chill the hell out. Grabbing her coffee and the remote, she flopped onto her couch and turned on the TV in hopes of finding something to distract her.

Two episodes of *Hoarders* later, she was on her third cup of coffee and glued to the television in fascination. Every now and then, her brain would forget that compulsive hoarding was a mental illness, not just messiness, and she'd glance around her first floor, looking for any signs of piles of useless things or trash she hadn't picked up. Then she'd remember she didn't actually have the disorder and go back to being fascinated.

The network was running a marathon of episodes, and she'd seen the third one, which was probably why she drifted off. That and the fact that she'd gotten about three full hours of sleep. Maybe. She must've been in that place where you're not quite asleep, but well on your way, that place where outside noises sounded like they were coming over a bullhorn, because when her doorbell rang, she woke up like she'd been poked with a cattle prod. Hand pressed to her chest, as if trying to keep her heart from hammering its way right out of her ribcage, she took a couple seconds to orient herself.

Living room. On the couch. Fell asleep.

Okay, good. Breathing and heart rate somewhat under control, she went to the front door and opened it, knowing in the back of her mind who she hoped it was.

No such luck.

"Hey, sis," Declan said as he pushed himself past her and into the house.

"No, really, come right on in," she muttered as she shut the door.

He looked like hell, which was no surprise, given his previous night, and she followed him into her kitchen directly to the coffeepot. His sandy hair was in serious need of a trim, and the spots that weren't matted into bedhead stuck out in all directions. He had about four days of scruff on his face, and his rumpled clothes gave off the distinct scent of *unlaundered*.

"Jesus, Deck, did you even pass by a mirror before you came? And might I suggest a shower? You smell like a brewery. It's coming right out of your pores." Unloading on him never helped, but Savannah was pissed, and the words were out before she could filter them.

He sipped his black coffee and shot her a glare. "I left the house this morning because I couldn't take Dina's bitching at me. I don't need it from you, too."

"Then maybe make some changes." She said it loudly. Actually raised her voice at him, something she rarely did. But goddamn it, last night had done something to her with him. Made her hit a wall. Reach her limit. She caught the volume, adjusted it, but still had some words for him. "God, aren't you tired of this? Of being"—she waved her hand in front of the mess that was her brother—"this? You're twenty-six years old. When do you think you might decide to grow up? Will it be soon? 'Cause I'm tired, Declan. Coming to your rescue is fucking exhausting." As if to demonstrate, she dropped into one of her kitchen chairs.

"Coming to my rescue?" he echoed, then added a snort. "Please. I don't need to be rescued."

"Says the guy who'd be waking up in jail this morning if it wasn't for me." She yawned. So tired.

"Who crapped in your Wheaties today?" he asked, but his sarcasm was less cutting than usual. Interesting.

"You did, little brother of mine. You did." She walked the handful of steps into the living room to retrieve her own coffee, then warmed it up in the microwave. As she waited for it, she turned to Declan, tipped her head to the side. "Do you even remember me telling you last night that I met someone?" She could tell by the blank look in his eyes that he didn't, and she sighed. "I'm not even sure if we're seeing each other yet. It's super new, and I'm still in that stage where you want to make a good impression. Know what I mean?"

He nodded and sipped his coffee, his expression clearly showing he had no idea where she was going with this. "I don't remember you telling me that, no."

"Well, I did. The owner of Martini's, in fact."

To the surprise of nobody, it took him a moment to catch up, and Savannah absently wondered if he was still drunk. Which then sent her brain over to *Did he drive here and should he be driving?* and she nibbled the inside of her cheek, willing her thoughts to slow down.

"Wait. The owner's a chick?"

Eyes closed, she exhaled, counted to five. Okay, maybe ten. *Stay calm.* "Yes, Declan, women can own bars, too."

His eyes went wide. "Is it that hot chick? The tall one with the sexy voice and all the hair?"

She almost got lost in that vision of Julia but was able to keep herself in the moment. She smiled, looking down at her feet.

"You're blushing, big sis." And Declan actually sounded sweet and kind and loving and all the things he was as a boy and as a teen before their mom died and he looked for ways to numb the pain.

"Well, I like her. And what I was trying to say is that she overlooked your actions last night. For me. And that was a *huge* ask. You know?" Somehow, the wind had left her sails. Yeah, her coping skills had definitely taken a nosedive in the past twenty-four hours. She'd started strong with him and then just…petered out. She sighed quietly, slowly shook her head. "I can't do this anymore, Declan. I can't."

"You can't do what?" he asked, and when she looked up into his blue eyes—eyes that, over the past few years, had become more familiar to her when they were glassy and swimming—she saw that he knew exactly what she meant.

"You need to do something. You need help. You know it and I know it and so does everybody else in the family." Her eyes filled with tears without her permission. It wasn't the first time she'd said that to him, and she had a million more things to say to him, things that encompassed anger and love and encouragement and frustration and hope. But again, it all felt so *heavy*. She swallowed, looked at him with as much clarity as she could find, and with a shrug, said simply, "I'm so tired."

Of course, what Declan did not do was set down his mug, put his hands on his hips like Superman, and tell Savannah she was absolutely right, he did need help, and he would run off and get it ASAP. Also, though? He didn't get mad at her, which was his usual go-to emotion whenever she called him out for his addictions. Instead, he became very quiet. She thought she saw him nod a little as he gazed into his coffee, took another sip, and looked out the kitchen window. His Adam's apple bobbed as he swallowed. Swallowed again. He was thinking about what she said—she knew it.

He was thinking about what she said.

Savannah wasn't an idiot. Things were not magically going to repair themselves. Declan wouldn't suddenly decide to make changes, and things would be better tomorrow. All she'd ever wanted from him was that first step—thinking about it. Actually hearing her words, listening to them, taking them in, and rolling them around. After nearly a decade of this, it was all she could ask for. And she didn't want to jinx it, but it seemed like he was actually doing exactly that.

The sound of the television seemed louder now that they weren't talking. She got up, found the remote, and turned the volume down. Declan still gazed out the window. She went up to him, laid her hand on his back. He was much taller than she was, but also way too skinny. He didn't eat enough, and when he did eat, it was rarely anything good for him. She made a mental note to cook a roast soon, so she could give some to him. His gangly form could use some meat and potatoes.

Still lost in food prep, she was surprised when Declan set his mug on the counter, turned around, and wrapped her in a hug. Not just a placating hug from one sibling to another, not quick and awkward. No, this was real. It was tight, and it was heartfelt, and his arms were strong around her, so much so that it brought tears to her eyes. Again. God, she had zero emotional control lately.

"I love you, Savannah." He said it quietly, right next to her ear, and she felt tears spill over and track hotly down her cheek, and he gave her one more squeeze. Then he let her go, kissed her cheek, and said, "I'll talk to you later."

She stayed rooted to her kitchen floor and listened as her front door clicked closed. The audio from the television was clearer now, somebody explaining that an item covered in rat feces was really not okay to keep, and if the person wanted to move forward, the key was going to be changing their behavior.

"A little too on the nose this morning, *Hoarders*," she muttered as she picked up the mugs and brought them to the sink. "A little too on the nose."

❖

Julia wasn't sure how long she'd been staring at her bedroom ceiling. She'd slept surprisingly well and for longer than five hours, which was almost unheard of. Bar hours were rough. Her spinning brain was rougher. Sleep wasn't a friend and hadn't been for a long, long time.

Savannah had texted her back very, very early, and part of Julia wondered if she'd had trouble sleeping. While she didn't actually know for sure, something told her Savannah was a pretty routine person with a regular wake-up time and a regular go-to-bed time, and she followed that schedule religiously.

Things felt better this morning. She could admit that and wondered why. Maybe she'd just been tired and stressed last night. It had, thank freaking God, been a very busy Saturday night and—despite the craziness with the crowd of drunk dudes and the awkwardness with Savannah—a good one as far as profits went. She was excited for family dinner because maybe her dad would finally be impressed.

Savannah wanted to talk. That's what her text said, and Julia thought that was a good idea. Plus, she wanted to see her face.

That was the thing that had her staring at the ceiling.

Even after last night. Even after the discussion with Amelia and her weak excuses, Julia still wanted to see her.

Unexpected hardly covered it.

She'd needed to roll it around before responding to the text, and while she was fairly sure Amelia would understand that, she could almost hear Vanessa's voice in her head. *Why? Why do you have to mull it over? What's so hard about texting back* I'd love to talk? *Why do you have to overthink everything?* Julia lay there grinning at the imaginary conversation, enjoyed it for a few minutes because driving free-spirited Vanessa insane with logic was one of her favorite pastimes. This time, though, imaginary Vanessa was right.

Her day was kind of packed, as she'd promised to go to her parents' house early and give her mother a hand with dinner. Then she worked that night. Much as she wanted to see Savannah, she wanted to talk to her without a bar between them and other patrons pulling her attention away. She reached to her left and grabbed her phone, opening Savannah's text.

I'd love to talk. Today's rough, but can you come by The Bar Back tomorrow night?

A small snort of a laugh left her, as it always did when she referred to her back room as something with a proper name, making it sound like she ran two bars. It was ridiculous, and also, she loved it.

The gray dots immediately started to bounce. Savannah was awake, as predicted.

I can. Time?

Well. That was less than enthusiastic. Again, she could hear Vanessa's voice telling her not to read into it, that she had no idea at all what Savannah was doing at the moment—plus, this was text, and there was no emotion or tone of voice or facial expressions over text…

Doing her best to listen to Imaginary Vanessa's advice, she shook off the weird feeling and sent back a time suggestion, said she was looking forward to it, and left it at that. She had other things to handle today, so she finally rolled out of bed and hit the shower.

Three hours later, she was elbow deep in pasta dough and ricotta cheese and ground beef, helping her mother make homemade ravioli for family dinner.

When she'd been younger—mid to late teens—she'd looked down a bit on the fact that her mom was a stay-at-home mother. She was embarrassed. Ashamed, if she was being honest. Her friends had moms that were doctors and lawyers and entrepreneurs. Julia's mom cleaned the house and cooked meals and baked cookies, but essentially had no career and did nothing all day. At least, that's what she'd thought, knowing nothing about how much work it was to run a household of seven and not at all interested in delving any deeper. They didn't have a lot of money. Raising five kids on a mechanic's salary wasn't ideal. They ate cheaply, got clothes from Goodwill sometimes—if there wasn't an older cousin in the family with hand-me-downs.

As she got older, of course, she understood not only how much work her mother actually did all day, cleaning up after five kids—four of them boys, discovering ways to stretch the food budget, and still finding some time for herself, but also that she wasn't the only one who looked down on women like her mother. Turned out, there were a lot of people out there who thought a woman without a job outside the home was lazy and old-fashioned, and that the stay-at-home mom went out with the seventies, and when Julia'd realized this, the guilt started to seep in. Thanks, Catholicism! While she'd never actually apologized to her mother for her own thoughts and shame, she made sure to celebrate her whenever she could. And learn from her. It wasn't lost on her that she'd ended up in a field where she served people. The fruit didn't fall far from the tree, as her grandma would say.

"Not too much filling, honey, or they'll break in the water." Her mom pointed to one pile of ricotta Julia had scooped. She took some away, then went on to the next until she'd done an entire row. Once she'd done three rows, her mother brushed an egg wash around each pile of filling, which would seal the edges. Then together, they laid another sheet of pasta dough over the top and carefully pressed down around each bit of filling, which now looked like bumps under a blanket. Her mother handed her the pasta cutter, which was like a pizza cutter with a wiggly edge.

"Just run it through the rows, up and down, until they're all separate."

Julia had helped make ravioli a hundred times—though admittedly, not for a while now—but she loved that her mom still felt the need to direct her, and she nodded as if hearing the instructions for the first time. She cut the dough, and her mom took the cookie sheet they were on and ran them down to the basement where it was cooler, until they were ready to cook. On to the next batch.

They found a rhythm, she and her mom—mixing, rolling, filling, cutting—and they worked well together. They always had. It wasn't often that she got her mom all to herself, so when the opportunity popped up, she tried to grab it. Even now that she was so busy.

"How are things at the bar?" her mother asked, not looking up from the sauce she was stirring on the stove.

How to answer? Total honesty? A slightly glittery varnishing of reality? Outright lie? She chose number one.

"Last night was great. Vanessa brainstormed with me, and we came up with some ideas for some theme nights and a select martini special each night on the weekends. We pulled in a lot of customers."

"That's great. I'm so happy to hear that." Her mom spooned up some sauce, gave it a taste, added some oregano. "What was last night's special martini?"

"Last night was the appletini. You'd like it."

"Yeah?"

"Definitely." She hesitated. "You and Pop should come in sometime." Her mother met her eyes and Julia said, "Let me rephrase that. Ma, can you please get Dad to bring you in sometime? He's been in exactly once, and he barely spoke to me."

She was holding it together well until her mother tipped her head sideways and laid a hand against Julia's cheek. Her palm was warm and soft, and her dark eyes were filled with love.

"Is he ashamed of me, Ma?" Julia's voice was barely above a whisper. "'Cause it feels like he is."

"Oh, sweetie, no." Her mother pulled her into a hug, wrapped her up tight. "Of course not."

But what else could she say, right? *Yes, he absolutely is. What did you expect would happen when you told your very traditional Catholic Italian father that you're gay? And you've used your fancy-schmancy business degree to be a bartender?*

Everybody else in the family seemed fine, but her father? He'd changed since that day. Not drastically, but there'd been a very slight pulling away from her. A stepping back of sorts. It might have been subtle, but she'd felt it like a slap.

Her mother pulled back enough to look up at her face, smoothing a thumb across Julia's brow. "Your father loves you."

She nodded. He did. She didn't doubt that. "I know."

"Give him some time."

That had been her mother's advice for a few years now. Seriously, how much time did the guy actually need?

CHAPTER FOURTEEN

N ext month is Pride month, you know." Vanessa was on the couch in The Bar Back, feet crossed at the ankle and propped on the coffee table, Diet Coke in one hand as she pointed at Julia with the other.

"I'm aware." Julia was playing with different martini recipes and had been for over an hour. It was going on nine on Monday night. Clea was tending to the customers—not a ton, but more than a handful, which was nice for a Monday—and Julia was vacillating between concentrating on the drinks and worrying that she should be manning the bar instead of paying a bartender.

"You need to capitalize on it." Vanessa's excitement was clearly growing as she set her soda down and raised her hands up together, then spread them apart like a banner. "Drink specials. Put up some Pride decorations. Maybe sponsor some part of the day or the parade..." Her brain was racing—Julia could tell. Then she gasped. "We could make a float!"

"No float."

A sigh. "You're right. It's probably too late this year. But next year, *definitely*."

"You've thought about this."

"You haven't?"

"I mean, I have..." Julia scratched her eyebrow as she remixed a limontini using Uncle Joe's homemade limoncello that Vanessa had brought with her, instead of the bottled limoncello from her distributor.

Vanessa sat up and pulled out her phone. "I did some googling, and listen to these martini names. The Ruby Slipper martini—Auntie Em! Auntie Em! The Purple Hooter martini—you should serve that one while showing ample amounts of cleavage. The In and Out martini." She looked up through her eyelashes at Julia. "Come *on*. If that one isn't made for a Pride festival, I don't know what is." She set down her phone. "Capitalize on the month. Draw a new crowd in addition to your current one. Flaunt your inclusivity, you know?"

It was a fantastic idea, and it was hard not to get caught up in Vanessa's enthusiasm. Which was par for the course with her. She could talk about anything and get you all worked up and ready to go, simply because her excitement was contagious. That was Vanessa.

A sip of the martini told her that Uncle Joe's limoncello was more tart, but also tasted fresher than the commercially produced liqueur. "How many bottles of this do you think your dad has?" She held up the bottle.

"Oh God, there have to be three or four dozen in the basement. And he'll get another batch started by August or September, probably." Limoncello had to sit for forty days before it was drinkable, and Uncle Joe liked to have it ready for the holidays and gave it out as gifts.

"Excellent. Tell him I want to buy ten bottles."

"Jules, he's not going to let you pay for them."

"Tell him I want to *buy* ten bottles."

A quiet knock on the outside door interrupted them, but Julia knew who it was, and her heart skipped a proverbial beat. "Come on in," she called.

"Hey," Savannah said, a tentative smile on her face. When she saw Vanessa, her brows rose slightly, and she added, "Oh, I didn't expect you to be here. Hi." Her tone said she was happy to see Vanessa, which was no surprise. Everybody was happy to see Vanessa.

"Hey there." Vanessa stood and gave her a hug. "And good-bye. I was just on my way out."

"Already?" Savannah slipped off the light jacket she was wearing.

"'Fraid so." And then Vanessa and Julia said in tandem, "School night."

"Well, I'm glad I got to see you for eleven and a half seconds anyway."

Vanessa waved, pulled the door open, and said, "Ask Savannah what she thinks of Pride month," as a parting shot. A wink, the door shut, she was gone.

Savannah turned to Julia. "I'm very fond of Pride month. Aren't you?"

Julia grinned. "I am. Vanessa wants me to use it to market, join in the local Pride stuff. Decorations. Special Pride drinks. Stuff like that."

"That's a fabulous idea. You could have a theme about everybody being welcome. Inclusion. That kind of thing."

Julia studied her as she walked up to the practice bar and took a stool. She looked beautiful, as always, despite her simple outfit of jeans, a long-sleeved black T-shirt, and black sandals. Her hair was pulled back in a ponytail, but there were lots of escapees around her ears, curled at the back of her neck, draped near her left eye. And she looked tired. Deflated. Something was bothering her, and Julia wondered if it was the whole thing with her brother or something more. Whatever it was, she wanted to help. That was the only clear thing in her brain. She wanted to fix whatever it was that was dimming Savannah's thousand-watt smile, and that was unexpected.

"Between the two of you, I think I have more than enough ideas." She grinned, sliding the limontini over to her. "Taste this and tell me what you think. And then tell me what's bothering you."

A split-second of surprise zipped across Savannah's face, and then she sat up a little straighter. Lifted her chin just a bit. In challenge? Defense? "I'm fine."

"You're not, though. Drink." She gestured to the glass, and Savannah took a dutiful sip. What Julia liked was that she didn't answer right away. She let the drink stay in her mouth for a beat. Swallowed it. Tipped her head in thought. Took another sip.

"That's delicious," she finally pronounced. "Really good. Lemony, but not cloyingly so like some citrusy drinks can be. Tart, but not puckery. Just enough. It's very refreshing."

A smile crept onto Julia's face. She could feel it spread. "I love how much you thought about it and how detailed you were. Thank you for that."

Whatever was holding Savannah down lifted just the smallest amount. "You're welcome."

Julia reached across the bar and covered Savannah's hand with hers. "If you're worried about the thing with your brother, don't be. I mean, it wasn't good, and we need to talk about how to deal with him in the future, but please don't let it pull you down." She cleared her throat, realizing what a big assumption she'd made. "If that's what's bothering you, I mean."

Savannah looked at her for what felt like a long moment, and yes, there was definitely something there. A shadow of some kind. Pain? It was hard to say because Julia didn't know her all that well yet, but there was something.

"What do you do when you need to blow off some steam? When you have something"—she swallowed and tapped her fingers against her chest—"sitting right here, and you don't know what to do with it?" And when Savannah trained her gaze on her, the blue of her eyes was so deep, but not deep enough to hide the pain in them.

"I mix." The simplest, most honest answer she had.

"You mix?"

"Come back here." She gestured for Savannah to join her behind the bar, which she did without hesitation. Standing that close to her felt so many things in that instant. Sexy. Warm. Right. With a shake of her head, she sent those thoughts scattering to the corners of her mind. "Okay. What shall we make? I'm going to suggest a martini of some kind, and you'll see why."

Savannah took in all the ingredients and tools Julia had still strewn about the bar. Mixer and strainer and lemons and little bottles of bitters and vermouths and such. A beat went by, and she looked up at Julia with those eyes. "Cosmo?"

"Good choice. Simple, easy, yummy. Okay." She grabbed the two-piece cocktail shaker and the strainer and put them in front of Savannah on the bar. Then she grabbed the ingredients—vodka, Cointreau, cranberry juice, and a lime—and added them to the supplies. "First thing to know about martinis of any kind—the colder, the better."

Savannah nodded. "Okay."

"That's why we chill the glasses." She pointed to the variety of glasses stacked in the freezer, then pulled out a tray of ice. "And that's why the ice is so important."

"It is?"

"Absolutely. Now, fill the glass part of your shaker about two-thirds full of ice."

"Two-thirds?"

"You wanna leave shaking room."

"Ah, makes sense."

Julia directed her on how much of each liquor to pour in, how to juice a quarter of the lime, and then taught her how to slap the stainless steel part of the shaker home so it fit tight.

"Now," she said, as she moved close behind Savannah so her front was against Savannah's back and her lips were near Savannah's ear, "roll up your sleeves." Savannah did as she was told, and Julia could smell the warm scent of cherries and almonds, and she did her best to stay silent as she inhaled deeply, took the essence of Savannah all the way in. "This is where you can take out some frustrations." She positioned Savannah's hands on the shaker, then pulled her arms up so she was holding it over her right shoulder. "Shake it. Everything that has hurt you or pissed you off or made you sad today, just shake it up. Hard. Shake the shit out of it."

Her words hit home—Julia could tell when she moved back and could see Savannah's face again. There was a strength there now. A determination. And pain. Definite pain. Savannah gritted her teeth and looked like she shook that damn shaker for all she was worth. Julia took two martini glasses out of the freezer and set them on the bar where they clouded up instantly.

"Most people don't shake hard enough or long enough," she said as Savannah kept shaking, and she tried not to get too distracted by the definition in her forearms or the slight flush in her cheeks. "But remember—I said it's all about cold with martinis. Which means it's all about the ice. And the longer and harder you shake, the more you get tiny ice chips from the cubes in there, which is what you want. Ten more seconds."

Savannah's eyes had watered up by the time ten seconds had passed. Julia taught her to smack the heel of her hand against the shaker to break the seal, then handed her the strainer and watched as Savannah filled both glasses with the pink liquid, all the while clearly struggling to keep her emotions at bay.

They picked up their glasses, touched them together in silent toast, and sipped.

"Oh, that's perfect," Julia pronounced with a grin. "You get an A-plus." Then she reached over, took Savannah's glass, and set them both on the bar. Knowing that this was a big moment, doing what she was about to do, Julia didn't care. She took both Savannah's hands in hers, held them, felt their warmth, their softness, even as she dipped her head to catch those blue eyes with hers. Very, very quietly, she said, "Now, please, tell me what's wrong."

That was all it took, apparently. The watering in Savannah's eyes increased and spilled over until teardrops were rolling down her cheeks. A small, quiet sob pushed its way out of her, and all Julia could do was pull her in, pull her close, wrap her up, hold her tight. Savannah sobbed into her shoulder as Julia stroked her head, caressed her neck, and rubbed her shoulders. "Shh," she said, pressing a kiss to Savannah's head, and let her cry. As desperately as she wanted to know what was causing so much heartache, she knew she needed to wait, that Savannah would talk when she was ready.

She couldn't see her phone or the clock on the wall, so she had no idea how long they stood like that. Savannah's sobs became small hiccups, then quieted, and once her breathing was less ragged and more normal, she lifted her head from Julia's shoulder—*No, come back, stay forever!*—and sniffled. Julia handed her a bar napkin and waited for her to blow her nose, dab at her eyes, and pull herself together.

"Okay now?" she asked.

Savannah nodded.

"Wanna talk about it?"

Another nod.

"How about we take our excellent drinks over to the couch?"

A third nod.

Once settled comfortably—or at least Julia was, sitting back on the couch, feet crossed at the ankle on the coffee table—exactly where Vanessa had sat not long ago, Savannah stayed perched on the edge of the cushion and took a very large gulp of her cocktail. Then she set it down, wiped her hands along her thighs, and picked it up and took another gulp.

"Easy there, Carrie Bradshaw," Julia said.

That got a tiny grin. "Sorry." Savannah nibbled on her bottom lip, and under any other circumstances it would've been devastatingly sexy. "Can you not judge?" she asked suddenly. Blurted really, and Julia felt herself flinch a bit in surprise. "Because it's really stupid. What's upsetting me."

"I can. Yes. I promise." This was important. She felt it as if it was hanging in the air somehow. She sat up, feet on the ground, and for the second time, took Savannah's hands in hers. "Talk to me."

Savannah seemed to study their hands, kept her focus there as she ran her thumbs over Julia's skin. She didn't look up as she spoke, and her voice was barely a whisper. "My baby sister is heartbroken. Her boyfriend broke up with her last week, and she needed me."

"Okay." She waited because there was clearly more to come.

"I've always been her surrogate mom. Ever since our mother died, that's been my role. With both her and Declan. I'm much older, and I do the mom stuff. I filled their Christmas stockings when they were younger—still do. I taught them how to cook. I taught Chelsea about birth control and educated them both on consent." Savannah finally glanced up from her hands. Her eyes filled with tears as she looked away from Julia's gaze. "This is so stupid," she whispered. "You're gonna think I'm pathetic."

"I would never think that." Julia waited, watched the internal struggle Savannah was going through.

"My dad has been seeing this woman, Dina, for a while now. She's the first long-term girlfriend he's had really, since my mom. And she's fine. She's a health nut and a little pushy, but she takes care of him, and he seems happy with her, so I put up with her."

Julia nodded, an inkling of where this was headed tickling along her spine.

Savannah took in a big breath and blew it out. "Well, it seems that Chelsea started talking to Dina about her breakup. I went over there to check up on her, see how she was doing, and she was sitting at the table with Dina, and they were laughing and joking about how guys are douchebags, and…and…" The tears spilled over. "And she didn't need me."

Julia didn't think twice. She reached out for her, wrapped Savannah in her arms, and held her while she cried some more, her face pressed into Julia's shoulder. She felt Savannah's arms around her, clenching her shirt in her fist, and Julia gently rocked them both back and forth like her mother always did.

Time passed. At one point, Clea peeked her head in, saw them wrapped up, and made eye contact with Julia, who raised her eyebrows in question. Clea waved a dismissive hand, silently telling Julia it was no big deal, but a glance at the clock told her it was going on eleven.

"All cleared out?" she asked quietly. Savannah stirred in her arms, as if to answer.

"Yeah," Clea said. "Last two people left about twenty minutes ago. Should I close up?"

Julia nodded. Customers until almost eleven on a Monday night wasn't bad, especially considering she often closed by nine on Mondays.

"I thought you were asking me if I was all cleared out." Savannah's voice was muffled from where she still lay tucked against Julia's shoulder. "I was thinking, *What an odd way to ask me if I'm done.*"

Julia grinned at the cuteness of her. "I would never ask if you're done. You can stay right here as long as you like." To punctuate that, she tightened her arms.

"Sure, you say that now. But what about when a beer truck comes? Or a liquor delivery? Or there's a barroom brawl?"

"I thought barroom brawls only happened in Westerns."

"Hey, you don't know. One could happen any day. Hell, my brother would probably be the instigator."

"Your voice is hoarse." Julia pressed a kiss to her head.

"I'm trying to sound as sexy as you do."

A little zap shot through her, and she pulled back enough to look in Savannah's red and swollen eyes. "You are way sexier than I am. Trust me."

Savannah barked a small laugh as she sat up. "Oh, I'm sure. I bet the puffy eyes and snot on my face seal the deal, don't they?"

"You have no idea." Julia reached for the tissue box on the coffee table and handed it over. "You've found my weakness."

That made Savannah laugh a little more, and Julia gave herself a point. A deep, slow breath in and then a slow exhalation, and Savannah met her eyes. "Thank you. I'm sorry to have melted down like that. I just…I haven't had anybody to talk to about it, and I feel kind of stupid anyway, but…"

"You are by no means stupid. It makes perfect sense that you'd feel the way you do. But can I say one thing?"

Savannah nodded. "Of course."

"Well, two things."

Another nod.

"One, you have not been replaced. Not even close. I have never met your sister, and I'm sure of this. You know that, right?"

Savannah tipped her head left and right, as if to almost but not quite agree.

"Second, what about looking at it as more of sharing the load? I can only imagine how hard it is to look out for your siblings with only one parent. I have two, and I worry about all of mine."

"Look at you," Savannah said with a grin. "Sexy *and* making excellent points." Seemingly in better control of her emotions now, Savannah said, "I didn't expect it to affect me like it did. I was not ready for that." Her small laugh held little humor. "I hope I didn't put you in a weird position. I mean, I'd prefer to know you for longer than a few weeks before I cry all over you. Sorry about that."

"Don't apologize. At all. You have nothing to be sorry about. I'm just sorry it stung so much."

This time when Clea came back, she knocked softly first and came into the room only after Julia invited her to. "All set," she said, gathering her things from the shelf against the wall. "Good night."

"I should go, too," Savannah said once Clea had left through The Bar Back's outside door. "It's late." She stood up, held out a hand to Julia, and pulled her to her feet so Savannah had to then tip her chin up to look at her. "Thank you," she said again, quietly, softly, and her eyes held more than gratitude. "Will you be here tomorrow night?"

Julia rested her hands on Savannah's hips and tugged her a little closer. "I'm here every night." She lowered her head to Savannah's, kissed her softly.

Savannah's hands were on Julia's chest, and she toyed with the buttons on the denim shirt she'd thrown on over her Martini's T-shirt when the night had cooled down. "Yeah, we're gonna work on that."

"Oh, really?" Julia raised her eyebrows and leaned back enough to see Savannah's face. She was equal parts defensive that somebody she hardly knew planned to mess with her schedule and thrilled that this sexy woman she wanted to get to know better planned to mess with her schedule.

"Yes, really. But first, we need to talk about my brother." Savannah closed her eyes and shook her head. "My siblings, man. Seriously." A small laugh through her nose. "And you need to teach me how to mix a martini again. And maybe other drinks."

"Yeah?"

"But just the ones where you have to stand really close behind me in order for me to get them right." She walked her fingers up Julia's chest to her neck, sending a pleasantly sensual shiver across Julia's skin.

"Oh. I see. Only the sexy drinks."

"Exactly," Savannah breathed as she lifted her chin and pulled Julia's head down to meet her.

The night had been a bit of an emotional roller coaster, and Julia hadn't even thought to take things in any kind of sexual direction after the meltdown, but it was like Savannah had grabbed her hand

and sprinted toward Let's Make Out town, tugging Julia along behind her. And, hell, who was she to argue? She let herself sink into the kiss, deepening it just a touch until Savannah's tongue was pressing into her mouth and bursts of arousal were shooting through Julia's body, settling low. Throbbing. A small whimper escaped Savannah, and it spurred Julia on, it was so sexy. She brought her hands up, cradled Savannah's face in them, kissed her deeply and thoroughly, explored every inch of her mouth. And oh my God, did she want more.

As if reading her mind, Savannah wrenched their mouths apart, took a small step back, and looked up at her. Blue eyes wide and dark. Breath coming raggedly. Hands on Julia's upper arms, rubbing up and down. "Holy shit," she said, and the lazy half grin she shot Julia then nearly turned her knees to jelly. "We have to stop, or I'm going to rip all your clothes off and have you right on this couch."

Danger! Danger! All the warning bells went off in Julia's head because holy hell, she would absolutely be down for hot sex on her couch with this beautiful woman. But she also knew Savannah deserved much better than that. Something less spontaneous and less frat-house living room and more…romantic.

"So glad to know we're on the same page," she said, then dragged her finger down the side of Savannah's face, across her lips, over her chin, and down her neck.

It wasn't until they'd kissed a little more and Julia'd helped Savannah out the door and closed it behind her that she was able to clear her head, think logically. Did she want to sleep with Savannah? What a stupid question! Of course she did. But there was more to it than that. She could feel it, and she didn't know what to do with it because it scared the crap out of her.

How did she even have room in her head—hell, in her life—for Savannah? There was so much already. She dropped back down onto the couch and took a sip of the room temperature limontini she'd left on the bar and grabbed on her way back in. A grimace sent her to the freezer to do something that would make every bartender who took an ounce of pride in her work wince in horror—she poured her drink into a rocks glass with ice and drank it that way.

The couch had been chosen for its comfort. Julia told no one that little tidbit, but it was true. She felt more at home at her bar than she did in her apartment, and she wanted it to be as inviting and comfortable as possible. Kicking off her shoes, she flopped down, leaned against the arm, put her feet up, and sipped her drink. Which was fucking delicious, by the way, and was going on the specials board on Friday.

Back to Savannah, though.

They could sleep together. It would be hot, definitely. Third degree burns hot. She knew that without a doubt. How, she wasn't sure, but she knew it. Julia had no trouble getting her needs met. She was on Tinder. No shame in that. She'd always found other women like her—busy, horny, wanting no strings—and it worked just fine. In fact, she saw a woman she'd met that way every month or two. They took care of each other's needs, both left satisfied, and they went on with their lives. It was the perfect arrangement. And not at all what she wanted with Savannah.

The limontini had begun warming her from the inside, and she pulled the fleece blanket she'd gotten from a company that made cordials—*Snuggle up and let us keep you warm* was their tagline— and draped it over her legs as she slid down into the cushions more and let herself relax. She could still smell Savannah. On her shirt. On her hands. In the air? Suddenly, it was like she was everywhere, and Julia loved it. *Loved* it.

Her eyelids grew heavy as she took in big, slow, deep breaths, her tired mind taking her back to the kissing. God, the kissing…

I hope I dream about the kissing, was her last thought before drifting off to sleep.

She totally dreamed about the kissing.

CHAPTER FIFTEEN

M rs. Richter had been a German-speaking Tasmanian devil on Tuesday, and Savannah was utterly wiped out from spending the day with her. Between trying to understand her using the two years of German she'd taken in high school and following her all around the house because Mrs. Richter was having one of those days where she couldn't sit still, Savannah didn't think she'd stopped working or moving for longer than a few minutes at a time all day. Her feet were killing her, and her brain was fried, but she wanted to check in on Chelsea before going home, see if maybe she wanted to come stay overnight with her, have a night of pizza, popcorn, and the show *Snapped,* which was having a marathon, and she'd set her DVR to record it all day. A sleepover, like they used to have, might be just what Chelsea needed.

Her father's car was missing, but both Dina's and Chelsea's were in the driveway. Savannah let go of a sigh. It was one thing to have Dina always there, but it was harder to deal with her when her father wasn't around. To be fair, she imagined Dina felt the same way about her. She shouldered her purse, locked her car, and went inside.

"Hello," she called as she dropped her purse onto a chair. She had no intention of knocking on her own parents' door, but also knew she needed to have a tiny bit of respect for Dina's privacy, even if she didn't technically live there.

"Oh, hi there, Savvy," Dina said from the couch where she sat with Chelsea. The TV was on, and Chelsea hit the pause button. A mug sat in front of each of them on the coffee table, along with a big bowl that looked like it might've had popcorn in it at one time. Chelsea was in pajama pants and a hoodie, her chestnut hair in a messy bun. Dina was dressed in yoga pants and a flowy shirt and waved her to come in. "Chelsea has introduced me to *Snapped*." She was breathy and excited, if her voice was any indication. "It's fascinating." Her eyes went wide as she turned back to the television.

"It's a marathon," Chelsea added. "Wanna join?"

It was hard to describe the myriad of feelings that rolled through Savannah then. *Snapped* was basically a true-crime show about women who'd reached their breaking points and usually murdered their husbands or boyfriends as a result. Savannah, Chelsea, and their mother used to watch it all the time, joking that Chelsea was probably too young for the show, yet letting her sit with them anyway. After their mother had passed, it was their go-to show, just the two of them. When one of them was feeling down, they watched *Snapped*. On their mother's birthday, they watched *Snapped*. On the anniversary of her death, they watched *Snapped*. And now, here was Chelsea, watching *Snapped* with Dina. Not only that, but looking comfortable and happy and not even a little heartbroken anymore.

She couldn't exactly turn around and leave now, could she? That would look weird. But she wasn't about to tell Chelsea how much she felt like she'd just been punched in the stomach. Instead, she forced a smile and took a seat opposite them in her father's recliner.

Chelsea smiled at her and held up her mug. "Dina's making me drink green tea, and if you put a little honey in it, it's not that bad."

"So full of antioxidants," Dina said with a smile.

Had she stepped into an alternate universe? One where Dina was the mom and Savannah was the interloper? Where green tea was delicious rather than tasting like grass? Where *Snapped* wasn't her thing with Chelsea but Chelsea's thing with Dina?

"Want some?" Dina was still smiling at her. "I can brew you a cup quick."

Savannah swallowed. Cleared her throat. "No. Thanks. I can't stay. I just wanted to stop by to see how you're doing." She shifted her gaze to Chelsea. "See if you needed anything."

Chelsea waved a hand at her. "Oh, I'm good. I think Dina's right—I'm better off. I mean, Parker and me? We've been together since we were *kids*." She stressed the word, as if she wasn't still a kid to Savannah. "Breaking up was hard, but maybe it's time to have a grown-up relationship. You know?"

Savannah nodded, made herself smile. After all, Chelsea was right. Which meant Dina was right. And was that such a bad thing? Really, was it?

Chelsea hit the remote, and the show started up again.

Savannah settled back into the chair and was telling herself she'd just hang out until this episode ended when the front door banged open and her father's booming voice entered before he did.

"Why am I just finding this out now?" he shouted as he stepped into the foyer and the three of them turned to look. "And not from you?" When Savannah finally saw him, she was shocked by his face. Red. Angry. Flashing eyes and clenched fists hanging by his sides. Part of the dementia he refused to see the doctor about sent his moods all over the place, and this was a prime example. Her dad didn't yell. He didn't get red-faced and look like he wanted to punch somebody. Ever.

The reason for his anger became clear as Declan walked in behind him but kept a good few feet between them until he could get past their dad. Then he began pacing back and forth in the living room, running a hand through his sandy hair that needed to be washed. His hands were busy, kept moving, and Savannah figured he was at least a little high, because when was he not? With an internal sigh, she noticed that Dina stood from the couch but didn't approach either of them, an expression of obvious concern painted across her face.

"What's going on?" Savannah asked, also standing, and deliberately kept her voice at a regular level. *Stay calm. By staying calm, you bring calm to the rest of the room.* Or so she told herself.

She could feel the warmth of Chelsea suddenly standing behind her, Chelsea's usual spot when things got tense.

"What's going on?" Her father looked at her, his anger coming off him in waves of heat. "I'll tell you what's going on. Your brother here nearly got himself arrested over the weekend." His gaze snapped back to Declan. "Again. Apparently, that's not something he thought I should know. I had to hear it from that goddamn Harvey Smith because he was there."

Oh, crap.

"Where?" Dina asked.

Oh, double crap.

"That goddamn Martini's." While Savannah knew her dad wasn't in great health, that the dementia was popping in more often, staying a few seconds longer each time, she was still amazed by how it could change his personality so easily. Instead of a friendly, cheerful guy, he was instantly cranky. Crotchety. Shades of *Get off my lawn!* "You kids know how I feel about that place."

"Dad," Savannah said, again doing her best to keep her voice calm and even, "we have no idea how you feel about the place or why."

"It shouldn't matter why!" He bellowed the words. Actually bellowed them. Savannah took half a step back, a little shocked by his volume, and felt Chelsea's hands on her waist. "I'm your father. If I say I don't want you going someplace, I don't want you going someplace. Or making a goddamn spectacle of yourself." He pointed a finger at Declan. "And I certainly don't want you getting arrested there. You stay away from that place."

"Tell her that," Declan shouted, pointing at Savannah, and while she'd seen him do it more than once, she still found herself shocked by her brother's ability to throw anyone and everyone under the bus to save himself. "She's dating the freaking owner."

Every eye in the house was suddenly on her, and despite knowing she had nothing at all to feel badly about, she still shifted uncomfortably, like a child caught in a lie. Declan looked far too pleased with himself, having shifted the focus elsewhere. Pleased with himself but, more than that, relieved. Like he could take a breath or two now.

"You're what?" Her father's voice was quiet.

"Dad." Savannah raised her hands, palms forward. "Just take a breath. Your blood pressure's gonna skyrocket."

"Don't you tell me to take a breath, young lady." He didn't yell it this time. He was calm, and it was weird. Dina took the opportunity to step closer and laid a hand on his arm.

"Honey, Savannah's right." She tried to pull him toward his chair. "Why don't you sit down?"

"Who are you dating?" he asked. Still calm.

"Julia Martini. She owns the bar." Savannah had seen this behavior many times in her various clients. The spike in emotion, an outburst, followed by a calm that she could see was already on its way. She kept her tone even.

"Which one of those bastards is her father?"

A furrowed brow and a shake of her head. "I don't know her father, Dad. I haven't been seeing her for that long."

Her father grunted.

"Kevin, sit down. Please." Dina continued to gently tug at him, her voice soft, until he finally listened, and as Chelsea and Savannah scrambled out of the way, he folded himself into his La-Z-Boy, his bluster suddenly gone.

Savannah went to him and squatted before him with her hand on his knee. "Dad? Why do you hate the Martinis so much?"

"Bah," was his reply, and he waved her away, looking and sounding much older than his seventy years. And that was the end of the conversation.

She glanced up at Dina, who gave her a half shrug and a small smile, as if to say *What can you do?* Issues Savannah had with her aside, Dina was beyond patient with her father. Obviously loved him a great deal.

"I'll fix you some green tea, Kev," Dina said and left for the kitchen.

Savannah pushed herself to her feet and ran her hand down her father's arm, unable to look at the blankness that had settled in his eyes. She knew from experience it would stay for several minutes, and then he'd be back to his regularly scheduled programming, smiling and happy.

"Man, it's weird when he does that," Declan said very quietly, still a good distance away from their dad, still fidgety, still needing a shower.

"Don't even talk to me right now," Savannah snapped at him. She turned and grabbed her purse from the chair where she'd left it and swung it over her shoulder.

"Aw, come on, Savannah, don't be like that," he said, a slight whine in his voice, and something in her cracked just a bit.

"You know what, Deck?" Savannah whirled on him and waved her hand in front of him, from his head to his legs as she said, "How about *you* stop being like *this*." She turned on her heel, kissed Chelsea on the cheek, whispering, "Text me," as she passed, and headed out the door. She needed different air. She didn't know how else to explain it. The air in her childhood home—in her mother's home—had changed somehow. Shifted. It didn't feel the same. Sure, it was still her childhood home. It still held warm, loving memories. It still held her father, her sister, her brother. But pieces of her dad were slipping away every day, she could feel it, even if she couldn't see it, like small particles were leaving, one microscopic bunch at a time.

It broke her heart.

That's why she liked to focus on her own house. On her houseplants and the color on the walls and the furniture layout. Her house was her home now, and she let those words sink in as she sat in her car in her father's driveway. It had to be because she knew she was going to lose this one eventually.

With a big sigh, she shifted the car into reverse, pulled out, and drove to the stop sign at the end of the street, where she clicked on her left turn signal toward home. She'd intended to text Julia and bow out of seeing her tonight, but actually? Now? Now she felt kind of energized. She'd been so tired after her shift that she'd just wanted to go home, put on some cozy clothes, and veg on the couch, give her brain a rest. But the arguments between her father and Declan, between Declan and her, they'd shot her with some weird adrenaline, and inexplicably, the only person she wanted to see was Julia.

She changed her turn signal. Turning right.

"Seriously, Jules, it's okay. I got this." Evan Daniels stood there, smiling at Julia as they stood behind the bar. He was cute. Tall and dark with a neatly trimmed beard and kind eyes. He was young, twenty-five. Clea had originally suggested him to help bring in a younger crowd. Julia wasn't thrilled at the idea of twentysomething college kids getting crazy in her bar, but she also knew they could help build her business simply by using their social media accounts. While Julia was pretty tech savvy, she was also busy, and the other reason for hiring Evan was that he was in IT. They had a meeting planned for tomorrow where he'd help her update her website, show her the consumer rating sites she should pay attention to besides Yelp, and take over running Martini's Instagram account, which Julia hadn't posted to in over a month.

"If I need you, you'll be right in the back." Evan's patient smile forced her into motion.

"Yes." A nod. "Okay." A rap on the bar with her knuckles. "Right."

For a young guy, Evan seemed very in tune with people. It was something Julia instantly liked about him. "Julia"—he put a hand on her arm and looked her in the eye—"it's okay. I got this."

She was being ridiculous, and she knew it. Overprotective. Worrying needlessly. Amelia would roll her eyes so hard at her right now. She gave him another nod, tossed her rag under the bar, and headed for The Bar Back.

Savannah walking in through the back door with a pizza was the happiest surprise she could've gotten, and she knew her face lit up at the sight. She could feel it. It was automatic, not anything she had a modicum of control over.

"Hi," Savannah said as she shut the door behind her. "I wasn't sure if you'd eaten, and I'm starving, so..." She held up the box. "Dinner?"

"Yes, please." Julia went to her, took the pizza from her hands, and kissed her softly. "Hi."

Savannah touched Julia's face as she looked up at her. "I knew I wanted to see you but didn't realize just how much until this moment."

"Yeah?"

"Yeah." Another kiss and then Savannah dropped her purse on the coffee table with a loud sigh. "It has been a *day*, let me tell you."

"Tell me." Julia put the pizza on the bar, opened the box, and inhaled deeply.

"Actually, no." Savannah's words surprised her, and she turned to meet her gaze. "I'd rather shake the hell out of some martinis and talk about anything else."

"I think we can make that happen."

Half an hour later, after they'd eaten pizza and kissed a little bit between slices, they were behind the bar together, martini tools spread out in front of them.

"I'm trying to decide on the special for Pride weekend." Julia had a list of the martinis Vanessa had mentioned, plus a couple she'd looked up herself. "I've narrowed it down to two. The naked martini and the In and Out martini."

Savannah tilted her head. "A naked martini? Color me intrigued."

"We'll start with that one, then." Julia grabbed a stool and pulled it around to the back of the practice bar. She took a seat and gestured with her chin. "Go for it."

Savannah's big eyes looked even bigger. "Me?"

"Yup. You said you wanted to make martinis again."

"I do, but"—she arched an eyebrow—"you have to help me shake."

That did things to Julia. Flutters low in her body. A tingle in her fingertips. "Deal."

"Good. Okay." Hands on her hips, Savannah asked, "What do I do?"

"You need Godiva liqueur and vodka."

"That's it?"

"And a garnish. It can be a lemon peel or a strawberry, and since we're talking about chocolate and it's strawberry season…"

"Strawberries it is."

Julia pulled a small bowl out of the fridge containing bright red strawberries she'd already cut slices in, so they'd fit over the edge of a glass.

Savannah picked up the martini shaker, filled it with ice, and followed the directions Julia gave her, and watching her work was more fun than Julia could've imagined. Her dark jeans did a terrific job displaying her ass—a part of her that Julia was growing very fond of—and her hair was down and wavy, and she blew it out of her eyes more than once.

"Okay," Savannah said as she slapped the stainless steel part of the shaker over the glass, then turned her gaze to lock on Julia's. "Help me." How it was possible to make those two words insanely sexy was a mystery, but she did.

Julia slid off her stool, took the three steps that separated them, and tucked herself up against Savannah's back. The cherry almond scent that she associated with Savannah filled her nostrils, and she inhaled as she wrapped her arms around her, placed her hands over Savannah's on the shaker, and got her started. Once the martini was being well shaken over Savannah's right shoulder, Julia slid around her left and backed against the bar, elbows bracing her body, and Savannah only had to lean slightly to meet Julia's lips with hers.

Impressed by the way Savannah managed to shake the martini and kiss her, Julia let herself drift, languish, in the feel of Savannah's mouth. The softness. The heat. The tang of tomato sauce still on her tongue. The kiss was leisurely. Gradual. Unhurried. Julia couldn't recall ever having been kissed that way, with such teasing promise of what might be to come. It was easy to drift, to lose herself in Savannah…

A knock loud enough to be heard over the shaker startled them both. Julia felt Savannah jump and she turned toward the door to the bar.

"Um, Julia?" It was Evan, face flushed, eyes darting. The kid who'd been so sure of himself less than an hour ago now looked nervous. "You have a visitor." Twitchy. When she looked beyond him, she saw why.

Her father.

Oh God.

"Pop." She did a crappy job hiding her surprise, and she knew it as she stood straighter and felt her face flush. It wasn't like her father didn't know she was gay, but he'd never seen her kissing another woman, and for some reason she couldn't quite specify, she was as shocked as he seemed to be by what he saw. Not to mention her surprise that he was there at all. "What are you doing here?" she asked as Evan left—no, *fled*—back to the bar, and her father walked into The Bar Back. Realizing how she'd sounded, she cleared her throat and went for damage control. "I didn't mean it to sound like that—I'm just surprised to see you. Here."

He was looking around, taking it all in, still dressed in his work clothes, hands tucked in his pockets. "I was on my way home from the shop," he said as his eyes roamed over her desk, the walls, the couch. "Thought I'd pop in, see how it was going." He paused, gazed around. "This part is new."

It was weird, right? She'd been open for months now, and he'd shown up exactly once. While suspicious, she also didn't want to ruin it, so she gave him a nod. Opened her mouth to answer him. Felt Savannah brush past her.

Savannah. Oh my God.

She'd nearly forgotten about her for a moment.

"Mr. Martini," Savannah said as she crossed to him, hand outstretched. "I'm Julia's friend, Savannah McNally. It's so nice to meet you."

His bushy salt-and-pepper eyebrows went up, and he shook her hand even as he gave what sounded like a sarcastic grunt. "Her friend, huh?"

Savannah's cheeks went rosy, and it was adorable, and she shrugged. "Well. She's a friend I *really* like a lot." A quick look to Julia, a small laugh, and damn if her father wasn't charmed—she could see it on his face, a very subtle softening of his gruff, hard features. Of course he was charmed by Savannah—how could he not be? His brows went back to their usual spot on his face, and he even looked like he might be smiling. Just a little. A teeny, tiny bit.

"McNally. That's familiar to me. What's your dad's name? What does he do?"

"Kevin. He's retired from the DPW." As he seemed to think about that, she gestured to the bar. "We're taste-testing martinis for bar specials." She reached for the shaker, popped the strainer on it, and poured it into two glasses. "This is called a naked martini," she told him as her blush deepened. Julia watched, kind of amazed at the ease with which she talked to her dad. Savannah garnished the glasses with the strawberries, then handed one glass to Julia's father and kept one for herself, which she held toward him. "I made these. Be gentle," she said with a smile. "Cheers."

And Jesus, take the wheel, her father touched his glass to Savannah's with a pretty little ping, and they both sipped. While Julia watched in...amazement? Shock? Delight? Horror? She couldn't decide.

He smacked his lips a bit, like he was really gauging the taste. He looked at Julia. "Your mother would love this."

"Wow," Savannah said and also turned to her. "This is *fantastic*." She held the glass out to Julia. "And deadly, 'cause I barely taste the alcohol." She clenched her teeth and made a face toward Julia's father, who—Did he? Yes, he did. He smiled at her.

"This was the storeroom?" her father asked, slowly walking around The Bar Back, drink still in his hand.

Julia joined him, pointing at different spots on the wall as she spoke. "Yeah, partially. And it was the break room and one of the employee bathrooms and a lot of wasted space. So I knocked out this wall and made this area bigger, changed the other employee bathroom to a unisex one and kept a private one in here. I wanted a practice bar where I could experiment with new drinks and also teach new employees how to make the specials." Was she talking too fast? Too much? She was. Definitely. But she was proud of the place, and he was asking, and it was so weird and so good at the same time, and she just couldn't seem to stop. "Vanessa has some great ideas for bringing in more business, and Savannah here has been a great help because she thinks similarly."

"To Vanessa?" Her father snorted. "Better not put them in the same room. Something might catch fire with those brains working so hard so close together."

Did her father just make a joke? She blinked as Savannah laughed. What was happening?

"The four-sided bar in the center was a smart change," her father said. His voice was low, gruff, and holy cow, was he still drinking the naked martini? "Your idea?"

Julia sipped the drink she was holding—actually, no, she took a big gulp of it—as Savannah hadn't taken it back yet, then said, "More seats if the bar's in the center than against a wall."

He nodded and said, "I remember you saying that," still wandering slowly as if in a museum, and the coffee table and barstools were exhibits on display. Before he could ask another question, the side door opened, startling all three of them.

"Uncle Vinnie," Vanessa said in surprise without looking at either Julia or Savannah. She threw her arms around him and, over his shoulder, widened her eyes comically at Julia and mouthed, *What the fuck?*

Julia grinned and shrugged and shook her head because honestly? She had no idea. *What the fuck* was totally accurate.

"All right, I gotta get home before this place bursts into flames," her father said, his demeanor light and fun. At Vanessa's puzzled look, he jerked his chin in Julia's direction and said, "She'll explain."

"Tell Aunt Anna Banana I said hi," Vanessa ordered as Savannah told him it was nice to meet him.

Julia turned to her dad and gave him a wave. "Thanks for coming, Pop."

He gave a nod. A grunt. "Can I use this door?" He indicated the one Vanessa had just entered and handed her his glass.

"Absolutely. You'll be right in the parking lot." Julia pushed it open for him, and he stepped out and was gone into the early evening.

She shut the door, and the room was quiet for several seconds. Savannah met her gaze, smiling. Vanessa looked from one of them to the other and back, clearly wondering what had happened. Julia pointed to the martini equipment and bottles on the bar.

"Yeah, I'm gonna need another one of those."

CHAPTER SIXTEEN

Things were going well. Like, really well. Especially considering Savannah hadn't been looking for a new relationship. Or, hell, any relationship. But Julia was…God, what was she? How could she describe what Julia did to her? Made her feel? There were words, but they didn't seem like enough.

Mr. Davidson was napping when her replacement arrived. She gave her report, wished them well, and headed out to her car just as her phone pinged. Tiffany.

RU alive?

Savannah grinned. It had been a while since they'd seen each other or even texted more than a quick check-in here or there. Instead of texting back, she got in her car, started the engine, hooked the phone up, and called.

"Okay," Tiff answered. "Who is this, and what have you done with my girl? 'Cause she doesn't call. Like, ever. Do your research next time, *imposter.*"

"It's good to hear your voice, too."

"You've obviously been too busy for me." It was meant to be light and teasing—Savannah knew Tiff well enough to know that— but that meant she also knew her well enough to catch the tiny edge of hurt. Before she could respond to it, though, Tiffany added, "Which I am willing to overlook if you've been busy, I don't know, say, naked and between some sheets with a hot bartender."

"Not yet," Savannah said, surprised by the suggestion. She pulled into traffic, adding in her defense, "It hasn't been that long."

"Yes, give me more excuses," Tiffany teased. "You met her in March, weirdo. It's almost June."

Savannah blinked. Wait, what? "Really?"

"Um, yes? Are there no calendars where you live?"

"You're hilarious."

"Listen, I'm not the one dating the hottest bartender in all the land and hasn't slept with her yet."

Savannah barked a laugh and was grateful. Tiffany could always do that, take a weird or awkward or too-serious subject and find the humor. "I know what the issue is," she said and was somehow startled when the words left her lips.

"Tell me."

"It's the bar. She's there all the time. We've had exactly one date that hasn't been either out front or in the back lounge area."

"Doesn't she have a manager or something?"

"I don't think so. I know her cousins have bugged her about it. I mean, she doesn't need to be there every second they're open, right?"

"In the beginning, maybe, but not now. This is why people hire managers and such."

"I think she sleeps there sometimes." Savannah hadn't voiced that to anybody before now, but it had occurred to her when she noticed a pillow and blankets piled in a corner. What kind of bar needed pillows and blankets?

"Get out. Seriously?"

"I mean, maybe?" And just like that, she was suddenly protective of Julia. "She's there a lot. Like, *a lot*."

"You need to get her away from that place. Take her out."

It was an idea that had been sort of floating around in the back of her head for a while, but she hadn't been able to find a night that worked and had kind of settled for seeing her at the bar whenever she could. A little making out here, a little cuddling and talking there. And it was great. But Tiffany saying out loud that she should find a way brought it to the forefront and somehow filled her with new determination. "I think you're right."

"Can you talk to her cousins? Or that bartender that's there so much? The one with the funky haircut?"

"Clea. I bet I could." She hit her turn signal and sat at a No Turn on Red. "Do you think she's not as into me?" Another thing she hadn't really meant to say out loud. She'd just been thinking it, but apparently, words had a mind of their own now.

"What?" Tiffany's voice said Savannah was being ridiculous, and if Savannah could've hugged her right then, she absolutely would have. "Why would you say that?"

A sigh. "I don't know. I'm just now thinking about how you said it's been nearly three months, and why don't we spend more time together, and my family is giving me stress, and my coping skills are in the toilet, and you should ignore me." A bitter laugh. Little humor. She suddenly wasn't feeling it at all, the humor. She'd always been good at finding it, a little ray of sunshine, something small to smile at. Not now. As if out of the blue, she felt weighed down. Like she was carrying too much on her shoulders.

"Take a breath," Tiffany said, and her tone held no sarcasm, no mockery. Only love and calm. "I've told you before that you take on too much of everybody else's burdens. It's okay to take care of Savannah, you know."

The car glided to a stop in her father's driveway, and she blew out a long, slow breath. "I know."

"Talk to the cousins. You need to go on a real date, away from your family and friends, away from her bar. Just the two of you. Then you'll know."

"I'll know what?"

"If it's time."

"Time for what?"

Tiffany's sigh was more like a groan. "Oh my God, I love you so much, but you need to get laid, my friend. Time for bumping uglies. Time to butter the biscuit, shuck the oyster, open the gates of Mordor, you know? Are you with me?"

Savannah was laughing so hard, tears had filled her eyes. This. This was what she needed. "You are the best, you know that?"

"Please." Tiff snorted. "Of course, I know that."

"I gotta go in and see my dad. I promise I will consider your advice."

"Do more than consider it, okay? You deserve to know if it's worth it to take things further with this girl. And if not, you deserve to have at least one hot night of spelunking in the Batcave."

They signed off, Savannah feeling a little bit lighter than she had when she'd begun her drive. She went into her dad's house, calling out a hello.

It seemed like it was easier and easier somehow to tell if her father was having a good day or a bad day or somewhere in between, and she wasn't sure that was a good thing. It meant his episodes, as she called them, had become more pronounced. She pegged that day as a tweener right away because his eyes were neither completely clear, nor totally dazed out, but when he turned and saw her, they seemed to clear right up. That was new. He was sitting in his recliner, MSNBC on the television, empty sandwich plate on the table next to him, and his smile was wide as she approached him.

"Hi, Dad." She kissed his stubbly cheek.

"There's my girl. How's life?"

Savannah glanced into the dining room where Dina sat at her laptop and gave a thumbs-up even as she met with her client virtually.

"Life's okay. How are you?"

"I'm great. It's gorgeous out, and I sat on the deck for a while. Worked in the garden."

"We started a new therapy, too," Dina said, coming into the room with her headset around her neck. With her chin, she indicated her father's laptop on the table. "When he's feeling anger or frustration, he writes a letter or a journal entry or even an article to the person or place he's fixated on."

Savannah furrowed her brow. "Really? Like…what do you mean?"

"Like, I got a burger yesterday from that new place on Pike," her father said, sitting forward in his chair and looked Savannah in the eye, his intensity rising a bit. "And it was *terrible*. Raw in the middle, the cheese wasn't melted, my fries were cold. Made me so mad." He cleared his throat and looked away. "I was having one of my spells."

They'd talked more than once about how he shouldn't criticize anybody during his spells because his emotions ran extra high, and he could end up saying something he couldn't take back. It was something that, at the time, made her grateful for Dina's presence because she'd helped convince him.

"So instead of just spending the day being mad about it," Dina said, "we opened the laptop and he wrote a review. We didn't send it, of course, because…"

"I got a little nasty," her father said, and one corner of his mouth lifted in a half grin, which made Savannah smile.

"Dad," she scolded, feigning horror.

"But it really seemed to help him," Dina said. "It calmed him right down."

"That's amazing." She meant it. One of the biggest changes in her father since showing the early signs of dementia had been in his temper. He'd never been an angry guy, not the kind of father who used volume to control his kids. So when he started to yell and say terribly mean things, she and Deck and Chelsea had been shocked. It had taken a while to understand that it was the disease and not him. If this new therapy, as Dina called it, helped to channel his anger into something creative, she was all for it. "Good for you." She gave a nod of thanks to Dina, who smiled widely.

"Just one more client and a few emails, Kev. Then I'm done."

"Well, hurry it up, woman. They've taken enough of you for today."

He was happy.

The simple statement of fact didn't hover in Savannah's brain often, so she was kind of surprised by it. She'd never been a fan of Dina. She could admit that. Dina was nosy and pushy and, okay, anybody standing in her mother's place wasn't going to earn big points right away. If at all. But she had to concede that her father loved Dina, and Dina loved him. And that was all that mattered, really.

She'd come by to check on Chelsea, but she wasn't home. Neither was Declan. She wasn't happy about the relief she felt over not having to deal with her brother or hear Chelsea talk about what other fun stuff she'd done with Dina. Instant guilt then set in for using the phrase *dealing with* when it came to her siblings, even if only in her head. But she was exhausted from work and had way too much on her mind, and that included Julia now. So she sat and chatted with her father for a while, did her best to push everything else aside. They laughed and joked, and when Dina told him dinner was ready—and Savannah had politely declined the invitation to stay—she kissed his cheek and left.

An idea had been slowly simmering in her brain since talking to Tiffany, and she was ready to put it into action.

"I don't understand what's happening here," Julia said. Anger was bubbling up in her gut, and she did her best to keep it contained as Vanessa tugged her by the hand into The Bar Back. "It's Friday. We're busy. I need to be out there." A jerk of her head indicated she meant the bar, as if there was any doubt.

"It's fine. It's covered," Vanessa said. Finally in the back, she dropped Julia's hand, and there was Amelia, holding out clothes on a hanger.

"Here. Put these on."

Julia blinked at her. "What is going on, you guys?"

Vanessa waved a hand at her. "Change your clothes, or you're gonna be late."

What the hell was happening? Julia held her arms out to the sides and let them drop, looking from one cousin to the other and back again.

Vanessa sighed as she exchanged a look with Amelia, clearly annoyed that Julia either couldn't read her mind or didn't have the patience to wait and see. Probably both. "I told you she'd fight us."

With a nod, Amelia turned to Julia. "Savannah is picking you up in twenty minutes. You have a date."

Both positive and negative emotions rushed through her system at the same time. A date was exciting! Especially one with Savannah. She wondered where they were going. What they were doing. Then, of course, her brain immediately shifted to wondering how long they'd be gone. What time would they be back? Who would take care of the bar? What if something happened?

"Stop it." Vanessa was seated on the couch now, scrolling on her phone, and Amelia flopped down next to her, folding her arms. "Everything is taken care of. Clea and Evan have things handled out front. We'll be right here in case they need something else, and we will take care of locking up."

Julia blinked at the two of them, trying to comprehend what she'd just said. "Wait, what?"

"Oh my God." Amelia blew out an obviously frustrated breath as she dropped both hands down to the couch. "You've got a really cool woman ready to sweep you off your feet and two cousins who love you and are doing whatever they can to help ensure that happens. Can you just trust us, take a fucking breath, and go have a good time? Please?"

A beat passed. Finally, Julia spoke. "I can. Yeah."

"Thank Christ."

"These are my clothes." Julia was startled to see that when she finally looked at what Amelia had handed her, even though she knew both of them had keys to her apartment, just like she had keys to their homes.

"They are," Amelia said. "By the way, when's the last time you did laundry? 2011?"

"Around then, yeah." Julia headed toward the small bathroom to change.

"And you should fire your housekeeper," Vanessa called as she closed the door. "She sucks at her job."

Julia pulled off her Martini's polo shirt. Vanessa had grabbed her a black tank top and then a sleeveless button-down in purple and black to wear over it. Dark jeans and black sporty sandals finished the outfit. It was nice. Casual, but put together. Not at all fancy, but nice.

Where was Savannah taking her?

Both of her cousins were texting when Julia exited the bathroom, and both looked up and smiled. "Perfect," Vanessa said as Amelia gave a satisfied nod. Popping up off the couch, Vanessa took out the black elastic that held Julia's hair back in a low ponytail. Then she fluffed it up, finger-combed it. "Here," she said, putting the elastic around Julia's wrist. "You might need it later."

"Well, that's cryptic."

A grin and a shrug from her cousin. Nothing more. She handed her a tube. "Gloss 'em up, baby."

As Julia did as she was ordered, running the gloss over her lips, still uncomfortable about leaving the bar, Amelia's phone pinged.

"Your chariot awaits."

Just like that, the thrill was back, elbowing the anxiety out of the way, and she was suddenly nervous, filled with that kind of anticipation that was uncomfortable in its excitement. Made her stomach feel a little woozy. Made her almost light-headed, but not quite. Started that sexy fluttering in her lower body. That kind of anticipation. She wasn't sure what expression she was making when she shot a look toward Vanessa, but her cousin smiled, added a head tilt, and reached out to squeeze her upper arm.

"We've got this. Okay? Don't worry about Martini's. It's in the hands of two other Martinis, and they will take good care of it. I promise you. Now go. Have a good time." With that, Vanessa pushed herself to her tiptoes, kissed Julia on the cheek, and ushered her out the side door.

"We mean it," Amelia said, dangling the keys to the bar from a finger as Julia stepped into the parking lot. "Don't you come back here. We won't let you in." Then she waved to somebody beyond Julia, winked at her, and pulled the door closed.

It was still light out and would be for a couple more hours, the temperature warm, that time of summer where the season was still just getting started and it had yet to throw the three *H*s—hazy, hot, and humid—at its people. Savannah was there, her car idling as she stood holding the passenger side door open.

"Well, hello there, sexy. Ready to have some fun?" She looked like...everything right. Absolutely everything. Beautiful. Sexy. Inviting. Mischievous. Sexy. Mysterious. Breathtaking. Sexy. And for that moment, that one beat in time, nothing existed but her. Not the bar. Not the rest of the people milling about. Not the sun or the moon or the trees. Only Savannah McNally, standing there in her jeans and green top, smiling at her and waiting patiently.

Julia stopped when they were face to face and placed a gentle kiss on Savannah's lips. "Ready as I'll ever be. You look amazing, by the way." She got in the car, and Savannah slammed the door shut, then zipped around and got in behind the wheel.

"*You* look amazing." Another kiss, this one a little less gentle, holding a little more promise. Then seat belts clicked, the car was shifted, and they were moving.

"Where are we going?" Julia asked, fighting the urge to look back at the bar as they pulled away.

"You'll see."

CHAPTER SEVENTEEN

"No way." Julia blinked in disbelief as Savannah searched for a parking spot because, oh my God, they were at Dasher Park. She turned to Savannah, stunned. "This is one of my favorite places on earth."

"I know that. I had help." Savannah grinned as she put the car in park and turned to her. Asking for guidance from Vanessa and Amelia had turned out to be an impressively supersmart move on her part.

"I haven't been here in forever."

"I know that, too."

Everything inside Julia softened. "I can't believe you brought me here."

"Well, believe it. Now let's get moving. We have rides to ride and crap to eat." A quick peck to Julia's lips and she pushed her door open.

"So much crap to eat," Julia said with relish.

Savannah wouldn't let her pay her way, reiterating that this was a date, and once they had their wristbands and had pushed through the turnstiles, Julia stopped and held her arms out.

"I am home, my friends." The smells were the same as they'd always been. The sweet scent of cotton candy floated all through the park as if purposely blown around by strategically placed fans. Which it probably was, 'cause that would be terrific marketing. To their left was a six-foot statue of the park mascot, Dasher the chipmunk, dressed in his bright yellow T-shirt with the big red *D* on the front. Fake antlers were on his head and a string of red garland was draped around his neck. Julia gasped, called his name, and hurried over to him to pose so Savannah could snap a photo.

"Um, isn't Dasher supposed to be a reindeer?" she asked as she jutted her chin toward the mascot. "And why is he decorated for Christmas? It's June."

"Oh, Savannah, you sweet, uninformed girl. Do you not know the story of Dasher Park?" At the shake of Savannah's head, Julia put her arm around her shoulders, hugged her close, and inhaled her cherry almond scent, which somehow paired perfectly with the cotton candy aroma of the air around them. "Dasher Park was built by the Mayfield family. You've heard of them? Wealthy entrepreneurs in Northwood? They have buildings and wings of hospitals and universities named after them?"

"I've heard of them."

They began to walk as she filled Savannah in. "Well, they called it Dasher Park after their youngest son, Dasher Mayfield. And he wanted to use a reindeer for their mascot because he's totally in love with Christmas. But his parents were not okay with that because it seemed weird to have a reindeer as a mascot for something that wasn't Christmas themed. Dasher himself is the one who chose the chipmunk, but he also wanted to keep celebrating his favorite holiday. Therefore, Dasher Park has several Christmas weeks a year." She made air quotes as she spoke. "One is the first week of June. Yay for us, right?"

Was she being a weirdo? Because she thought maybe she was, but she couldn't help it. She was so happy to be there, and she felt like a kid again. "I can't believe you brought me here," she said again and would probably say it several more times throughout the night.

It was warm and the sun was heading toward the horizon. The park was busy. Bustling. The customer changeover was beginning. Families with little ones who'd likely been there in the afternoon were heading out, and teenagers in flocks were coming in. Lights turned on, and the Christmas carols over the loudspeakers got a little louder. Julia pulled out her phone, checked it, saw nothing from Vanessa, but sent a text anyway, asking if everything was going okay. Then she turned to Savannah, whose smile was amused and had been since they'd arrived.

"There's a method to seeing the park that I came up with when I was eighteen," she told her. "Do you have a plan?"

Savannah laughed through her nose and her blue eyes sparkled in the park lighting. "Nope. You lead and I'll follow."

"Excellent. Okay." Julia indicated to their left. "We go counterclockwise to start. Merry-go-round, Shotgun, Tilt-A-Whirl, all in that direction. Then we cut down the center, hit the Slingshot." She stopped, found Savannah's eyes with hers. "How are you with roller coasters?"

"Love 'em."

"Excellent. We hit the Slingshot, then keep moving that way. The Funhouse. We can grab food and beer or whatever at any point. Play some games. And then we end with the Ferris wheel. It'll be fully dark, and you can see the entire city from up there. Yeah? Sound good?"

"Sounds amazing."

Julia clapped her hands together once, trying not to dwell on the surge of adrenaline that shot through her, the joy she felt in the moment, and trying to ignore the fact that this woman had gone out of her way to bring her to a place she loved. All of it, it was a lot. Giving herself an internal shake, she vowed to enjoy herself, not worry about the bar—even though she was going to text Vanessa very soon—and she grabbed Savannah's warm hand. "Follow me."

"Anywhere," came the soft reply from Savannah. Julia held her gaze, touched her face tenderly. Somebody shrieked a laugh nearby and made them both flinch, which then made them both laugh.

"Let's go." Julia gave Savannah a tug, and they were off.

Amusement parks were not at all Savannah's thing. She didn't hate them—that was too strong a word. A more accurate description—going to an amusement park would never, ever be at the top of her list of things to do. She liked them fine. She loved the food. Carnival food truly was one of the best things about summer. Funnel cakes and candy apples and cotton candy and please, God, give her all the deep-fried Oreos. She could walk around, happily stuffing her face for hours.

The rides, though. The rides hated her. Which was fine because the feeling was so very mutual.

Even as a child, Savannah didn't love amusement park rides. She went on them because she loved her brother and sister, and they loved rides. They would beg and plead and pull her by the arms, and how could she say no to those adorable faces? You could say she'd become a pro at riding rides if somebody she cared about asked her to.

She could do it again. Right?

Besides, it was worth it to see Julia's face, to feel the excited anticipation rolling off her in waves. She was a different person in Dasher Park. Well, not completely different, because she was checking her phone every other minute, but…Savannah suspected this Julia, this happy, joyful, bouncy Julia, was actually much closer to the real Julia than bar-owning, drink-mixing, budget-worrying Julia. And Savannah liked bar-owning Julia. A lot. That was how this whole thing had started. But this Julia? This fun, sparkly eyed Julia? Oh, Savannah *so* wanted to keep her.

Even if it meant riding a roller coaster called the Slingshot.

She eyed it warily, recalling a horror movie she'd seen once where a roller coaster malfunctioned and flew apart midride, flinging bodies of screaming teenagers through the air like hormone-laced confetti.

"Ready?" Julia asked, yanking her out of her daydreams. Or day-nightmares. Daymares? Were those a thing?

Julia slipped her phone back into her pocket, having checked it yet again, and turned to her, so clearly excited, as she pulled her dark hair back and held up the elastic she'd had around her wrist. "Vanessa told me I'd need this, and I had no idea why. Remind me to thank her."

And then they were in line.

Julia bounced on the balls of her feet like a kid, and honestly, it was so adorable, it made Savannah work harder to set aside the fear that had started to simmer in her stomach.

They showed their bracelets to the ride operator, who looked like he was nineteen and still couldn't grow a beard, his stubble in weird patches on his face like a young and gangly Keanu Reeves.

Julia tugged her to the very front. The first car in line. They'd be the first people at the top of the shockingly high hill. They'd be the first ones plunging to their inevitable deaths...

Stop it.

She swallowed. Stepped into the car. Pulled the safety brace down and heard it click into place. Broke out in a cold sweat.

"You okay?" Julia asked, her giddiness almost contagious. Almost. Savannah forced a smile. Nodded. The car began to move. She managed not to throw up.

She didn't remember much of the ride at all.

Before she knew it, they were slowing down, easing into the loading and unloading area once again, thank fucking God.

Julia's face was flushed. Some of her hair had escaped the ponytail and brushed along her face, her neck, and she looked invigorated. Alive. Those dimples were on full display, and she turned to look at Savannah.

"Oh my God, that was—Are you okay?"

Savannah felt herself nod, swallow, blink. A lot. A lot of blinking.

Julia reached toward her. "Sweetie, let go. It's over. You're good. Let go of this."

She felt Julia pry her fingers off the safety brace, and she pushed it up. Her heart rate began to slow as she took in a huge breath of air. "Wow." She managed to get that word out. One word. That was progress, right? She flexed her fingers, took Julia's hand when she offered it, and stood. They didn't speak until they were back out onto the fairway. Solid ground. Savannah somehow managed to keep herself from dropping to her knees and kissing the asphalt. Then Julia turned to face her, her expression soft, her smile gentle.

"Why didn't you tell me you were scared of roller coasters?"

"I'm not." Savannah looked away, a little embarrassed, then turned back. "Okay, I am. Terrified, actually."

A beat passed.

And then she laughed. It bubbled up out of her like she had no control over it. "They scare the crap out of me. I was sure I was going to die." She kept laughing until Julia joined her, and they were both cracking up like lunatics.

"Why wouldn't you tell me?" Julia asked when they'd finally calmed down and were walking by unspoken agreement toward a beer and wine booth.

Savannah shrugged, buying time while she tried to decide how to answer. Tell the truth? Make something up that made her look less...hooked on Julia? Not answer at all? They got in line and she inhaled deeply. Blew it out. "Because you were so excited and..." Cleared her throat. "I didn't want to put a damper on that. It was too cute." Another shrug, just to prove how nonchalant she was being, 'cause yeah. Almost died. No biggie.

Julia's hug came out of nowhere and surprised her enough to startle a small yelp from her lungs. A kiss was pressed to her temple, and when she finally looked at Julia, her eyes were wide with what seemed to be wonder.

"Help you, ladies?" The woman behind the counter pulled them back to the reality of life.

They strolled for a long time, warm cups of mulled wine in their hands, which only felt weird for a minute or two, given that it was June and they were in tank tops and sandals, and then it felt perfect. The warmth of it as Savannah sipped and felt it sort of seeping through her body, the wonderful scents of Christmas— cinnamon and nutmeg and allspice. It was like Christmas in a cup. The evening had cooled a bit, and their shoulders touched, rubbed here and there, as they walked, taking in various Christmas trees around the park, each decorated in some kind of theme.

"I still like the dog one," Julia commented as they strolled, recalling a tree they'd passed that must've been twelve feet high, every ornament a dog or having to do with dogs.

"Me, too," Savannah said as Julia took out her phone and gave it a quick check. "Don't you think they'd let you know if something was wrong?"

Looking the smallest bit scolded, Julia gave a quick nod and slipped the phone into her back pocket once again. "How do you feel about Ferris wheels?" she asked, changing the subject quickly and completely.

"I actually love them."

"Truth?"

"Truth."

"Not afraid?"

Savannah shook her head as she tossed her empty cup into a nearby garbage can. "Nope. I'm not afraid of heights. I'm afraid of hurtling through the air at a million miles an hour with nothing but a foam-covered metal bar holding me in place."

Julia's laugh was big. Loud. Came from deep in her belly as she tossed her head back. "Fair enough," she said and grabbed Savannah's hand. "Let's check out this view then, okay?"

There was a line, and they stood and waited. The woman behind them coughed. Loudly. Wetly. Savannah grimaced and turned subtly to Julia, whose expression probably mirrored hers, and they both grinned. The woman coughed some more, off and on, with little apparent regard to those around her.

Once they'd settled into their car and it moved a few positions as the rest of the cars were filled, Julia gave a full-body shudder. "Why don't people cover their mouths when they cough? Is it so hard to not infect everybody with your germs?" Her voice was low enough that nobody but Savannah could hear her.

"Agreed. Though I think I have a fortress of an immune system."

"Yeah? How do you figure?" The car moved again, and Julia slid closer until their thighs touched. The heat was instant.

"I mean, I'm a home health aide. I'm around sick people all the time, and I never get sick."

Julia's eyes went comically wide. "I cannot believe you just said that out loud."

"I see you believe in jinxes."

"Of course I believe in jinxes. Who doesn't believe in jinxes?" Savannah raised her hand slowly, waved it a bit, and Julia gasped extra loudly, making her laugh. "Do you get sick a lot?"

"I hope not," Julia said. "I don't have time to be sick."

"I would take care of you if you did." Savannah held her gaze, and Julia gave her a quick peck on the lips.

"You take care of everybody—I'm beginning to understand."

A shrug. "Always have." She liked the way Julia was looking at her then. Softly. Tenderness in her dark eyes, her nearly black brows accenting the concern in her expression.

"Well, *I* would take care of *you* if you got sick."

"Good thing I don't get sick then. You just said you didn't have the time." It was an attempt at lightening the mood because the air suddenly felt heavy, weighted with something important.

Julia's turn to shrug. "I'd make time," she said quietly, and then the wheel picked up speed and the ride had begun.

When Savannah had said she wasn't afraid of heights, that wasn't the whole truth. Because the whole truth was that she loved them. She loved being up high and getting a bird's eye view of the world below. She loved seeing everything in one snapshot. The tops of buildings. The lights of the city. The people on the fairway, nothing more than dots of color from up there. "If you could have one superpower, what would it be?" She held out her arms and leaned her head back. "I'd want to fly."

"Yeah?" Julia was gazing at her with that look in her eye—deep, dark, and sexy as hell.

"Yeah. And stop looking at me like that, or I'm going to rip your clothes off right here on the Ferris wheel for all the world to see."

A barked laugh. "Scandalous."

"You have no idea." The look that passed between them was beyond hot. So much more than scorching. Oh yes, Savannah was taking her home tonight. Not a doubt in her mind. That thought settled, she said, "But back to the conversation at hand, Sexypants. Superpower?"

"Time travel," Julia said, voice firm.

"Really?" Savannah drew out the word. "Interesting. What would you change? And aren't you concerned about the Butterfly Effect?"

The night air was gentle, and it picked up some of Julia's hair and rearranged it before letting it settle back down against her head. "While I'd definitely do my best to change some bigger things in history, I actually want it for selfish reasons."

"Like, fixing a bad haircut you had in seventh grade?"

Julia snorted a laugh. "Yes! Or not doing that last shot of tequila at the keg party my sophomore year in college." She clenched her teeth, made a face.

"Worst hangover of your life?"

"Worst night, worst morning, worst shift at my work-study job…"

"Lotta worsts there."

"So many."

The wheel began to slow, and Savannah had mixed feelings about the ride ending. There was something about being in that car, feeling like it was just her and Julia in the world, that made her want to stay longer, ask more questions, twirl that dark hair around her finger while she listened to Julia's soft husky voice. At the same time, she was ready to get off the ride because the night was so far from over.

Back on the fairway, they strolled, their pace a pretty clear indicator that they weren't ready to go quite yet. At least, that's how Savannah looked at it. This time, they held hands as they walked, the darkness and the late hour whittling away any worries about who might see and have an opinion. It was closing in on eleven, and things were shutting down, booths closing, the lights of some of the kiddie rides turning off. Something else about the darkness and the hour and the mood—they gave Savannah courage.

"So," she said quietly as they continued to walk. "You should check in with Vanessa one more time, make sure everything's good, and then you're not going to check again."

"I'm not?"

"Nope."

"Why not?"

She stopped walking, then waited until Julia looked at her and she had her full attention. "Because I'm taking you home with me and you'll be busy. Very busy."

Julia's eyes went wide, a beat passed, and a slow, lazy smile spread across her face. "I see," was all she said, but it was all she had to say because those dimples spoke volumes.

"Come with me." Savannah led the way to the park exit.

CHAPTER EIGHTEEN

Any other time, Julia would have taken the time to look around, to absorb the decor, to wander slowly through Savannah's house and get to know her more by taking in the place she called home. She would take the time to look at Savannah longer. Sure, she'd feasted her eyes on the ass-hugging jeans she wore. She'd tried not to stare at the tank top and the way it liked to slide down a bit to give a tantalizing peek of cleavage before Savannah adjusted it again. Yeah, Julia owed that tank top a hefty tip.

But that night was not any other time. It was going to be *the* night. Their first night together. And despite being surprised by the boldness of Savannah's invitation—well, it had been more of a command, hadn't it, an insanely sexy one—she'd known this was the direction they'd been heading. And then it was more like hurtling, on fire, like a comet across the dark, star-filled sky.

The drive had been silent, but not awkwardly so. Julia's mind had been filled with possibility. The promise of what was to come, as well as the nerves that promise brought along with it. She wondered what Savannah was thinking but had felt weird asking.

Now, Savannah led her up the front stairs to the open porch and slid her key home. She glanced over her shoulder at Julia, and her eyes were filled with arousal, desire, and maybe the tiniest flicker of worry, but honestly, she just looked crazy sexy to Julia. It surprised her that the air around them wasn't audibly sizzling because it sure felt like it was.

"This is my place," Savannah said as she shut the door behind them, her quiet voice almost too loud in the silent sensuality of the moment. "You can look at it tomorrow."

And that was it. No more words. Just the kissing.

So. Much. Kissing.

Kissing, touching, seriously making out.

It was different this time, different than their previous kisses. Because this time, it was just them. Only the two of them. Nobody about to walk in on them. No chance of being startled or discovered. They had all the time in the world, and they kissed like it.

One small lamp gave off the only light, the rest of the living room dim. Savannah's mouth was hot and soft, and Julia knew she could get lost in kissing her, just stay there always, her mouth exploring Savannah's, for the rest of her life. Even though she wanted more. Even though she was going to need more very, very soon, kissing Savannah gave her something she hadn't felt in longer than she realized: peace. Like she was exactly where she was supposed to be. It was a confusing, weird, wonderful feeling, and while she had no idea where it had come from, why this woman had shown up and shaken everything in her world, she never wanted it to end. She dug both hands into Savannah's hair, holding her head as her tongue battled Savannah's for the lead.

When air became an issue, they parted with just enough space between their mouths to breathe. Savannah slid her arms up and around Julia's neck, and her normally bright eyes had gone dark—Julia could see the desire in them like it was standing in a spotlight. The arousal. The primal *want*, and oh my God, she knew that feeling intimately because it mirrored her own.

But her nerves. God. It had been quite a while since she'd been with a woman that had *meant* something, and a much longer while since she'd wanted one this badly. She wanted to be sexy and flirtatious, to whisper, *If you don't take me to your bedroom, I'm going to rip your clothes off right here in your living room.* But something held the words locked tightly in her head. Confidence had never really been an issue for her with regard to most things, and certainly not around sex. Why now? What was it about Savannah that made her nerves rattle inside her? Even as she asked herself the question, a full-body tremble rolled through her.

"You okay?" Savannah asked softly, bending herself back enough to look up into Julia's face. "You're shaking." Her arms were around Julia's neck, and she dug her fingers into the hair at her nape, scratched lightly, and Julia felt goose bumps break out across her skin.

"I just..." She looked away, nibbled on her bottom lip, then cleared her throat. "It's been a while for me." Glad the lighting was dim, she felt a blush heat her cheeks, swallowed down a lump of embarrassment.

"A while since what? Since you've had sex? Oh God, me, too. Please." She waved a hand.

Julia let it go, let Savannah think that's what she meant because she didn't want to make the moment any heavier than it already was. Still, she tipped her head to one side as she felt a grin she had zero control over blossoming. "How do you do that?" she asked quietly.

"Do what?" Savannah seemed genuinely confused by the question, furrowing her light brow, and it made her that much more wonderful.

"Make me feel better in, like, two and a half seconds."

This time, the smile that appeared was Savannah's. Bright. Gorgeous. Made everything in the entire world perfect in that moment.

"How about we go upstairs, and I make you feel a lot better?" she asked, and the sexy glint in her eyes, the way she arched one eyebrow, had Julia's underwear suddenly very, very wet.

"Yes, please," she whispered, then bent to kiss Savannah once again.

They parted, eventually, and Savannah took her hand. Eyes never leaving Julia's, she lifted it, pressed a warm kiss to it, then headed toward the stairs, tugging her gently behind. They didn't speak. Simply walked. But the air was so thick with anticipation that Julia wondered if she could reach out and touch it, hold it in her hands and examine it from different angles.

The wondering stopped abruptly, though.

At the door of her bedroom, Savannah looked over her shoulder. Held Julia's gaze. Gave her a slow, sexy smile.

And tugged her toward the bed.

❖

Had she ever been this hot in her life? This turned on? This ready to shed all her clothes in record time and lie down naked with somebody? No. The answer to that was definitely no. And Savannah was pretty sure she wasn't going to survive it. She was either going to burst into flames, melt into a useless puddle, or explode into a million pieces. One of those things was bound to happen because, oh my God, she was so hot.

Hadn't she been in control of things? Like, from the beginning of the evening, hadn't she been in the driver's seat? Because she certainly wasn't now—Julia was everywhere—and she couldn't pinpoint when the shift of power had happened. They were in her bedroom, and they'd kissed all the way up the stairs and into the room, which was spotless because Savannah had planned this. Sex with Julia had been the endgame since she'd spoken with Vanessa about what her cousin's perfect date would be. And things had gone exactly according to plan. Except now, she couldn't think. Couldn't see. Couldn't focus. All she could do was feel, and holy good God, the things she was feeling...

"You are so fucking sexy," Julia whispered, her mouth close to that spot where her neck and shoulder met, and Savannah was so lost in sensation that it took her a beat to fully comprehend or respond to the words. But once they hit, once she absorbed them, they acted like a zap of electricity, spurring her into action. With Julia's face in both her hands, she turned them in a half circle, kissing Julia fiercely as she walked her backward. *God, she tastes so good.* Julia's mouth was a combination of cotton candy sweetness and hot, wet passion, and Savannah couldn't get enough as she pushed her tongue in deep, and Julia's legs hit the edge of the mattress, and she dropped to sit.

Savannah took her in. She could feel the desire, the arousal, the sheer want coursing through her and knew it was visible on her face by the way Julia's eyes widened slightly. Savannah motioned with one hand, and Julia slid her behind backward, Savannah following her on hands and knees, crawling up that long, gorgeous body until Julia stopped, and Savannah was on all fours above her. Looking down into the most beautiful face, the sexiest eyes she'd ever seen.

"*You* are so fucking sexy," she said, and her own voice was hoarse, gravelly. "And I need you naked. Right now." Upper hand fully back in place, she wasted no time undressing Julia. She wanted to do it slowly, to savor the revelation of each expanse of that sensual, olive-toned skin, but her hands were traitors. Wouldn't listen to her brain's commands. Practically ripped the clothing from Julia's body until she lay beneath her in just her black bra and matching bikinis. Savannah pushed herself up to her knees and just stared. No, ogled, really. She ogled the mostly naked woman beneath her, and the words left her lips before she was able to filter them.

"How the hell did I get so lucky?" It was a whisper, but enough, and Julia's face softened, reddened just a bit, as she raised her hand to lay her palm against Savannah's cheek.

"I was going to say the same thing."

"You, too, were wondering how I got so lucky?" She rolled her lips in, and Julia barked a laugh, and the heaviness, the seriousness in the air dissipated until they were left with each other and comfort.

"Come here, smart-ass," Julia ordered and pulled Savannah down for a kiss that seared every cell within her. "Your turn," Julia whispered as she tugged Savannah's tank top over her head, then went to work on unfastening her jeans. She pushed her hand down the front of them without even attempting to pull them off. "I can't wait any longer to touch you."

And at those words, Savannah felt a surge of wetness at her center. She'd been damp before. She was soaked now, and bursts of sensation shot through her legs and lower body as Julia's fingers found her, stroked her, and Savannah had zero time to even comprehend that her orgasm was that close before it ripped through her. Colors exploded behind her eyes as she closed a handful of Julia's hair in her fist and clenched her teeth, unable to contain the cry of surprise that rumbled up from her throat and forced its way out of her mouth.

"Well," Julia said simply, gazing up at Savannah with a satisfied grin on her face.

Savannah covered her eyes with a hand. "Oh my God."

"That was..." When Savannah opened her eyes, Julia was still grinning and just shaking her head as if at a loss for words. And something about that grin, that sexy expression on her face, spurred Savannah into action once again.

"Yeah, well, we're not done." And just like that, she took the upper hand back once more. In fact, she took that upper hand and slipped it right along the crotch of Julia's very wet bikinis—she could feel the damp heat even through the fabric—pulling an erotically charged gasp from her. Torn between wanting to take her time and wanting to dive right into the sexiness of Julia's body, Savannah managed to corral her brain and think clearly for a split second. Long enough to utter one line. "Um, we're both way overdressed, you know."

"I completely agree with that. We should fix it."

"We should." Savannah laughed at the speed with which they each removed their remaining clothes. "We look like cartoon characters."

"Clothes flying everywhere?" Julia's eyes sparkled even in the dim light of the small lamp on the nightstand.

"Yes," Savannah agreed, and then they were naked. Both of them. Naked and breathless and looking at each other. Julia was even more gorgeous than Savannah had expected. That olive skin glowed in the low light, her breasts small, her nipples brown and standing at attention, all that hair cascading over her shoulders as she leaned back on her forearms and didn't seem the least bit shy about her nude body. Why would she be? She was stunning.

At the same time as she let her gaze roam slowly over Julia's body, Julia's dark eyes were doing the same to hers. She could feel them—Savannah would swear to God in that moment. Like fingertips, trailing softly from her shoulders down over her bare breasts, circling a nipple, then continuing down her stomach to the apex of her thighs. She felt the pressure building in her once again, like a pot on the stove, steam released, but now the lid was back on, and it was starting again.

"Oh no, you don't," Savannah said and stretched her body over Julia's, forcing her onto her back. A knee between her thighs made Julia gasp, and Savannah decided that sound had quickly become one of her favorites ever. That sharp little intake of breath that let her know Julia was turned on. Savannah pressed her knee up, just enough to tug another gasp, this one with some volume to it.

She captured Julia's mouth with hers once again.

Details went hazy then, everything blending into one giant wave of sensation. Her hands explored Julia's body as if they had minds of their own, coursing along skin that was even softer than it looked. Warm and smooth. Like velvet. Like silk.

Julia's small breast fit perfectly in her hand, as if it was measured just for that, for sitting against her palm. She kneaded it slowly, rolled the nipple between her thumb and forefinger, before dipping her head and pulling it into her mouth.

So sweet.

Somehow, Julia's skin tasted as sweet as she smelled. Like warm brown sugar and a hint of vanilla and Savannah was sure she could run her tongue around that nipple all day long, just lie there for hours, licking, sucking, tasting.

But there was so much more of Julia to explore.

Stomach, hips, sides, legs, and then an entire other side.

"I could spend forever just touching your skin," she whispered as Julia writhed gently beneath her.

"Not if you don't want me to burst into flames you can't."

Savannah was at her stomach, her tongue circling Julia's belly button, and she looked up. Their eyes met. Held. The room crackled with arousal and desire and sheer, unbridled sex. Without breaking eye contact, Savannah slid her hands under Julia's thighs and pushed them up and apart. Spread her open completely.

"Oh God," Julia whispered.

How she was able to take her time then, Savannah didn't know, but she did. With her tongue, she made lazy trails up and down the insides of Julia's thighs, moving in closer and closer to her center, but circling around it. The increasing wetness only spurred her on until she felt Julia's fingers in her hair, clenching, grabbing a handful. She glanced up into dark, hooded eyes, Julia's head was raised, and she was gazing down her body.

"Please, Savannah. I can't take any more. Please." Her voice was soft, but strained. Steady, but also pleading. It was erotic and sensual and sexy as hell, and all Savannah wanted then was to give the woman what she asked for.

The first slow swipe of her tongue over Julia's hot, wet center cranked Julia's hips up off the bed and pulled a long groan from her throat. After that, Julia devolved into soft, throaty whispers of, "Oh God. Yes. There. Please. Right there. Don't stop. Please don't stop." And Savannah didn't stop.

It only took a few short minutes before the orgasm crashed over Julia, and Savannah watched as her muscles tightened, her mouth opened silently, the vein along her neck standing out in bas relief as she pushed her head back into the pillows, one hand still in Savannah's hair, fingers clenched tightly, the other gripping the sheets as if holding on for dear life.

Savannah held her hips, did her best to stay with her moving, writhing form, until she felt the contractions ease against her tongue and only tiny aftershocks were left, little pulses that made Julia's legs twitch sporadically. The hand in her hair tugged gently, silently telling her Julia'd had enough and to come join her.

Was there a glow in the room? Because it felt like there was. Which was corny, she knew, but still. She crawled up Julia's body, simultaneously sad to leave the glorious space between her legs but thrilled to be face to face with her once again.

"Hi," she said quietly and touched her lips to Julia's. It was meant to be a quick kiss, but Julia cupped the back of her head and held her there for a long moment.

"Hi," Julia said back, finally, after releasing Savannah's mouth. "That was…You were…" She exhaled in defeat.

"So much for us being two women who were worried we'd forgotten how to do this, right?"

Julia's laugh filled the room, and Savannah realized right then how much she loved it. More, how she loved being the cause of it. Julia was so serious most of the time. Being the person who could get her to relax and find humor in the world was a pretty awesome feeling, and she wanted to hold on to it. Tight.

They curled up by unspoken agreement, Savannah's head tucked under Julia's chin and against her shoulder, her leg thrown over Julia's. She couldn't remember ever feeling so...content. Like she was exactly where she was supposed to be. Julia's heartbeat pulsed softly in her ear, and she felt her entire body relax, become one with Julia, and then the mattress.

"Hey." Savannah was just drifting off when Julia spoke, nudged her gently. "Don't you fall asleep. I just needed a minute to recover from what you did to me, but we're not done."

"We're not?" Savannah lifted her head so she could look down into Julia's eyes, and that sexy sparkle was still there.

"Really? You think that orgasm from thirty seconds of my hand in your jeans was the best I've got?"

Savannah grinned down at her. "You mean it wasn't?" A snort. An arched eyebrow. And then before Savannah could utter another word, Julia had flipped their positions, and she was lying underneath her for the first time. An incredibly sexy place to be, she realized immediately. *I could get used to this.* She managed to not say the words aloud, but it took effort. It was too soon to be thinking in terms of down the road or in the future. She needed to focus on today. Tonight. This moment right here. And as Julia lowered herself, set her full weight deliciously on Savannah's body, the thought hit again and played through her head on a loop.

Yeah, she could get used to this.

CHAPTER NINETEEN

"And everything went okay? No issues? Did it stay busy?" Julia kept her voice low as she talked to Vanessa on her cell and rooted quietly through Savannah's kitchen looking for coffee makings.

"Yes, yes, I told you. Everything went fine." Vanessa was trying to hold on to her irritation, Julia could tell.

"I'll get back over there by late morning. I want to check the receipts and stuff."

"I told you, it was fine. Relax. I want to hear about your night. Tell me every teeny, tiny, sexy detail." Her voice went all dreamy and Julia couldn't help but smile as her cousin went on. "Was it amazing? Did you have fun? Was there kissing? Were you surprised when you got to Dasher Park? I helped with that. She really wanted to take you someplace you'd enjoy."

"It was great." Julia looked around and lowered her voice a little more, forcing herself to shift from the work mode she'd been sliding into since she woke up back to regular dating person. "She told me you helped. Thank you for that."

"Why are you whispering? Where are you?"

"In her kitchen. She's still sleeping." She held the phone away from her ear as Vanessa squealed her delight.

"Oh my God, you stayed over. Thank freaking God! I mean, I love you, Jules, but you seriously needed to get laid."

"Gee, thanks." Then Julia snort-laughed. She couldn't help it. "I did. It's true. I can admit it."

"And?" Back to the dreamy voice. "Was it wonderful? Were you up all night? How many orgasms did you have? Is she as beautiful under her clothes as she is with them on?"

"Careful now," Julia teased.

"Oh, sorry. I'll pretend I haven't noticed that she's gorgeous."

The happy sigh left Julia all on its own. Yeah, regular dating-person mode was a nice place to be. "It was pretty incredible," she said as her brain tossed her images from only a few hours ago. Savannah beneath her, arching her back, her breasts the most perfect Julia had ever seen. And the sounds. The sounds she made. *My God.* Maybe the sexiest part of the entire night. Julia wanted to hear those sounds again, to cause them. As often as possible.

"I am so happy for you, Jules. Seriously." And Vanessa was. Julia knew her cousin well and could hear it in her voice. "So, do you think you'll..." She could almost hear the wheels turning as Vanessa seemed to search for the right words. "Get married and have babies and live happily ever after?"

Julia laughed quietly. "I mean, I've spent one night with her, but sure. I was thinking of ring shopping later today."

"Perfect. Let me know where, and I'll meet you." A squeak of wood made Julia turn to find Savannah leaning against the doorjamb, hair tousled, wearing pale pink pajama bottoms with Winnie-the-Pooh and Piglet on them and a white T-shirt that left nothing to the imagination. Julia's gaze fell to the very prominent nipples that apparently wanted to wish her a good morning of their own.

"I'll call you later, Ness. Bye." She hung up, met those blue eyes, and her entire body felt like it was on fire all over again. "Good morning, sunshine."

"Hi," Savannah said as a yawn cranked her mouth open, and she pushed off the doorjamb. "I like platinum better than gold. And a good-sized stone I can show off, but not so big that it's pretentious." She pressed a kiss to Julia's lips as she passed. "Did you find the coffee?"

"Not yet."

Savannah pulled down the coffee makings from the only cupboard Julia hadn't checked and got things going while Julia propped her elbows on the counter, her gaze moving from Savannah to her phone and back.

When the coffee was brewed, poured, and doctored, Savannah held her cup in both hands and leaned a hip against the counter. "What should we do today?" A sip, sleepy blue eyes watching her.

"Oh, I need to go back to the bar," Julia said.

Savannah's disappointment was clear in an instant. "Really?" Savannah said, her pitch a little higher than normal. "I thought we could spend the day together. Get lunch. Find other ways to amuse ourselves." She drew out the word *amuse* and waggled her eyebrows, and Julia couldn't help but laugh.

"Oh, sweetie, I'd love that. But I need to work. I should probably scoot after I have my coffee."

Savannah's shoulders drooped, and her face fell. "Seriously?" She blinked at her a few times before asking, "Is everything okay?" Her voice had gone quiet, uncertain.

Jesus, Jules, reassure the poor girl, her brain shouted at her when she realized Savannah's confidence was likely shaken. "Oh my God, yes," she said, stepping close to Savannah. Hand on her face, she felt the warmth of Savannah's skin and bent her head down to catch her eye. "Everything is amazing. *Amazing*. I had the best time last night, at Dasher Park and here." In an almost whisper, she added, "If I had to choose, the best time was here." A kiss to punctuate that statement because it was absolutely true.

"I was really hoping to spend the day with you."

"I'm sorry. Life of a small business owner, I'm afraid." Mentally, she smacked her own forehead. Vanessa and Amelia would both slap her if they heard that. She sipped her coffee and—fully aware that she was doing so—changed the subject. "Hey, how are things with your sister?"

Savannah studied her for a beat before gazing into her cup as if her thoughts were all congregated there. "You know, I haven't had a ton of contact with her in the past couple of days. Dina seems to have things covered." She cleared her throat. "Maybe I'll try to see her today." She gave a small nod, like she'd just decided that was the plan.

They sat together at Savannah's small kitchen table, but something had settled over them, something uncertain and somewhat awkward. Julia could feel it because she knew she'd caused it, and it was all she could do to keep from giving a full-body shudder to try and shake it. She reached across the round surface and closed her hand over Savannah's smooth wrist, gave her a gentle smile, and when those blue eyes met hers, there was something slightly different about them. They were—she studied them for a moment before finding the word—guarded.

"I'm sorry," Savannah said and one corner of her mouth lifted in a small smile. "I'm being a little clingy. I don't mean to be." She gave a laugh and waved a dismissive hand. "Ignore me. Go do what you've got to do, and call me when you can."

"I absolutely will." Her body was a weird mix right then. Relief. Surprise. Guilt. Lots and lots of guilt, thanks to her Catholic Italian heritage. But she swallowed it down, managed a smile. "Promise."

❖

Wrapped in a towel, her skin bright red from standing under a super hot shower for longer than she probably should have in an attempt to loosen up her tense shoulders, Savannah walked into her bedroom to get dressed.

The bed was unmade. Rumpled. The heady scent of sex still hung in the air. Warmth flowed through her body as her brain tossed her flashbacks. Images. Julia, naked and writhing beneath her. On top of her. Behind her while Savannah pushed her ass against Julia's probing fingers.

A sigh and she dropped the towel and pulled out clothes for the day.

Shame had flowed through her since Julia had left. No, fled. She'd fled. Seemed happy to be given permission to go. What the hell was she thinking? That thought ran through her head on a loop all morning, poking at her, mocking her. She'd been *so* needy. God. What a fucking turn-off that was. No wonder Julia'd been in a hurry to get out of there. Yes, they'd been talking, meeting, whatever you wanted to call it, for a couple months now, but they'd really only gone out together twice. Slept together once. Julia didn't owe her anything.

Her cheeks puffed as she blew out a breath, and she grabbed her phone to text Chelsea, see if she was around. The only thing that was going to keep her from dwelling on this topic all damn day was finding something else to occupy her mind. And Julia had reminded her that she could check up on Chelsea.

Another glance at the bed.

What a night it had been. God.

Another sigh.

Less than ninety minutes after leaving Savannah's, Julia was walking into The Bar Back through the back door. She didn't have to open for another couple hours, and she always felt a sense of calm and content when she walked in, set her stuff down on her desk, and took her laptop to the couch to handle the day's orders.

Today felt different.

It felt different and weird and she didn't like it. At all. What the hell?

Her phone rang from her back pocket as she walked out into the bar, and she pulled it out to see who was calling. Amelia.

"Hey, Meels."

"Oh my God, tell me all about it." She was eating something, the sound of her chewing clear.

"Talked to Vanessa, did you?" Julia laughed softly as she walked farther into the bar to check things out.

"I did." A pause. "Where are you? It's echoey."

"The bar." Chairs were up, floor was clean. Everything looked great. Clea and Evan had done a nice job cleaning up after closing.

"The bar?"

"Yeah. Gotta get ready for today."

Silence.

"Amelia? I lose you?" Julia pulled her phone from her ear to look at the screen. The timer continued to click forward below Amelia's name. Still connected. "Hello?"

"What are you doing?" Amelia's voice was low. Steady. Firm. A smart-ass comment lingered on Julia's tongue, but Amelia's tone kept it in her mouth.

"I just told you. Getting ready to open."

"I don't understand you." She could picture Amelia shaking her head, that crease she got above her nose when she was thinking hard or annoyed by something. "Why?"

"Why what?"

"For fuck's sake, Julia, stop being purposely hardheaded." Julia blinked in surprise at the sharp tone. "Did you seriously spend the night with an incredible woman you really like and then sprint away from her on a Saturday morning because you needed to get ready to open your bar in another three or four hours? Un-fucking-believable."

"Wow, Meels. I mean, tell me how you *really* feel."

"I really feel that you're being an idiot, and I can't even deal with you right now."

The line went dead.

Julia blinked and a small gasp escaped her lips. She looked at the screen in disbelief. Sure enough, Amelia had ended the call. Anger surged as she hit the right button. Directly to voice mail. She didn't leave a message, just dialed again and kept doing so every time she went directly to voice mail. She put it on speaker and set it on the bar so she could walk around and check all the tables and chairs, doors, windows, lights. Each time she passed the bar, she dialed again.

Finally, it rang more than twice, and Julia picked it up, put it to her ear. As soon as the line opened, she let loose. "Did you seriously just hang up on me? Are you that petty?"

"Are you that selfish?" Amelia snapped back.

"What? How am I being selfish? You're the one who hung up on *me*."

"I'm not talking about you and me, dumbass. I'm talking about you and Savannah."

"Look, I—"

"Save it." Amelia cut her off. "We'll be there in a minute."

"We?"

"Me and Ness. We're coming over."

"Now?"

"Now.

Chapter Twenty

Julia loved the smell of Martini's.

That may have sounded weird to many people because a bar? Gross. Bars traditionally smelled like stale beer and cigarette smoke and desperation. And maybe she was biased, but Martini's didn't smell like that. To her, it smelled like fruit and perfume and invitation and fun with a tinge of alcohol thrown in, just to remind you that it was, in fact, a bar. She wandered around some more, stopping to look at the photos on the wall. They'd been around forever. She knew each of them well. But still, they fascinated her. Black-and-whites Uncle Tony'd had in the back in a box. But they represented the history of the place, and she felt it was important to embrace that. When something has been in a family for generations, it was to be celebrated. Her gaze roamed over shots of regulars sitting at the bar in the late seventies and early eighties. The limited number of bottles behind the old bar. Only three beer taps then, compared to the fourteen she had now, and they changed regularly. She could see her father in the background of one shot, beer in hand, smile on his face, Uncle Tony behind the bar. Her heart warmed every time she let herself get lost in those snapshots of the past, long before she'd come along, but her eyes kept taking her back to the photo with her dad. The good time he was having was obvious, and she felt that pang once more. But then she recalled his second visit, how it was really obvious he was making an effort, and she told herself to chill out. Maybe he'd come by again soon. Or maybe she should invite him, make it clear he was welcome, and he'd love it.

She'd come out into the main bar to calm herself, but she couldn't seem to ease her own nerves, and confusion about her dad only added to the sour churning in her gut.

She blew out a breath, and a groan came with it. She could pretend not to understand why her cousins were coming to talk to her, but she knew. Of course she knew. Not wanting to face something wasn't the same as not knowing. She shook herself, decided she needed something to busy herself, and flitted around the bar, needlessly straightening bottles and wiping nonexistent spots off the bar top. She could feel her own stress crawling up her throat like it was an actual, physical thing, and she swallowed it down more than once.

And then Savannah's face popped into her head. The soft eyes, the gentle smile, and just like that, everything in her went calm. Relaxed. She exhaled. She let the feeling cover her, like warm honey, and when she closed her eyes, she could see Savannah's blue ones, the way she made it so clear that you had her full attention. The way she'd tip her head just a bit and *really* listen.

Jesus, what is wrong with me?

Before she had a chance to dwell on that very complicated—and also very simple—question, she heard noise coming from the back.

The cousins had arrived.

"Where are you?" Amelia's voice arrived before she did, then she peeked her head in from the back and gestured wildly with an arm. "Get back here, young lady." It was meant to carry a little humor, but all Julia could think was if Amelia'd had kids, that tone would make it very clear they were in trouble.

"Hey," she said as she entered the room and immediately felt two pairs of eyes on her. Could looks actually *feel* disapproving? Because they absolutely did.

"Sit." Amelia pointed to the couch, and Julia obeyed. Behind the practice bar, Amelia poured herself a Coke from the nozzle. "Anybody else?"

"Diet, please," Vanessa said. The wheels of Julia's desk chair felt loud as she tugged it across toward the couch and sat.

As Vanessa took her glass from Amelia, she said, "We love you. You know that, right?"

"Is this an intervention?" Julia went for levity, grinned as she looked from one cousin to the other. Amelia was stone-faced. Of course. Vanessa allowed a small smile to appear. "Oh, wait. It's good cop, bad cop. Right?"

Amelia sat on the coffee table, elbows on her knees. "You've got daddy issues. Bad ones."

"Amelia," Vanessa said, her voice hushed as if she'd be overheard. "Easy."

"Um, ouch." Julia's unease increased.

"Well, it's true." Amelia huffed.

"What's your problem, Meels?" Julia asked, feeling just this side of attacked.

Amelia stood up and began to pace. Not something she usually did. Her light hair was in a ponytail. She wore jeans and a white T-shirt and her eyes were hard. To be fair, her eyes had been hard since her wife left her, but this was different somehow. They were hard and…something else.

Vanessa, on the other hand, stayed seated and quiet, her gaze moving slowly and almost carefully from Amelia to Julia and back.

"Okay, you two are freaking me out with the role reversal here."

"We want you to be happy," Vanessa began, her eyes darting back to Amelia as if waiting for approval.

"But there's a pattern." Amelia stopped pacing.

"A pattern," Julia said with a squint.

"Yes." Vanessa again. "You meet someone. They flirt. You sometimes flirt back. There's clear interest."

"And you use the bar as an excuse to not pursue anything further." Amelia exhaled and sat back down on the coffee table, apparently having harnessed her nerves. Or whatever.

"I don't think that's true," Julia began.

Vanessa started ticking off on her fingers as Amelia muttered, "Oh, it's *so* true."

"There was that woman in the Realtor's office when you were first looking to buy this place. Then the liquor distributor who kept bringing you lunch."

A snort. "She's a salesperson," Julia said. "Salespeople bring food to schmooze you." Please. She'd dealt with enough of them to know.

"She brought you food when she wasn't working, Jules." Amelia arched an eyebrow at her, expression unamused.

Yeah, okay, that was true. That girl had abruptly stopped coming, a new guy in her place, she remembered.

"And the softball team chick that came in a couple months ago." Vanessa ticked another finger.

"She wanted me to sponsor her team!" This was getting ridiculous. Julia sat forward on the couch, felt her own brow furrow as she felt irritation building.

"Julia. She came by in January." Amelia's stare was intense. "When you were here working for my dad and talking about changes you wanted to make. *January*. The middle of winter. For softball. And then again in February."

"Twice," Vanessa added. "I even told you it sounded like she had a crush on you."

"I don't have time for a relationship," Amelia said in a mocking tone.

"Was that supposed to be me? 'Cause I don't sound like that. At all." Julia folded her arms, fully aware of how that looked, but too self-conscious not to do it.

"Don't forget the Tinder account." Amelia pointed at Vanessa, who grimaced with distaste.

Vanessa used her feet to roll the chair closer and rested a warm hand on Julia's thigh. "Then you meet this great girl, and we can tell she's different than all those others."

Even Amelia's face brightened a bit at the mention of Savannah. "*You* were different with her."

Vanessa's nod was vigorous. "So different. And Savannah is…"

As Vanessa's voice trailed off, Amelia picked up the thread. "Perfect for you. She is perfect for you. Do you know how much time and effort she put into last night's date? And then this morning happens." She shook her head and blew out a hard breath. "What are you doing?"

For the second time that morning, Julia was very aware of the fact that she could pretend not to know what they meant. She could shrug. Act perplexed. Hold up her hands, puzzled by the whole thing. But—

"We know you, okay?" Vanessa said, taking the exact thought right from Julia's head. "We know you and we're worried about you."

Amelia slapped her hands against her thighs, and it seemed like irritation ejected her from her chair, and she started to pace again. "We don't want you to screw this up. Hell, *I* don't want you to screw this up." She softened slightly. "As someone who isn't sure she'll ever have something like that again, I want to make sure you take care of it. I know it's early. I know it might feel like rushing things, but..." She looked to Vanessa as if asking for help, and Vanessa took up the explanation.

"First of all, you do like this girl. Despite your...other issues"— Julia squinted and made a mental note to be sure and circle back to *that*—"you've made time for her. Given the way you've been over the past six or seven months, that's big. And second, she is into you. In a big way. My God, she contacted *me*, a person she doesn't know well at all, to ask for guidance on how to create the perfect date for you. You don't do that if you're not into somebody." She seemed to give Julia time to absorb her words before continuing. "And you went. You went! We know you and you would've fought us harder, unless you're also very into her."

Goddamn them and how well they knew her.

"But now? You're here on a Saturday morning instead of lounging around with her, having lunch together, and all those stupid lovely things couples do after the first time together." Amelia waved a dismissive hand and snorted, and Julia would've laughed if she wasn't feeling so uncomfortably exposed. "Because you have daddy issues."

"I was here when your dad came by, remember?" Vanessa said. "I saw how your face lit up. How nervous you were. How you watched every move he made and every place he looked. The reason you work like a crazy person is to get the thing you want more than anything—his approval. Everybody knows it but you."

A lump had formed in her throat, and Julia nodded, even as she tried to swallow it down, clear it out.

"Your relationship with Uncle Vinnie has been rocky your entire adult life." Amelia's voice had gone gentle, so uncharacteristic for her when she was trying to make a point. Vanessa finessed things. Amelia pounded them with a hammer. "Maybe it's time you sat down and had a real talk with him."

The snort ejected itself before Julia even knew it was there. "Easy for you to say. Your dad is like a saint, a king, and a teddy bear all rolled into one."

"Truth," Vanessa agreed. "But Amelia's right. If you let your need for his approval ruin what might be an amazing thing for you, you'll regret it forever. And he liked her! I saw it with my own eyes."

Julia had to laugh at that. "He did, right?"

"Time to shift your priorities." Amelia. The three of them were quiet for several beats before Amelia spoke again. "Tell me something. How do you feel about this girl?"

"Savannah?" Julia asked.

"No, the chick on the beer poster out front." Amelia rolled her eyes. "Yes, Savannah. I know it hasn't been that long, but like we said earlier, we know you, and you seem to really be into her. True?"

"Set aside everything else," Vanessa suggested. "Your dad. The bar. Just focus on her and how you feel about her."

And for a reason she couldn't put her finger on, Julia did just that. She did her best to take the other things out of the equation—no easy feat—and think about Savannah. *Really* think about her. To her shock, it took barely a couple seconds before she spoke.

"I feel safe with her." Boom. Julia blinked in surprise at her own words, then met Vanessa's gaze and repeated it. "I feel safe with her."

"That's a pretty good endorsement," Vanessa said with a gentle smile. "What else?"

"I have fun with her." She was on a roll now. "I'm not so serious. I relax. Loosen up."

"Crazy important right there," Amelia said. "Does she make you laugh?"

"She does." Julia grinned. "She really does."

"Does she get you?" Vanessa asked.

That one brought her up short, but she forced herself to be honest. "I haven't given her much of a chance to, but..." A swallow because that stupid lump was back. "I have a really solid feeling she would. She listens. And she's smart."

"How was the sex?" Amelia asked, then, "What?" at the look Vanessa shot her.

"Oh my God." Julia let herself go boneless and fell back and sank into the couch. "*So* good. So, so, so good."

Amelia stood up, shaking her head. "Speaking as a woman who hasn't had sex in more than two years, how you didn't drag her back to bed this morning, I'll never understand. You're an idiot."

Another scolding look from Vanessa, but Julia laughed. Loudly. Her cousins snapped their heads around to look at her.

"She's right," Julia said to Vanessa. Then to Amelia, "You're absolutely right. I'm an idiot. A huge one." And suddenly, everything was so clear. How? How was it all so foggy mere hours ago, and now, as if the sky had cleared and the sun came out, she could see everything laid out in front of her. What did they call that? An epiphany? Is that what was happening?

"You look weird," Amelia said, hands on her hips.

Vanessa burst out laughing.

❖

Savannah missed her mother.

She missed her every day, so it wasn't unusual, but that day, she was missing her even more strongly. A dull ache had settled in her chest, and she felt like her emotions were just behind her eyes, too close to the surface for her own liking.

"Hey," she said to Chelsea as she entered her dad's house and saw her sister sitting in the living room watching dogs on the television. "Where is everybody? It's quiet in here."

Chelsea answered while keeping her eyes on the screen. "Dad and Dina are taking a walk. No idea where Deck is."

"And how're you doing?"

Chelsea turned to her then, obviously recognized the deeper question in her voice, then saw it in her eyes, because she gave a nod, a half shrug, and lifted one corner of her mouth just a bit. "I'm good today." Then she sighed and said, unprompted, "I miss Mom, though."

Savannah blew out a breath, set her purse down, and plopped herself on the couch next to her sister. Wrapping an arm around her, she pressed a kiss to her temple. "Me, too, kiddo. Me, too."

They spent the next half an hour in silence, cuddled together like they used to do when Chelsea was little, and watched dogs with cool jobs. Savannah couldn't describe the genuine relief she felt.

"How are things with the new girl?" Chelsea asked once the credits rolled. Savannah gave her a startled look, to which her sister replied, "I heard Declan talking about it."

"They're fine."

Chelsea made a face, tipped her head to one side, and lifted an eyebrow, then pointed at her own face. "This is the look you give me when you ask me a question and I give you a stupid answer."

A soft laugh bubbled up out of her. "You make a valid point."

"So?"

When Savannah sighed, it felt like she'd been holding it in since the moment she realized Julia was actually leaving to go to work. "The problem is, I really like her. A lot." She met Chelsea's eyes. "Like, really a lot."

Chelsea seemed to come to life then. She sat forward and turned so her body faced Savannah's. "I mean, isn't that usually a good thing? Why's it a problem?"

"Because of her job."

A furrowed brow. "Doesn't she own a bar? Or did I hear wrong?"

"She does. But she has no bar manager. It's all her. She's got employees, but—and I don't know why this is yet—she does it all on her own. It's like she thinks she has to." It was like once she'd started thinking about Julia and her situation, once she'd started to analyze it, it all came tumbling out. "I know she's got an apartment somewhere, but I've never seen it. I don't think she even goes home often. She's got this back room in the bar, and if she's not out front and actually working behind the bar or dealing with orders, she's in the back, practicing making drinks or creating new ones." There were so many things she'd started thinking about after Julia's departure that morning, the apartment being one, the fact that she'd never seen anybody behind the practice bar practicing except Julia. "I think she's afraid to let go of some of the control."

Chelsea tipped her head one way, then the other. "That's not uncommon for a small-business owner." Savannah tried to hide her surprise, but her sister caught it and shrugged. "What? I've been reading up on small business lately," she said, so nonchalantly that it made Savannah squint at her. More seriously, she added, "I needed something to occupy my mind. You know?" She shrugged like it made perfect sense, and it did, and Savannah nodded her understanding. "Back to you. So what are you going to do?"

That was the question, wasn't it? The one that had been on her mind—if she was honest—before they'd spent the night together. "I don't know," she said slowly. "Sex makes everything so much more complicated."

"I was gonna ask, but now I don't have to."

Savannah grinned. "Yeah."

"Good?"

"Incredible."

"Wow. That's a big deal." Chelsea studied her for a beat. "How did you get to that?"

Savannah told her the whole story, and as she did, she realized how much she'd wanted to share it. Bounce it off somebody else. She planned to call Tiffany later, get some much-needed guidance, and here was Chelsea. Unexpected, but open and calm and shockingly wise. It was perfect.

"So...what now?" Chelsea asked after Savannah finished her story.

That was the question, wasn't it? The big one. The one that had been hanging out in her mind for hours, but before she could answer, the door opened and their father and Dina entered.

"Hi, Savvy," Dina said in her high-pitched voice. "My God, it's gorgeous out."

Behind her came Savannah's father, looking fresh, his eyes sharp. "Hi, sweetheart," he said when their eyes met.

"Hi, Dad. Good walk?"

"Great."

The fresh air seemed to help him, she'd noticed. Which made sense, really. Staying cooped up in the same handful of rooms didn't allow for much stimulation.

"What brings you by?" he asked as Dina headed for the kitchen and he dropped into his recliner. "Both my girls are here. I like it."

Dina appeared with two water bottles and handed him one as Savannah said, "I just popped by to see you guys, say hi."

"And to tell us all about her new *girlfriend*." Chelsea said it in a teasing tone. Meant to be light. Put it right out there.

"Judging by how wide her eyes just got, I'm gonna guess she didn't come to tell all of us." Her father's voice was light, and his eyes danced. Not something she'd seen a lot lately, and she stared at him. "What? I can't want my girl to be happy?"

"First of all, of course you can, but she's not my *girlfriend*." She used the same tone Chelsea had, kept it teasing and playful as she bumped her sister with a shoulder. At the same time, she decided maybe it was a good time to address the weird elephant in the room, while everybody was happy. "And second, her last name hasn't changed, you know. She's still a Martini, and if I recall correctly, you were not a fan."

"Oh!" But it was Dina and not her father who held up a finger, and said, "I think we've figured that out."

It was the strangest thing, to actually witness her father's face turning red. The color—and she had to assume heat—crawled slowly up his neck, spreading out from the top of his T-shirt to his face, his ears, his wide forehead.

"Dad? You okay?" she asked. He seemed acutely embarrassed, and the last thing she wanted to do was embarrass her father.

He grunted but looked at her almost bashfully. Then he shook his head and sighed. Waved a hand at Dina, obviously giving her permission to explain.

"Remember I was telling you about the writing? That we've been having him write things down when he's worked up to keep him from lashing out verbally when he's not quite himself?"

A nod. Savannah remembered it well, liked the idea. "I do."

Dina came farther into the room and took a seat on the arm of the recliner, put a hand on her father's shoulder while he studied his own hands. "It's been working really well for him. His outbursts are less." A shrug that seemed almost self-conscious. "At least I think they are."

The need to reassure this woman was a foreign one for Savannah, but she went with it. "Well, you're around him more often than the rest of us, so you'd probably know best." It hadn't even killed her to say something nice. And Dina's smile was wide. Bright. Like Savannah had made her day.

"To make a long story short, it turns out when your dad was young, just before he met your mom, he was smitten with a young lady named Anna Carducci. She was"—she glanced down at Savannah's dad—"was it three years younger than you?"

"Two," her father supplied. "I was a senior when she was a sophomore in high school, but we didn't really know each other then."

"Right. And it was later that they met up again."

It would've had to have been, Savannah thought, as there'd been a solid ten-year age difference between her father and her mother.

"Apparently, your dad asked her out, they went on a date—"

"Two. Two dates." He harrumphed in his chair, and Savannah had to smother a smile because the harrumphing reminded her so much of her grandfather, it was comical.

Chelsea must've thought the same thing because she said, "Dad. Don't grunt like that. You're seventy, not ninety-five. You sound like Grandpa."

Bracing for an outburst had become second nature since her dad had started with his episodes, so it came as a surprise when he chuckled, and her body relaxed. Dina rubbed her hand from his shoulder across his back, and Savannah could see that it calmed him. Or kept him calm.

"Anyway, long story short," Dina said, "it seems your father was quite taken with Anna. Planned on seeing her regularly—"

Her father grumbled, "Until she met that damn Vince Martini."

Savannah blinked at them, stunned. "That's Julia's father."

"Holy shit," Chelsea chimed in, looking wide-eyed at Savannah. "Small world, huh?"

Savannah knew from her job that for people who suffered from any kind of dementia, severe or mild, the past was often more prevalent in their minds than the present. So it made sense that, at the mention of the name Martini, her father would zero in on something that happened more than forty years ago. "When did you meet Mom?"

Her dad's blue eyes focused on the ceiling and he pursed his lips. "A year later, I think?"

"So weird to think we were almost Martinis," Chelsea teased. "Chelsea Martini...Chelsea Martini..." She rolled the name around as if she was trying it on, and their father shot her a mock glare that made them all laugh.

Her father became serious then, settled his gaze on Savannah, and smiled tenderly. "So, tell me about this girl."

Chapter Twenty-one

The buzzing of her phone woke Savannah up. Who the hell was texting so early? She reached toward the nightstand, not wanting to open her eyes because her head felt like it was stuffed with cotton, and its ache ran through her ears, down her neck and into her body.

9:47 a.m.

Wait, what?

How could it possibly be going on ten in the morning? Savannah was a morning person, always up by seven at the latest, even when she didn't have to work. She rarely slept past then. A full-body shiver hit her next, and she felt her own forehead. Did she have a fever? Her mother told her once that you couldn't gauge your own fever by feeling your own forehead, but she tried anyway. Definitely hot. She should take her temperature. But the thermometer was in the bathroom, which was miles away, and she could not bring herself to get out of bed yet.

She squinted at her phone, looked through the slits of her eyelids to read.

What are you doing today? Julia. They'd texted yesterday. A lot, actually, given that Julia was working, and it had been a busy Saturday night. But Savannah had purposely kept things kind of surface, figuratively keeping Julia at arm's length until she could figure out the best way to handle the concerns she had. She was surprised to hear from her this early. Trying to decide if that meant something, if it was some kind of good sign, was too much for her, though. Her brain didn't have the capacity to do complicated things like think. She rolled onto her back and held the phone above her so she could type.

Was going to run errands. Dying instead. Still in bed.

Her arm and the phone flopped down to the bed while the little dots bounced. Focusing on them was too much for her and she closed her eyes. Her mouth felt like something had crawled inside and died overnight, her entire nasal cavity congested.

Her hand buzzed, but this time it wasn't a text. Julia was calling. Savannah croaked a hello.

"Oh, wow, you aren't kidding. You sound awful."

"Thanks. I feel like crap."

"So would that mean, like, I'm just trying to clarify…Would you venture to say that you're…" A long pause. "Sick? 'Cause, if I remember correctly, you don't get sick."

Their conversation at the amusement park Friday night came roaring back to her. The coughing woman. "I don't," she said, trying to inject some vehemence into her words but tipping over the edge into a whining coughing fit instead.

"And you don't believe in jinxes either."

"No."

"I see." The smile in Julia's voice was clear, but Savannah couldn't be mad at the light teasing. "I suggest you stay in bed. I'll be right over."

"Wait. What?" She was having trouble concentrating on the words.

"I said I'm coming over. And look, don't bother arguing with me. I don't know if you've ever argued with an Italian, but you can't. I'll just get louder until you let me win, so that I'll lower my volume."

Savannah smiled at the logic. And despite the fact that she was certain she looked like roadkill, the thought of seeing Julia again was…It made her warm inside. In a good way, not in an *I have a fever* way. At least she didn't think so. "Fine," she finally said. "But you can't get close, and you can't stay long. I don't want to get you sick."

Julia scoffed as if that was the silliest thing she'd ever heard and told her she'd see her soon.

There was no way she was going to manage a shower yet. Standing up made her feel dizzy and uncertain, but she managed to scuff her way to the bathroom and at least brush her teeth and wash her face. Seriously, though, who was the woman in the mirror with the gray skin and dark circles? A sneeze and a blow told her she'd add red nose to those descriptors by the afternoon.

Dragging a pillow and an extra blanket—a super soft fleecy one Chelsea had given her for Christmas last year—Savannah made her way downstairs, unlocked the front door, and collapsed on the couch like she'd been walking for days. In the desert. With no food or water. She fought with the blanket until it covered her feet as well as the rest of her, another full-body shudder confirming that she likely did have a fever. She was just drifting back off when the doorbell rang, shocking her back awake, her pounding heartbeat throbbing in her head.

The door pushed open, and Julia's face came into view. That beautiful face with those beautiful dimples and all that beautiful hair, and when those beautiful dark eyes met hers, Savannah almost cried with relief. Something she didn't expect, that. Relief to see Julia. Relief to lay eyes on her and have her standing in the same space as her once again. Despite everything that had happened the last time she was there, the relief washed over all of it. It was all that mattered.

"Hey," Julia said. She came right to the couch and perched on the edge next to Savannah's hip, laid her hand across her forehead, and the coolness of Julia's skin was like some sort of balm. A salve. It felt indescribably good, and she closed her eyes and sighed quietly. "Oh, baby, you look like hell."

"Mean," Savannah managed, not opening her eyes.

Julia's cool fingers stroked her flaming cheeks. "Not at all. I just feel bad for you. Have you taken your temperature? You definitely have a fever. Where's your thermometer?"

And just like that, Julia took over. Everything. Savannah drifted in and out of sleep for the next few hours, but every time she opened her eyes, Julia was either sitting nearby or she could hear her in the kitchen.

❖

A dark head peeked around the doorjamb. "Well, hi there. How're you feeling?"

Savannah pushed herself to a sitting position for the first time all day. It took effort, and she felt like a fawn, had trouble using her limbs, as she considered the question. An attempt swallow felt like she was eating razor blades.

"My throat is on fire," she said quietly, worried that any kind of volume would make it worse.

"I thought that might be the case." And then she was there, perched on the edge of the couch again, right next to Savannah's hip again, a mug in her hand this time. "Here. Tea with honey and lemon. My grandmother's solution to a sore throat." A lopsided grin and she added, "Except she used brandy instead of tea."

Swallowing in any way, shape, or form sounded like torture, but she took the mug, inhaled deeply the scent of warm lemons and honey. Sipped. The razor blades dulled a tiny bit, and she looked up into those beautiful eyes.

"Don't you have to work?" Her intense effort not to sound accusing seemed to work, and her question came out as a simple inquiry.

"Nope." A simple response to that simple inquiry. Interesting.

Savannah squinted at her. "I want to delve deeper into this, but I also don't want to jinx anything."

"Oh, sure, *now* you believe in jinxes." They both grinned and their gazes held, and Savannah worried that this was some kind of wonderful dream, that she'd wake up any moment in her own bed, alone, sick, and without the magical mug of throat-soothing goodness in her hands. But she blinked. Several times. And Julia stayed. Not only did she stay, but she reached out, brushed some of

Savannah's hair—which had to be approaching the category of rat's nest by now—off her forehead, ran the backs of her fingers down her cheek.

"I'm going to warm you up some of my mother's chicken soup. I know you may not be hungry, but it's after noon, and you haven't eaten today, so I want you to try a little, okay? Even if you just sip the broth. It's like magic, I promise. Cures everything."

"You brought soup?" Savannah hadn't seen a bag or anything. And bringing supplies had taken time. Thought. What was happening here?

"I told you I'd take care of you if you got sick." She stood up and pressed a kiss to Savannah's forehead. "It's a good thing you don't."

For the next twenty minutes, dishes clattering in the kitchen served as her soundtrack, her background music, and Savannah basked in it as if it was a symphony, an entire orchestra in her house. There was something oddly comforting about the sound, and she simply…listened.

"Here we go." Julia came back with a bowl and a spoon and a dish towel to drape across Savannah's front. "In case of drippage," she explained.

God, had anything in her life ever smelled better than that bowl of soup? If something had, Savannah couldn't think of what it was. She took the bowl and spoon. "Isn't it feed a cold, starve a fever?" she asked.

"Listen, I'm Italian. The word starve isn't even in my vocabulary. We feed everything. Plus, I googled. Apparently, starving anything is never the answer. My grandma would be thrilled to be right. You need the protein. Eat what you can, okay? I'm gonna go clean up."

The delicious and mouthwatering smell of the soup had nothing on the taste. Absolutely nothing. It was rich and seasoned to perfection with big chunks of chicken and egg noodles, and before she even realized it, she'd gone from gingerly spoonfuls of just broth to giant scoops and slurps. By the time Julia returned, the bowl was empty, and Savannah was pleasantly full, as well as exhausted.

"Well, look at that." Julia took the bowl. "My mom would be happy."

"That is by far the best soup I've ever had. And I am a soup connoisseur."

"I'll pass that along." More face touching from Julia, which Savannah could admit felt wonderful, Julia's fingers cool and soft against her skin. "You're still warm. Want to sleep some more?"

Savannah pursed her lips. "I'm not sure. I don't want to move, but not sure I'm sleepy."

"Movie?" Julia indicated the television with her eyes, and nothing had ever sounded more perfect.

"Yes, please."

Fifteen minutes later, her head was resting comfortably in Julia's lap, which Julia insisted on even after Savannah expressed worry about getting her sick. Julia's socked feet were perched on the coffee table, crossed at the ankle, and her fingers played lazily in Savannah's hair, and when was the last time somebody had played with her hair? And how had she forgotten how wonderful, how relaxing it felt?

A slight turn of her head and her gaze met Julia's, her eyes soft and looking at her with such tenderness, and what the hell had happened? Savannah wanted so much to know. To ask what had changed. But she was so damn tired now, and the fingers gently scratching at her scalp were literally lulling her toward slumber. She vaguely recalled seeing Sandra Bullock and Ryan Reynolds on the TV screen, but that was it before she drifted off.

❖

Julia was exactly where she was supposed to be.

When was the last time she'd been able to say that when it didn't revolve around her business? The last time she'd felt this content with a woman? Normally, she'd have gotten antsy way before now. Fidgety. Checking her watch. Her phone. Counting down how much longer she needed to stay before she could escape and not be thought of as cold or, her personal favorite, emotionally unavailable.

It was too long ago for her to even remember because it might've been never. She might've never felt this totally at ease, this satisfied. This at peace.

How, though?

How had she made such a one-eighty in so short a time?

As a Catholic, she'd had God and angels drummed into her head her whole life. As a gay woman, she also had a healthy wariness of them. But there were times, she had to admit, when she was fairly sure *something* was looking out for her. How else could she explain her cousins' words actually getting through, making sense? How else could she explain the peace she felt right now?

Savannah had been sleeping in her lap for almost two hours. Beads of sweat had appeared on her forehead about forty-five minutes earlier, telling Julia the fever had likely broken. As she flipped channels, trying to find something to watch, she was torn between wanting Savannah to wake up, so she could get lost in the ocean blue of her eyes once again, and wanting her to stay sleeping because having her this close was giving Julia life.

Still sleeping? A text from Vanessa.

Julia sent back an emoji with Zs. They'd gone back and forth a couple times, Vanessa having been the one to encourage her to go over. She'd also texted with Clea a few times, as she was running the bar. And while she still felt a bit of agita around it, she was doing her best not to worry or micromanage. Clea could handle it. She had handled it. More than once now. Tomorrow was Monday, and Julia was going to sit down with her to discuss a management position.

There were more important things in life besides work.

"Oh my God, who am I?" she asked aloud at the thought.

Savannah stirred. Blinked. Wiped a hand across her face and furrowed her brow. Met Julia's eyes—and her entire expression relaxed. "Hi," she said, sounding less hoarse than earlier.

"Hey there." Julia brushed hair off her forehead. "How do you feel?"

"A bit better, I think." Savannah made a move to sit up, and Julia helped her. "God, I'm gross," she said, and her cheeks got rosy.

"Your fever broke." Julia laid the backs of her fingers on Savannah's forehead. "Oh yeah. Much better."

"How long did I sleep?"

"Couple hours."

Savannah's eyes went wide. "Oh my God, I'm so sorry."

"For what?" Julia smiled at her, at the horrified look on her face, and held up the remote. "I was fine."

"You were trapped."

"If I'd wanted to get up, I would've gotten up."

Savannah seemed to study her. "Really?"

"I promise. I was perfectly happy to serve as your pillow."

A glance down at her hands as Savannah seemed to think, but when she looked up, she said, "I'm going to take a shower and put on some actual clothes."

Julia nodded.

"If you need to go, you can."

"I have nowhere else to be."

This time Savannah squinted at her, suspicion clear. "You've been away from the bar for a long time."

"Clea's got it under control." Julia held up her phone, tipped it from side to side. "If she needs me, she'll call."

"Okay, who are you, and what have you done with Julia? Julia Martini? 'Cause you're not her."

"I'm her. I promise. Go shower. I'll be right here when you're done."

Savannah continued to eye her suspiciously as she stood. As she moved to the stairs, she squinted at her some more until it became almost comical.

"Go," Julia ordered, shooed her with a hand, and laughed.

God, this felt good.

She heard the water turn on upstairs, and that contentment settled over her again. *I could get used to this.* No sooner had the thought run through her mind then she blinked rapidly and wondered what the hell was happening. Needing to move, she stood up and wandered around the living room, taking the time to get close-up looks at things she'd noticed from the couch. A framed photo of

Savannah and her siblings. She'd never seen her sister, but they looked a lot alike, though the sister had brown hair. A photo of a woman who could only be Savannah's mom because it was like looking at a photo of Savannah if she'd been a young woman in what looked to be the seventies or eighties. The same wide-set eyes, slightly tipped up at the outer corners, the same shade of ocean blue, the same angled eyebrows. She ran her fingertips over the glass, somehow sad that she'd never get to meet her.

One thing she'd noticed immediately about Savannah's house was that she had a lot of plants. They gave the place a cozy, inviting feel, all the lush green at different heights and levels of fullness. All the leaves were shiny and dust-free, the soil dark, and it occurred to her that the plants were well taken care of, which was no surprise since that was what Savannah did. It was who she was. The caretaker. A big part of the reason Julia had come over in the first place—because nobody ever took care of the caretaker, and nobody deserved being taken care of more.

"Julia?" Savannah's voice coming down the stairs cut into her thoughts.

"Yeah?"

"Just checking."

She felt her own smile blossom across her face. "Still here. I'm not going anywhere," she called up.

"Okay. Good."

She rolled up the blankets from the couch and took them to the basement stairs where she assumed Savannah's washer and dryer lived. Fluffed the throw pillows.

"Julia?"

Julia grinned. Same tone. Same inflection. "Yeah?"

"Is there more soup?"

"There is. Would you like some?"

"Yes, please."

"You got it."

In the kitchen, she took a second bowl of soup out of the fridge, super glad she'd thought to bring two. She had it warming on the stove and was mixing up batter for biscuits with the Bisquick she'd brought, just in case, when Savannah came into the kitchen. Without a word, she walked right up behind Julia, wrapped her arms around her, and laid her head against Julia's back.

"Thank you," she whispered.

Dropping everything she was doing, Julia turned in the embrace and wrapped Savannah in her arms, tucking her head under her chin. "You don't have to thank me. I just want you better." A kiss on the top of her slightly damp head. "You smell good." She did. Like warm cherries and almonds.

Savannah's arms tightened and she let out a sigh that sounded very much like contentment to Julia. "Can you stay a while longer?"

"Absolutely."

And for the first time in…pretty much ever, she texted her mother and told her she was going to miss Sunday dinner.

Seriously, who the hell was she?

Chapter Twenty-two

S weat-slicked skin against hers.
Hips arching up off the bed.

Fingertips digging into her shoulder.

And that cry. That gasp-groan-whimper sound that Julia made when she came. It was pretty much the most amazing sound Savannah had ever heard in her life, and it kept her feeling alive. It was like a drug, something she wanted more and more of. Something she'd become addicted to. When she wasn't with Julia, she was counting the days, hours, minutes until she would be. And then when they were in the same room, she found herself counting the days, hours, minutes until she could undress Julia, have her naked body in her arms, joyfully pull those sounds from her throat.

It had been nearly a month now. Almost four weeks since she'd had that awful twenty-four-hour bug. Since Julia had seemed to have some sort of epiphany. That was the only way Savannah could describe it. There had been bumps, and Julia could easily lose herself in the bar, but it was clear to Savannah that she was trying, that building something with her was important.

Julia dropped her hips back down to the bed, and Savannah slowed the stroking of her fingers, moving them in and out, in and out, and absolutely *not* wanting to leave the wet heat of this woman she was falling madly in love with. Pfft. Please. Who was she kidding? This incredibly sexy woman that she *already* had fallen madly in love with. Like, weeks ago. If she was being honest.

Julia opened her eyes and smiled, and Savannah wondered if she'd ever not melt at the sight of those damn dimples. That's what she called them now, those damn dimples. Because Julia could get anything she wanted from her just by flashing them. Did she know that? Maybe not yet, but she was a smart woman. She'd figure it out.

"God, that one almost killed me," Julia said, and her normally gravelly voice was even more hoarse.

"No way." Savannah kissed her softly. "I very carefully monitor things. I'd never let you be killed by an orgasm. I mean, I'd let you get close, 'cause that's half the fun, but no death. Promise. I'd like to keep you around a while longer."

"Well, that's a relief." Julia grinned and held her gaze for a beat before looking past her to the clock on the nightstand. "I gotta go, babe."

"I know. Just…kiss me one more time."

"I know this one," Julia said, arching one dark eyebrow. "This is a trap."

Savannah mock gasped. "How dare you?"

And then they made out for a good fifteen minutes before Julia wrenched her mouth free. "See? I knew it. Trap!"

Their laughter filled the room, and Savannah couldn't remember the last time she'd laughed so much with one person. "Fine," she said as she rolled off Julia, huffed, and let her arms flop out to the sides in surrender. "Go. Be free. But come back to me." She was playing. Pretending to be annoyed. It was their thing. But Julia seemed to get suddenly serious if the expression on her face was any indication.

"Always," she said softly and leaned down to kiss Savannah with a tenderness she hadn't felt before. "Always."

Forty-five minutes later, Julia was showered and on her way to Friday night at Martini's. While she'd gotten much better at letting Clea do her job and manage, she hadn't quite yet been able to stay completely away. They were working on it.

Savannah was still in a bit of a postsex haze as she showered and made the bed. Still getting used to the weird hours they sometimes kept, Savannah with a day job and Julia working nights, she'd come home from a long shift with Mrs. Richter to find Julia in her driveway. They'd made it in the front door and had headed directly up the stairs, mouths fused together, undressing each other along the way. She was pretty sure her bra was on the stairs and her underwear was in the hall someplace.

True happiness wasn't something she'd felt, like really felt, in a long time. Since her mother had died? That seemed awfully dramatic, but it might also be true. She was exceedingly, completely, happily in love with Julia. And while neither of them had actually used the *L* word, Savannah felt it in her heart, knew it was coming, thought about the right time, the right way to say it. And even though she was reasonably sure Julia was feeling it, too, she hesitated. Because what if she wasn't? What would she do then?

Before she could analyze herself into insanity, her phone pinged. *Still on?*

A big grin spread across her face because she hadn't seen Tiffany in almost three weeks and was looking forward to dinner with her. *Yes! I miss your face!* she typed back.

Saaaaaaaaame came Tiff's reply.

They were going to a nice place, and then they'd probably stop by Martini's after, so Savannah chose her outfit carefully. Summer was in full swing, complete with temperatures in the eighties and humidity that stole any and all body from her hair, and she picked a lightweight summer dress in deep green. It had capped sleeves and a V-neck that wasn't so much revealing as it was enticing, and she could already picture Julia trying—and failing—not to look, not to follow it to her cleavage. Julia was a breast woman, something Savannah had come to find out in the most delicious of ways over the past few weeks, and this neckline was going to mess with her.

Savannah couldn't wait.

❖

Summer brought out the crazies.

It was a lesson all bar owners learned. The heat, the longer days, the outdoor seating in some cases. It all made for customers who stayed longer and drank more. Good for the books. Could get dicey at times for places that played fast and loose with rules, though.

Julia was eternally grateful she had Terry as a bouncer, and she sent up a prayer of thanks as she drove by the front of the bar and saw a handful of folks hanging out on the sidewalk. They couldn't have their drinks out there by law because she didn't have a permit for outdoor seating, but they'd go out to smoke, congregate there until they finished, and went back inside. Julia'd had an aversion to smoking ever since she was little, when her dad was still a smoker. She'd poke holes in his cigarettes with pins, *accidentally* crush his packs, in covert protest. When he'd finally quit, and it stuck, just five years ago, she'd run around her mother's living room squealing in delight and dancing to no music. She hated sweeping up the cigarette butts that littered the front of her business each day—why was it so hard to use the ashtray on top of the garbage can out there?—but anything was better than people smoking inside.

She drove around the corner and parked, then sighed. Sat there for a beat. Another dis from *Northwood Nightlife*, the lifestyles blog. It was the second one in a month, and both had been one-eighties from the earlier reviews. Now her drinks were uncreative? Seriously? She was flighty? Yeah, this one had dissed her personally and had her feeling more defensive than usual. She hadn't told Savannah because she didn't want cheering up. She wanted to be mad about it. Wanted to stew and grind her teeth about it. Which was stupid and did no good, but so what? It was what she needed to do. It was how she absorbed. Blogs shouldn't be anonymous. She should have a chance to sit down with the blogger and talk.

Savannah would roll her eyes right out of her head if she heard her say that, and the thought made Julia grin, and just like that, she felt better.

Savannah.

Jesus, the things she did to Julia. Holy out-of-body experiences, Batman. Her legs *still* felt a little rubbery, and a very subtle pulsing started up between her legs when she thought about the position she'd been in a mere ninety minutes ago. Naked. Legs spread. Begging. Wow.

A full-body shake was needed before she could actually get out of her car and walk on those noodly legs. Yeah, Savannah did things to her. Naughty, wonderful things.

She pushed through the back door, and Clea yelped in surprise, barely managing to catch the bottle of what looked to be vodka as it flipped through the air. "Jesus, Jules. You scared the shit out of me." She was behind the practice bar in the back room.

"Did you watch *Cocktail* again?"

Clea laughed as she flipped the bottle again, caught it, and filled a shot glass, all in one smooth motion. "No, but I fell down a rabbit hole of bartending videos on YouTube this afternoon." She slapped the glass onto the stainless steel shaker and went to work on it.

"Ah, yep. That'll do it. Whatcha makin'?"

Clea finished shaking and strained the mixture into a martini glass that looked to be rimmed with cocoa. The drink was pink and creamy. "That, my friend, is a raspberry truffle."

"Gimme." Julia sipped, let the flavors coat her tongue. "Wow. That's delicious. Add that to the possible martini specials." Back at her desk, she put down her bag and sifted through the day's mail.

"You see *Nightlife*?" Clea asked.

A groan. "I did."

"I figured." Clea shrugged, focused on her bottle flipping. "You can't let it get to you. Everybody gets bad reviews."

"But a good one and then two downslides from there? From the same blogger? They obviously have a problem with me."

"Look on the bright side. That reviewer is obviously in here often. So even though they don't seem to like it, they keep showing up." She caught a bottle and poured, making it all one smooth motion.

"Nice work there." Julia hadn't tried the bottle throwing and catching, but she loved to watch Clea do it.

"Any publicity is good publicity."

She thought about that. "You know, you make a good point."

"Happens once in a while."

Two hours later, Friday night at Martini's was in full swing. Beyoncé was singing about being crazy in love, and when Julia realized she was smiling at the idea, a rush of adrenaline shot through her body. Not panic. Not fear. Just excitement. Simple, uncomplicated excitement. A flash of her mom meeting Savannah zipped through her mind, and even that didn't scare her. Weird.

She stood behind the bar, out of the way of Evan and Keisha, the newest bartender, as they worked, and surveyed her kingdom, arms folded across her chest. The bar was packed. Finally. This was what she'd been hoping for when she'd first approached Uncle Tony with the idea to buy the bar. She'd managed to transform it from an old, rickety almost-dive bar to something classy and popular. The decorations from Pride month were still up, flags and ads and streamers featuring all the colors of the LGBTQ+ rainbow, and the crowd was a mix, if her gaydar was working correctly. Evan was making a group of nicely dressed young women laugh as he fixed their drinks. Keisha had a martini shaker over her shoulder, her customers riveted to her nicely defined arms. It was perfect, and Julia felt herself swell up with pride. This was her place. The stupid *Northwood Nightlife* blogger could kiss her ass—business was good tonight.

"That's one creepily big smile," Dante said from her left.

"Oh, hey. I didn't know you were here." Julia leaned her elbows on the bar. Dante had a half-finished beer in front of him, and two of his buddies were talking baseball.

"I don't like to show off how I know the owner." He grinned at her as he tipped his head to one side. "How are you? Missed you at Sunday dinner last week."

Julia clenched her teeth and made a face. "How mad was Ma?"

"She lived. Pop was quiet."

"Yeah."

"That's what, three times now?"

A grimace was all Julia could manage.

"Might be time to bring your girl home, introduce her."

Normally, the suggestion would fill Julia with fear, have her launching protests and offering excuses why that was a terrible idea. But this time, she only felt agreement. She gave Dante a nod because maybe it *was* time.

A commotion near the door interrupted her thoughts. Shouting, Terry standing, customers' attention drawn that way. Glass shattered, and gasps ran through the crowd as shouting was heard. Julia quickly went around the bar to see what the hell was happening. She had zero time to assess the situation because as soon as she got close to the action, something hard—a bottle?—flew at her and cracked her right in the head.

She went down like she'd been clotheslined.

Chapter Twenty-three

Savannah waited for Tiffany to park her car. They'd had to find spots on a side street, as Martini's lot was full, and most of the spots on the street were taken. It was a Friday night in summer, after all, and Jefferson Square was hopping. On nights like this, people would wander from establishment to establishment. Drinks for happy hour here, dinner a few doors down, after-dinner drinks at yet another place that had live jazz. It was the beauty of the square, that you could hit so many different spots without having to move your car every time.

"That was a tight squeeze," Tiffany commented as she met Savannah on the sidewalk. "Do SUVs really need to be *that* big?" She'd gone home after work and changed out of her business suit into a gorgeous summer-weight dress in a mint green that Savannah could never wear without looking sickly. It was perfect on Tiffany, who shook her head as they started walking. "God, I'm full."

"Ugh. So full. I didn't really need that chocolate mousse pie, you know." Tiffany had insisted she help her eat the decadent dessert.

"Dessert is never about need. It's about want to and should. Besides, it was totally worth it, wasn't it?"

A sigh of defeat. "I cannot argue with your logic. Totally worth it."

Tiffany bumped her with a shoulder. "Ready to see your girl?"

The blush happened like an explosion of heat on her face, she could feel it.

"I'll take that as a yes," Tiffany said with a laugh.

The noise hit them as they turned the corner onto the main drag, before they could even see anything. A commotion. A ruckus, as Savannah's dad would call it. Right in front of Martini's. A bad feeling instantly dropped over her like a lead blanket.

"Uh-oh," Tiffany said as they picked up their pace by unspoken agreement. "What's going on?"

A crowd was in the doorway of Martini's. A few people were on the sidewalk, but most seemed to still be inside. Voices rose. Shouting. Arguing. Savannah could see Terry, eyes sharp, trying to control the problem, but it wasn't until she got directly in front of the bar that the niggling fear she'd had in the back of her brain burst forward like a football team busting through a banner and onto the field.

"Oh no."

Declan was shouting. His arms were flailing like a rag doll's—a sure sign of his intoxication. She could make out both Gator and Timbo and a couple other buddies she'd seen in passing, but she couldn't tell if they were trying to get him out of the bar or if they were part of the problem. The crowd was large, and the music was loud, and this was so very, very bad.

"Is that your brother?" Tiffany asked.

"Yes," she replied, hearing the defeat in her own voice. "I have to get him out of here. If he gets arrested, he's gonna have to stay for a while. He's out of favors with everybody. He's not even supposed to be here. Goddamn it. I told him that." Her heart was pounding, and her worry surged, and you'd think she'd be used to this by now, but she wasn't. It freaked her the hell out. Every time. She dived in, pushing through spectators of all kinds. Some were clearly fascinated. Some were egging on the problem folks, which Savannah would never understand. She felt like a salmon swimming upstream until she finally got into the bar far enough to see Declan, their eyes meeting for a brief moment, before her attention was drawn to her right. On the floor. Julia sat there, a rag pressed to her temple, a thin stream of blood running down the side of her face, and she wanted to run to her, kneel down, be the one to hold the rag and tell her it was fine, it was all going to be fine. But when Julia looked up and those dark eyes met hers, everything in Savannah dropped like a stone. Everything. Every emotion. Every ounce of energy. Every word of apology or explanation. It all just...fell. There was so much on Julia's face then. Sadness. Anger. Exhaustion. Disappointment.

And the sight of her blood?

God, Savannah wanted to go to her, but Dante was with her, and Savannah could tell just by the crackle in Julia's eyes that she shouldn't do that. Not yet. Not until she did something she should've done many times before. Not until she did what needed to be done.

"Savannah!" It was Declan's voice, but slurred and extra loud. It occurred to her right then that his drunk voice had become more common to her than his regular voice. "My big sister," he went on, trying to wave toward her, but inhibited by those who seemed to be trying to remove him. "Would you please tell your dyke girlfriend to let me have a drink? Please? I can be good." His words would've been laughable if they weren't breaking her heart. Tiffany was suddenly standing next to her, hand on her arm. Savannah looked at Julia again, who wasn't looking back at her, and slid her phone out of her purse. Certain she likely wasn't the first to do so, she dialed.

"9-1-1, what is your emergency?" the operator asked.

"I need the police, please."

❖

Julia's apartment smelled un-lived-in. It was the first thing Julia noticed when Vanessa let them in and walked her to a chair.

As if reading her mind, Vanessa wrinkled her nose. "God, when's the last time you opened a window in here?" Then she crossed the small living room and hauled one up. "It smells like dirty socks."

She wasn't wrong, but Julia was too tired to defend herself. It had taken a good twenty minutes for the police to arrive and haul away Savannah's brother, then another hour sitting in the emergency room before she was finally seen. Ninety minutes and six stitches after that, Vanessa was driving her home.

"How do you feel?" Vanessa parked her hands on her hips as she stood in the center of the room. "Dizzy? Light-headed? Nauseous?"

"None of the above," Julia replied, then sighed. "Just tired and sad. I guess it was fun while it lasted." She pushed herself to her feet, which wasn't as easy as it should've been, and turned toward her bedroom.

"Wait." Vanessa touched her arm. "What does that mean? *I guess it was fun while it lasted?*"

She didn't want to think about Savannah, was annoyed at herself for even letting the line slip out. "I'm tired, Ness. I just want to go to bed."

Vanessa glanced at her watch. "Okay. It's been long enough. You're allowed to do that."

"Gee, thanks, Mom." Julia was being a bitch and she knew it.

"But I'm going to be right here on your couch. And I'm going to check on you every couple hours just to make sure you're, you know, still breathing."

In her bedroom, Julia unfastened her jeans and stepped out of them. "You don't have to do that."

"You have a concussion."

"So I was told."

Vanessa stood in the doorway and pointed a finger at her. "Well, I'd prefer you don't die in your sleep, so I'm going to monitor you. Don't try and stop me. You're tall, but you're a wuss, and I'm stronger than I look."

She had a point. It was a fact—and something the whole family marveled over—that Vanessa was freakishly strong for such an average-sized woman. Julia knew better than to test her. "Fine." She finished undressing, put on a washed-to-the-point-of-being-see-through T-shirt, and crawled slowly under her rumpled covers of her unmade bed.

Vanessa fussed over her, making sure she took some Tylenol and not Advil, put a plate of graham crackers on the nightstand in case she got hungry. When Julia picked up her phone, Vanessa frowned.

"I'm going to grab you some water. Probably not great for your head to be looking at screens," she said over her shoulder.

Again, she wasn't wrong. Even on the nighttime setting, the screen seemed painfully bright. She reread the text Savannah had sent earlier.

I'm so sorry! I don't know what else to say. Declan was arrested. My family will pay for the damage he caused. Are you all right? You left for the ER before I finished with the police and then I had to do some paperwork, call my dad, tons of fun stuff. But I've been worried about you the whole time. I don't know where you are. ARE YOU OKAY?

The text had come almost a half hour ago. Julia knew she was being unreasonable by holding Savannah accountable for her brother's behavior, but her head hurt too much to think that all through. She just needed to be away, stay a few steps back from the McNallys for a while. At least until she could think clearly. Still, she couldn't just not answer.

I'm okay. Home. Talk tomorrow.

It was vague at best. Impersonal, which was worse. But her energy level had bottomed out and the throbbing in her head was only getting worse from the screen exposure, so she sent the text, turned the phone completely off—something she rarely did, and set it aside.

Even if she'd tried to, she couldn't fight the desire to sleep any longer, so she gave in and closed her eyes. She was out before Vanessa returned with the water.

Oh my God, who was shining a spotlight on her eyes?

Julia tried to close her eyes harder, but they were already scrunched as closed as possible. Luckily, a free pillow was within reach, and she grabbed it, clamping it tightly over her face. The idea to scream into it slid into her head, and she shoved it right back out again, fearing whatever kind of pain that pretty much guaranteed. She groaned instead.

"What's wrong?" Vanessa's voice was so close, so fast, that Julia jumped and yanked the pillow away.

"Jesus, were you lying on the floor next to the bed?" She squinted, annoyed, then blinked and squinted some more.

"Just attuned to any sound you make."

All right, fine. How could she possibly be mad about that? She forced herself to stop scowling at her cousin.

"Any nausea? Light-headedness? Headache?"

"I haven't even sat up yet. Gimme a minute." Again with the snark. She sighed as she pushed herself to sitting. "I'm sorry, Ness. I'm not trying to be a bitch. It's just kind of happening."

Vanessa made a *pfft* sound and waved a hand. "I teach elementary school. You don't scare me. Plus, your head's gotta be pounding. I'd be a bitch, too." She held out an arm, clearly offering Julia help if she needed it. "Go slow."

"No choice," Julia said as she maneuvered her legs off the bed and stood. Her body felt fine, but her head was throbbing, and her stitches hurt.

Vanessa stayed very close as she took the handful of steps to her small bathroom. "Your meds are out on the counter. I don't think you should shower, but if you must, just know I'm going to sit on the toilet lid while you do."

"In case I've fallen and can't get up?"

"Exactly that."

"I can shower later. I just want to wake up first."

"Hungry at all?"

Julia took stock of her body and realized yes, she actually could eat.

"Good. I'm on it."

Once she'd relieved herself, washed her face—carefully!—and brushed her teeth, she put on some clean cozy clothes consisting of leggings and the Adidas T-shirt she'd live in if she could, and padded barefoot out into the main living space as the smell of bacon tugged at her.

The living space was open, basically all one not terribly big room that encompassed a living room, an eat-in area, and a kitchen along the back wall. Vanessa was busy at the stove but glanced over her shoulder to see Julia's approach.

"Sit," she said. "I'll bring it to you."

A few minutes later, as she sat on the couch, she was handed a plate of scrambled eggs, three slices of bacon, and some toast.

"Just eat what you can and take your time," Vanessa ordered, then sat with her own smaller plate. They ate in silence for several minutes, and Julia was shocked not only at how good the food tasted, but by how hungry she actually was. She was on the last bite of her eggs when Vanessa spoke. "I'm kind of surprised she didn't show up here last night."

Julia knew exactly who she was referring to and lifted a shoulder in a half shrug. "She doesn't have the address. She's never been here."

Vanessa didn't seem surprised by this. "She hasn't? Why not?"

A snort. "Would you bring a girl to this dump?" As Vanessa seemed to study her face like she was looking for something, Julia waved her off. "I'm at the bar way more often than I'm here. And she has a house. Like, an honest-to-God house. It was better for us to be there." She was forcing the matter-of-fact tone, and she knew it.

"Have you talked to her?"

"I turned my phone off so I could sleep." She looked down at her plate, picked up an absolutely fascinating piece of bacon, and studied it carefully.

"Mm-hmm. You don't think she's probably texting to check on you?"

"I mean, maybe?"

"No. No maybes. She has been. She is. And she's texting me because you're not responding. I reassured her that you're fine, that you're here, and I gave her the address."

Julia flinched as if Vanessa had slapped her. "You what?"

"Relax. I told her not to come over until later. Give you time to shower and maybe grab a nap and to give me time to clean up this college dorm room."

"I have to get to the bar and see—"

"No." Julia flinched again because Vanessa's tone was sharp. Almost angry. "Look at me." Julia felt a bit like one of her cousin's students but did as she asked. "You have a fucking concussion, Julia. You're staying right here. Clea can handle the bar, just like she did when you went to Dasher Park. This is why you made her the manager, remember?"

She was right. Of course she was right. That didn't stop her from worrying, though. "I'll call her in a bit."

"Fine."

"And I can clean up my own place. I don't need you to do it."

"Too bad. I'm staying anyway, so it'll give me something to do."

"What do you mean, you're staying?"

Vanessa blinked at her. "Pretty simple sentence. I. Am. Staying. You have a concussion, and you need to be watched for at least twenty-four hours. Preferably forty-eight. So hi." She gave Julia a small wave, picked up the plates, and took them to the sink, then glanced over her shoulder. "I mean, unless you would rather I call your mom. I'm sure she'd be happy to come stay with you."

"No!" Julia jumped to her feet—an alarmingly bad idea, as her head swam, and little stars burst in her vision. A hand on the back of the couch helped her keep her balance as she squeezed her eyes shut, then opened them and met Vanessa's amused face. "No, thank you, please don't call my mom. You can stay."

A nod, a wry grin, and Vanessa went back to doing dishes. "Thought you'd see it my way."

Julia had to sit down again for a moment. Who knew a knock in the head with a bottle could take so much out of you? She inhaled deeply and let it out very slowly, suddenly feeling confused and overwhelmed.

A shower would help. Then she'd go from there.

CHAPTER TWENTY-FOUR

The white house with navy-blue trim didn't look large enough to hold that many apartments, but if the row of doorbells was to be believed, there were actually five of them in addition to Julia's. It was a nice enough street, kind of plain, slightly old. Savannah took a deep breath, replayed her speech in her head, and pushed the doorbell to apartment C.

The front door buzzed, and Savannah pulled it open. The entryway couldn't be referred to as any kind of lobby, just an entryway with deep maroon carpeting that had seen better days. A bank of six aluminum-looking mailboxes was on the wall to her right, and the stairs dead ahead.

She climbed up a flight. The door to apartment C was ajar, so she rapped her knuckles on it as she pushed it open. "Hello?"

"Hey," Vanessa said, her smile big. Genuine. It was something Savannah really liked about her—she never seemed to be faking it. "Come on in. It's good to see you." A hug—again, genuine. She smelled a little like lemon Pledge, and Savannah wondered if she'd been cleaning.

"How's she doing?" Savannah asked, setting her purse down on the counter, since the kitchen was right there as she walked in. A glance around was really all it took to see the entire place, aside from one doorway which she assumed led to a bedroom and bathroom. Maybe?

"She fine," came Julia's voice from the couch. Its back was to the kitchen, creating a bit of room separation, and Savannah hadn't seen her. The second she heard her voice, though, she hurried over, didn't wait for an invitation, and sat right down on the edge of the cushion near Julia's hip.

"You look tired," she said quietly and, before she could stop herself, reached out to Julia's face and touched gentle fingertips to the bandage on the side of her forehead. Something tugged at her, at her heart, and she trailed her fingers down the side of Julia's beautiful face, then horrified herself by letting her eyes well up. What the actual hell? This wasn't how the visit was supposed to go, damn it. She was mad. Mad at Declan. Mad at Julia. Mad, mad, mad.

"Hey," Julia said softly as she grabbed Savannah's hand in hers. "I'm okay. I promise. This head is way too hard to be hurt by some measly bottle."

Levity. Or at least an attempt at it. Okay, that was good. Savannah swallowed down the lump, cleared her throat, and met Julia's dark gaze. "Okay, listen. You can't ignore texts from me, not when you've been hurt. Understand? I didn't know if you were okay, and I was texting poor Vanessa at five o'clock this morning."

"Truth."

They both blinked as if they'd forgotten Vanessa was actually still in the room.

"I'm very sorry about that," Savannah said.

Vanessa waved it off. "I'd have done the same thing. No worries. I scolded her."

"I appreciate it." She gave Vanessa a grateful nod. "She needed scolding."

"Excuse me, *she* is right here." Julia pushed herself to a sitting position, and Savannah could tell the move was harder than she'd expected it to be. "I turned my phone off because I couldn't look at it with my head the way it was, and I just needed to sleep."

A terribly weak excuse and Savannah could tell by the uncertain expression on Julia's face that even Julia knew it. Whatever she needed to tell herself. "Okay. Fine. But I need to say a few things, and I need you to listen."

Their gazes held.

"I'm gonna"—Vanessa jerked a thumb over her shoulder at the door—"go for a walk or...something."

She and Julia continued to keep eye contact until the door clicked shut behind Vanessa and Julia gave her a nod.

"Okay." Savannah stood up and began a slow pacing as she tried to remember everything she wanted to say, everything she'd practiced on the way over. Nothing. It was gone. Left her to fend for herself extemporaneously. Terrific. She took a breath, stood tall, and did her best to put her thoughts into actual words. "First and foremost, I am so, so sorry about what happened. I apologize for my brother, something I've been doing most of his adult life." She stopped in front of a bookshelf, reached for a book and touched it, while she sorted through her thoughts. She gave a bitter laugh and turned to face the couch. "I have so much to say." She took a beat, rolled her lips in. "And I'm afraid to say half of it."

That seemed to get Julia's attention, and she tried to sit up even straighter. "Why are you afraid?"

More pacing. More thinking. And this time, when she looked back at Julia, met those soft, chocolate brown eyes that were so focused on her, she knew she had to just talk. Tell her exactly how she was feeling. Take the leap. She took a seat on the coffee table facing Julia.

"It hasn't been that long for us." *Oh, yeah, good start, Savannah, way to begin on a positive note.* She internally rolled her eyes. "It's a fact. And while we've made out a lot and we've had some"—she swallowed hard—"I can't think about it or I'll get hot all over again *amazing* sex, we haven't said anything about being exclusive. We haven't used the *L* word. We've done nothing to classify ourselves as a couple."

Julia seemed to deflate the tiniest bit at her words. Her shoulders dropped just a smidge. The corners of her mouth followed suit, ever so slightly.

"But." She held up a finger. "We feel like that to me. We *feel* like a couple. I feel more grounded with you than I've felt in longer than I can remember. I feel safe with you. I feel happy with you. And yes, I'm gonna say it—I feel loved with you."

Her words had the opposite effect this time. Julia puffed up noticeably, and the beginnings of a smile tugged the corners of her mouth upward. It gave Savannah hope, the energy to press on.

"I'd like us to explore, well, us. I'd like us to be exclusive. I think we have something here." She moved a finger back and forth between them. "I hope you feel that way, too..."

Julia nodded, her smile growing.

Oh, thank God. "Okay, good. Then I need you to understand one very important thing."

"Tell me."

Savannah took a deep breath. "I am not my family."

The expression on Julia's face then was hard to describe. Savannah watched carefully and saw so many emotions make themselves known in that moment. Chastised. Ashamed. Renewed. Determined. In that order. Savannah watched them march across Julia's face, one after the other.

"You're right," Julia said after several seconds of silence. "You're *so* right."

Savannah moved back to her original spot on the couch near Julia's hip and grabbed her hand, held it in both of hers. "I am so sorry about my brother. I'm so sorry for the commotion he caused. The damage. And I'm so sorry that he hurt you. You have no idea what that did to me." She paused. "I've never called the police on him before. I've always been the one to swoop in and clean up his mess, talk people out of pressing charges, smooth everything over. It's been my job since my mom died."

"Savannah—" Julia began, but Savannah stopped her.

"No. No, it's okay. Because that's the thing I have finally realized—it's not my job and I'm tired and I love him so much..." Her throat closed for a second or two, and she waited until her emotions waned just a bit. "It needed to be done. Maybe he can get the help he needs now. Or maybe he won't. But if last night taught me anything, it's that I can't spend the rest of my life rescuing him. I just can't." The stupid tears were back, but she couldn't seem to keep them in their place, and they spilled over, coursed down her cheek.

Julia reached out and caught a tear with her thumb, laid her warm palm against Savannah's cheek. "How do you do that?" she asked on a whisper.

"Do what?"

"Make me feel like everything's going to be okay?"

"I did that?"

Julia's smile was soft, and it was clearly her turn to have wet eyes. "You did. You've done it before. I was pretty sure this was it, that you were coming over here to say good-bye because I was an asshole last night, and this is all too hard. Instead, you just made me feel like it's totally safe to admit what's in my heart."

Speaking of hearts, Savannah felt hers kick up to beating double time. "And what's in your heart?"

"Love. For you. That's what's in my heart."

She'd said it. Just like that. No hesitation. No stammering. Savannah blinked at her. "Really?"

Julia barked a laugh, then winced and brought a hand to the bandage on her head. "Not *quite* the response I was hoping for, but yes, really." Those dark eyes seemed to look right into her soul, and Julia's face grew serious. "I know it hasn't been that long, you're right, and maybe it's way too soon, but you should know something about me—I don't toss the *L* word around lightly. When Vanessa gets back, you can ask her."

"It's true!" came Vanessa's voice through the door, and both Savannah and Julia burst out laughing.

"Oh my God, my family," Julia said, shaking her head.

"Is amazing," Savannah finished.

Julia inhaled and let it out slowly. "And you did say you felt loved when you're with me."

"I did. And I do." Nothing had been truer in the past several months, and letting that feeling come in and wash over her was nothing short of wonderful.

Julia adjusted her position, like she wanted to sit up straighter than she already was. She waved a hand between the two of them. "So, what do you think? Wanna give this a shot?"

Savannah grabbed her hand, held it in both of hers, reveled in the warmth of it, the strength of Julia's grip. "I want to give it more than a shot. I want to give it everything I have. I love you so much, Julia Martini."

"Yeah? How much?" Oh, Julia was playing, being a smart-ass, was she? Well, two could play at that game.

"Enough to help you with your daddy issues."

"Oh, ouch." Julia clamped both hands to her chest and fell back against the couch. "Direct hit!"

The front door opened then, and Vanessa breezed back in, laughing as she looked at her cousin, and pointed at Savannah. "I like her. She doesn't take your crap. Keep her. Pretty please?"

When Julia looked at her then, it felt like nothing else in the world existed to her, like Savannah was the sun, the moon, and the stars. How long had she been waiting for somebody to look at her like that? Months? Years? Her entire life? "I can't get rid of her now," Julia said quietly. "I love her too much."

Pretty sure her heart melted right there in her chest, the tears filled Savannah's eyes once again as she leaned forward. "I love you, too," she said, just before kissing the woman she hoped to kiss for the rest of her life.

"You guys," Vanessa said, her voice cracking as she waved her hands as if trying to dry her face. "I'm gonna cry."

EPILOGUE

Three months later

So much of her family was present, and it warmed Julia's heart. The Martini clan was huge and loud and took up a lot of space, both figuratively and literally. But having everybody—or everybody who lived close—together at the same time was something that didn't happen a whole lot since Julia's grandparents on her dad's side had been gone. So she was not only thrilled, but felt honored somehow, that she had them all in one place.

Business had been good, steadily picking up through the summer as word of mouth got out. The less-than-favorable reviews on the *Northwood Nightlife* blog had disappeared, and it took Julia more than two months to realize something else had as well— glamorous flower-sending, inappropriate email-writing customer Chris Norton. She'd just stopped showing up, and Julia often wondered if she could be the anonymous blogger. Her notorious crush on Julia plus the timing of the bad reviews—right after Julia'd started seeing Savannah—seemed beyond coincidental. But she didn't know for sure and likely never would.

Given the good business, and with Savannah's encouragement, by the time October rolled around, she decided to close on Sundays for the late fall and winter months.

But here they were, on a Sunday, and the bar was full. Also Savannah's idea. A Martini Family open house, she called it, suggesting Julia invite her extended family to come see the place.

After all, it had been in the family for three generations, and she should be proud of what she'd done with it. So said Savannah. She said it would be a great way to get her whole family together. Spoiler alert—she'd been right. She and Vanessa had made a big sandwich board that stood on the sidewalk out front. It read: *Closed for Private Event.* Inside, Halloween decorations were everywhere. Cobwebs and a giant spider hung in one corner. Skeletons dangled over various tables. Jack-o'-lanterns flickered on the corners of the bar, which was draped with black and silver garland.

Now Julia stood behind the bar, unable to curb the smile that had been on her face for the past hour. Uncle Sonny and Uncle Joe were debating the football season, arguing over who was worse, Uncle Sonny's Buffalo Bills or Uncle Joe's Cleveland Browns. Aunt Monica and Izzy, Vanessa's mom and sister, chatted with Julia's brother John and his wife, Sarah. Uncle Paul and Aunt Eva were in deep conversation with Aunt Maria about something that looked super important. So many of her relatives and their significant others had come, and Julia felt so filled with pride, she wanted to burst.

At one corner of the bar sat her father and mother, and just the sight of them, smiling and talking, her mother with a glass of cabernet, her dad with a whiskey, neat—that was new—filled her with a level of joy she hadn't expected. She had the music tuned to some soft rock, and Hank was helping pour drinks, since he knew half her family and all her uncles.

Vanessa and Amelia and Dante and Savannah were at a table together, and Julia was relieved to see the very clichéd but incredibly accurate deer-in-headlights look on Savannah's face had finally eased away. She grinned as she recalled how Savannah's blue eyes had gotten bigger and bigger as family members kept coming. She'd met Julia's immediate family—and could not have been a bigger hit with her mom, not that it surprised her at all—but the actual scope of the Martini clan had gone way beyond what she'd envisioned. Julia could tell and found it endlessly amusing.

"How's it going?" she asked as she approached the table where her cousins, brother, and girlfriend sat. "I'm glad to see you looking more relaxed," she teased as she kissed the top of Savannah's head.

"You were *not* kidding when you said your family was huge. Holy crap."

"Please," Amelia said, waving her off. "Everybody has loved her."

"Like, immediately," Vanessa chimed in. "It's like they're all smitten with her. I thought Uncle John was going to stand next to her and talk her ear off all day."

"Aw, he was nice," Savannah said, then sipped her club soda.

"Things are winding down some," Julia said, glancing at her watch. They'd been going strong for a couple hours now. "You ready for a drink yet?"

Savannah hadn't wanted to risk getting tipsy in front of any family of Julia's she was meeting for the first time, which Julia found super sweet. She'd done some mingling, introducing herself to many family members, and spent a good amount of time chatting with Julia's parents. Not that Julia had been spying on her or keeping track of her movements. Okay, fine, she totally had.

"I am, but it looks like your dad wants you." Savannah was looking past her toward the bar where, sure enough, her parents were beckoning to her.

"They're probably ready to leave. Be right back." She headed their way, and when she got close to them, her father cleared his throat, looking very serious. "Pop? Everything okay?"

"Yeah. Fine. Can we go talk in private for a minute?" His eyes found the sign marking The Bar Back.

Julia blinked her surprise while she tried to tamp down the nerves that had seized up in her belly. "Sure. Of course." She led them to the back room, gestured to the couch, the barstools. "Have a seat. Are you sure everything's okay? You're scaring me a little bit. You're not sick or something, are you?" Funny how that was the first place her mind went now that her parents were beyond age sixty-five.

"Oh, honey, no." Her mother took a seat at the practice bar and waved a hand, smiling. "We're fine. Your father wants to talk to you."

"Oh." A hard swallow, likely a throwback from childhood. The words *your father wants to talk to you* were rarely good when you were a kid. "Okay." She turned to him, noticed for the first time that he looked nervous. Toeing the floor. Eyes darting. Hands stuffed in the pockets of his coat. "What's up?"

He took a deep breath, seemed to collect himself, and looked up at her. His almond-shaped dark eyes that people said she'd inherited held something Julia rarely saw in her dad—emotion. Lots of it.

"Pop?" Her voice was small. She knew it and couldn't seem to make it bigger.

"I owe you an apology, Princess."

Julia felt her own eyes go wide. He hadn't called her that childhood nickname in ages, and only now, hearing it for the first time in years, did she understand how much she'd missed it. Her eyes welled up immediately. Damn it. "An apology for what?" She honestly had no idea where this was going.

He sighed, looking around the room, and kept his hands in his pockets as he rolled from the balls of his feet to his heels and back. "For being a horse's ass." Julia followed his gaze to her mom, who smiled and nodded at him in what seemed like encouragement. "I was jealous."

Julia blinked at him, shook her head. "I am so lost right now, Pop. Jealous of what?"

"Of you! Of your…your…tenacity." He took his hands out of his pockets and held them in front of his body, balled them into fists, and shook them. "I wanted to buy this bar. For years. And when the time came, when your uncle Tony said he was ready to sell? I chickened out." He dropped his hands and sighed. "I came up with so many excuses, so many reasons why I couldn't do it, but it really came down to not having the balls."

"Vince," her mother scolded.

"Sorry. Courage. I didn't have the courage to take the risk." When he looked at Julia this time, his eyes went soft. "But you know who did have the balls—err—courage? My girl. My only daughter stepped up and took a risk and"—he held out his arms again—"look at this place. It's magnificent!" His smile was wide, and his pride in her was so clearly written on his face, that Julia almost sobbed. He stepped toward her and cupped her face in both his hands. "I'm sorry for being an ass to you, Princess, and letting my pride keep me away. I am so very proud of you. Next time Uncle Tony comes back from Florida to visit, he's gonna be so impressed with you and everything you've done to the place."

Julia was Italian, and speechless wasn't something that could often describe her. But it did right then. She didn't know what to say, but her father wasn't done. He gestured with his chin toward her mother, who pulled a large envelope out of her ridiculously large purse and handed it to him.

"I found this in some of my stuff and had it blown up and framed. Thought maybe you could hang it someplace. Out there." He handed it to her, and she let out a quiet gasp.

It was a black-and-white photo taken in the bar many years ago, way before Julia was even a twinkle in her parents' eyes. Sitting at the bar in a row were her father and all four of his brothers. They all looked so handsome with their slicked hair and big smiles. Behind the bar stood her grandfather, also mid-laugh.

"Pop, oh my God, this is amazing!" She brought it closer to her face, studied the faces. "When was this taken?"

"I'm not completely sure, but I think I'm about twenty-five there. So forty, forty-five years ago? So nineteen seventy-five? Eighty?"

"This is…" Julia shook her head. Such a gesture from her dad was so unexpected. "It's perfect. I know right where it's going to go. Out in the front where people can see the history of this place." She met his gaze. "Thank you, Dad. This means more than you know."

It was kind of crazy how quickly walls could come down or how fast negative emotions could be banished, but she threw her arms around her father and nothing was the same between them. In a good way. In the very best of ways.

Later that night, once all the family had gone home, the music silenced, the floors mopped, the bar dark, it was just Julia, Savannah, Amelia, and Vanessa in the back room.

"I would call that one very successful open house," Amelia said. "I hope the liquor bill doesn't kill you."

Julia hadn't charged her family for wine or beer, and liquor had been half price. She knew going in that she'd have a loss but decided that word-of-mouth advertising from her sizable family would make up for it in the future. It was something she'd learned in the online marketing course Savannah had encouraged her to take—you had to spend money to make money.

"I planned for it." She shot a look toward Savannah, who grinned at her. She was behind the practice bar, working on a drink that she'd planned to share only with Savannah. But the time felt right, and her cousins were fixtures anyway. "Hey, I want you guys to try something."

"Ooh, taste testing," Vanessa said as she jumped off the couch and grabbed a seat on a stool. "My fave."

Julia added vodka, some peach nectar, and a generous splash of peach liqueur to the shaker with ice and shook, her eyes locked with Savannah's.

"Are you guys gonna do that the whole time?" Amelia asked.

"Do what?" Julia whacked the shaker with the heel of her hand to break the seal.

"Make goo-goo eyes at each other."

"Probs," Julia said and looked to Savannah, who nodded her agreement.

"We do excel at goo-goo eyes," Savannah noted. "It's true."

Amelia sighed. "Fine. Just"—she waved a hand—"don't get it on me."

Vanessa pushed at her playfully. "You're such a fun-killer."

"It's my life now, apparently," Amelia said, and though it was clear she was playing along and not fully serious, there was a sadness in her eyes that Julia wished she could erase.

Savannah stepped behind Amelia and wrapped her arms around her. "In no way is that your life," she said softly, then squeezed and kissed Amelia on the temple. "You're wonderful, and there's so much more in store for you. I just know it." Amelia's cheeks reddened as Savannah winked at Julia over her shoulder.

Martini glasses were lined up on the bar, and Julia strained the drink into them, its color a very pale golden. She then garnished each glass with a slice of fresh peach and twisted a fresh-picked basil leaf over it, getting the essence of the herb into the liquid before floating the leaf on top. She waved a hand, presenting the drinks. "Please. Taste."

She watched as the three of them each took a sip. They looked at each other as they seemed to gauge the taste.

"Oh," Vanessa said and went for a second sip before making any more commentary.

Amelia did the same, sipping again.

"Oh my goodness, that's fantastic," Savannah said.

"It's the basil," Amelia concluded. "It really gives it...depth."

Vanessa pointed at her. "That's the perfect word. Depth. It's a much more complex flavor than I was expecting. I love it."

"What is it?" Savannah asked, and they all turned their attention to Julia.

"That, my friends, is what I have named the Savannah Martini."

There was silence for a beat, and then Vanessa and Amelia fell into a tandem "Ooh!" of joy and delight. Savannah, on the other hand, just looked at her, eyes shimmery.

"You named a drink after me?" she asked in a small voice.

Julia lifted a shoulder in a half shrug that was meant to seem totally nonchalant, all oh yeah, the drink has your name, no big deal. "I mean, I kinda liked the way it sounded."

"It does have a ring to it," Vanessa said, catching Julia's drift as usual.

"And if anybody deserves to have a drink named after them," Julia added, "it's you."

Savannah used her forearms to stretch her body across the bar and kiss her, the flavor of peaches still clinging to her lips. "Thank you, baby. I love it." Another kiss. "And I love you."

"I love you back," Julia said.

"Ugh, I told you not to get it on me," Amelia whined, wiping at her shoulders and arms, making the others laugh. "It's everywhere!"

It occurred to Julia in the moment how perfect her life was. Right then, at that very second, she had everything she'd ever wanted. A successful business that allowed her to be creative, the approval from her father—finally—that she'd been craving so badly, and the love of an amazing woman. If somebody had told her eight months ago that she'd have it all, she never would've believed it. She would've laughed because nobody gets to have it all.

Never in her entire life had she ever been so happy to be wrong.

"Hey," she said, then waited until all three were looking at her. "I love you guys."

A beat passed, then they herded around the bar. "Group hug," Vanessa announced. They surrounded her, the three women she loved most in the world, wrapped their arms around her, until they were one living, breathing mass of affection. She looked down at Savannah, who'd ended up directly in her arms and was looking up at her with those beautiful baby blues, wide and watery.

"I love you," Savannah whispered.

"I love you, too," Julia whispered back. "I'm keeping you."

This time when they kissed, Amelia had no snarky comments. She just smiled as she and Vanessa hugged them tighter.

About the Author

Georgia Beers is a writer of romance, a sipper of wine, and a lover of animals. Residing in upstate New York with her cat and her puppy, she is currently hard at work on her next novel. You can visit her and find out more at georgiabeers.com

Books Available from Bold Strokes Books

Busy Ain't the Half of It by Frederick Smith and Chaz Lamar Cruz. Elijah and Justin seek happily-ever-afters in LA, but are they too busy to notice happiness when it's there? (978-1-63555-944-6)

Calumet by Ali Vali. Jaxon Lavigne and Iris Long had a forbidden small-town romance that didn't last, and the consequences of that love will be uncovered fifteen years later at their high school reunion. (978-1-63555-900-2)

Her Countess to Cherish by Jane Walsh. London Society's material girl realizes there is more to life than diamonds when she falls in love with a non-binary bluestocking. (978-1-63555-902-6)

Hot Days, Heated Nights by Renee Roman. When Cole and Lee meet, instant attraction quickly flares into uncontrollable passion, but their connection might be short lived as Lee's identity is tied to her life in the city. (978-1-63555-888-3)

Never Be the Same by MA Binfield. Casey meets Olivia and sparks fly in this opposites attract romance that proves love can be found in the unlikeliest places. (978-1-63555-938-5)

Quiet Village by Eden Darry. Something not quite human is stalking Collie and her niece, and she'll be forced to work with undercover reporter Emily Lassiter if they want to get out of Hyam alive. (978-1-63555-898-2)

Shaken or Stirred by Georgia Beers. Bar owner Julia Martini and home health aide Savannah McNally attempt to weather the storms brought on by a mysterious blogger trashing the bar, family feuds they knew nothing about, and way too much advice from way too many relatives. (978-1-63555-928-6)

The Fiend in the Fog by Jess Faraday. Can four people on different trajectories work together to save the vulnerable residents of East London from the terrifying fiend in the fog before it's too late? (978-1-63555-514-1)

The Marriage Masquerade by Toni Logan. A no strings attached marriage scheme to inherit a Maui B&B uncovers unexpected attractions and a dark family secret. (978-1-63555-914-9)

Flight SQA016 by Amanda Radley. Fastidious airline passenger Olivia Lewis is used to things being a certain way. When her routine is changed by a new, attractive member of the staff, sparks fly. (978-1-63679-045-9)

Home Is Where the Heart Is by Jenny Frame. Can Archie make the countryside her home and give Ash the fairytale romance she desires? Or will the countryside and small village life all be too much for her? (978-1-63555-922-4)

Moving Forward by PJ Trebelhorn. The last person Shelby Ryan expects to be attracted to is Iris Calhoun, the sister of the man who killed her wife four years and three thousand miles ago. (978-1-63555-953-8)

Poison Pen by Jean Copeland. Debut author Kendra Blake is finally living her best life until a nasty book review and exposed secrets threaten her promising new romance with aspiring journalist Alison Chatterley. (978-1-63555-849-4)

Seasons for Change by KC Richardson. Love, laughter, and trust develop for Shawn and Morgan throughout the changing seasons of Lake Tahoe. (978-1-63555-882-1)

Summer Lovin' by Julie Cannon. Three different women, three exotic locations, one unforgettable summer. What do you think will happen? (978-1-63555-920-0)

Unbridled by D. Jackson Leigh. A visit to a local stable turns into more than riding lessons between a novel writer and an equestrian with a taste for power play. (978-1-63555-847-0)

VIP by Jackie D. In a town where relationships are forged and shattered by perception, sometimes even love can't change who you really are. (978-1-63555-908-8)

Yearning by Gun Brooke. The sleepy town of Dennamore has an irresistible pull on those who've moved away. The mystery Darian Benson and Samantha Pike uncover will change them forever, but the love they find along the way just might be the key to saving themselves. (978-1-63555-757-2)

A Turn of Fate by Ronica Black. Will Nev and Kinsley finally face their painful past and relent to their powerful, forbidden attraction? Or will facing their past be too much to fight through? (978-1-63555-930-9)

Desires After Dark by MJ Williamz. When her human lover falls deathly ill, Alex, a vampire, must decide which is worse, letting her go or condemning her to everlasting life. (978-1-63555-940-8)

Her Consigliere by Carsen Taite. FBI agent Royal Scott swore an oath to uphold the law, and criminal defense attorney Siobhan Collins pledged her loyalty to the only family she's ever known, but will their love be stronger than the bonds they've vowed to others, or will their competing allegiances tear them apart? (978-1-63555-924-8)

In Our Words: Queer Stories from Black, Indigenous, and People of Color Writers. Stories selected by Anne Shade and Edited by Victoria Villaseñor. Comprising both the renowned and emerging voices of Black, Indigenous, and People of Color authors, this thoughtfully curated collection of short stories explores the intersection of racial and queer identity. (978-1-63555-936-1)

Measure of Devotion by CF Frizzell. Disguised as her late twin brother, Catherine Samson enters the Civil War to defend the Constitution as a Union soldier, never expecting her life to be altered by a Gettysburg farmer's daughter. (978-1-63555-951-4)

Not Guilty by Brit Ryder. Claire Weaver and Emery Pearson's day jobs clash, even as their desire for each other burns, and a discreet sex-only arrangement is the only option. (978-1-63555-896-8)

Opposites Attract: Butch/Femme Romances by Meghan O'Brien, Aurora Rey, Angie Williams. Sometimes opposites really do attract. Fall in love with these butch/femme romance novellas. (978-1-63555-784-8)

Swift Vengeance by Jean Copeland, Jackie D, Erin Zak. A journalist becomes the subject of her own investigation when sudden strange, violent visions summon her to a summer retreat and into the arms of a killer's possible next victim. (978-1-63555-880-7)

Under Her Influence by Amanda Radley. On their path to #truelove, will Beth and Jemma discover that reality is even better than illusion? (978-1-63555-963-7)

Wasteland by Kristin Keppler & Allisa Bahney. Danielle Clark is fighting against the National Armed Forces and finds peace as a scavenger, until the NAF general's daughter, Katelyn Turner, shows up on her doorstep and brings the fight right back to her. (978-1-63555-935-4)

When in Doubt by VK Powell. Police officer Jeri Wylder thinks she committed a crime in the line of duty but can't remember, until details emerge pointing to a cover-up by those close to her. (978-1-63555-955-2)

A Woman to Treasure by Ali Vali. An ancient scroll isn't the only treasure Levi Montbard finds as she starts her hunt for the truth—all she has to do is prove to Yasmine Hassani that there's more to her than an adventurous soul. (978-1-63555-890-6)

Before. After. Always. by Morgan Lee Miller. Still reeling from her tragic past, Eliza Walsh has sworn off taking risks, until Blake Navarro turns her world right-side up, making her question if falling in love again is worth it. (978-1-63555-845-6)

Bet the Farm by Fiona Riley. Lauren Calloway's luxury real estate sale of the century comes to a screeching halt when dairy farm heiress, and one-night stand, Thea Boudreaux calls her bluff. (978-1-63555-731-2)

Cowgirl by Nance Sparks. The last thing Aren expects is to fall for Carol. Sharing her home is one thing, but sharing her heart means sharing the demons in her past and risking everything to keep Carol safe. (978-1-63555-877-7)

Give In to Me by Elle Spencer. Gabriela Talbot never expected to sleep with her favorite author—certainly not after the scathing review she'd given Whitney Ainsworth's latest book. (978-1-63555-910-1)

Hidden Dreams by Shelley Thrasher. A lethal virus and its resulting vision send Texan Barbara Allan and her lovely guide, Dara, on a journey up Cambodia's Mekong River in search of Barbara's mother's mystifying past. (978-1-63555-856-2)

In the Spotlight by Lesley Davis. For actresses Cole Calder and Eris Whyte, their chance at love runs out fast when a fan's adoration turns to obsession. (978-1-63555-926-2)

Origins by Jen Jensen. Jamis Bachman is pulled into a dangerous mystery that becomes personal when she learns the truth of her origins as a ghost hunter. (978-1-63555-837-1)

Pursuit: A Victorian Entertainment by Felice Picano. An intelligent, handsome, ruthlessly ambitious young man who rose from the slums to become the right-hand man of the Lord Exchequer of England will stop at nothing as he pursues his Lord's vanished wife across Continental Europe. (978-1-63555-870-8)

Unrivaled by Radclyffe. Zoey Cohen will never accept second place in matters of the heart, even when her rival is a career, and Declan Black has nothing left to give of herself or her heart. (978-1-63679-013-8)

A Fae Tale by Genevieve McCluer. Dovana comes to terms with her changing feelings for her lifelong best friend and fae, Roze. (978-1-63555-918-7)

Accidental Desperados by Lee Lynch. Life is clobbering Berry, Jaudon, and their long romance. The arrival of directionless baby dyke MJ doesn't help. Can they find their passion again—and keep it? (978-1-63555-482-3)

Always Believe by Aimée. Greyson Walsden is pursuing ordination as an Anglican priest. Angela Arlingham doesn't believe in God. Do they follow their vocation or their hearts? (978-1-63555-912-5)

Best of the Wrong Reasons by Sander Santiago. For Fin Ness and Orion Starr, it takes a funeral to remind them that love is worth living for. (978-1-63555-867-8)

Courage by Jesse J. Thoma. No matter how often Natasha Parsons and Tommy Finch clash on the job, an undeniable attraction simmers just beneath the surface. Can they find the courage to change so love has room to grow? (978-1-63555-802-9)

I Am Chris by R Kent. There's one saving grace to losing everything and moving away. Nobody knows her as Chrissy Taylor. Now Chris can live who he truly is. (978-1-63555-904-0)